A
WHISPER
IN THE
SILENCE

Published by True Will Publishing

ISBN 978-1-84396-660-9
Also available as a Kindle ebook
ISBN 978-1-84396-645-6

A catalogue record for this book is available from
the British Library and American Library of Congress

Cover design by Adrian Dobbie
Aleister Crowley material used by kind permission of Ordo Templi Orientis

Typesetting and pre-press production
eBook Versions
127 Old Gloucester Street
London WC1N 3AX
www.ebookversions.com

This book is dedicated to ROSIE, my wife
and soulmate, my brother Brian and sister Veronica,
and all endangered monkeys and apes.

With special thanks to Adrian for his
cover design, to Nick, Chief Pilot of Pacific Island Air,
Fiji, and Sani of Turtle Airways, Fiji, for their
information on seaplanes,
and to Ray for his proofreading.

A
WHISPER
IN THE
SILENCE

Trevor Gray

TRUE WILL PUBLISHING

1

Noise! The dreadful droning sound of the seaplane's turbine engine and spinning propeller escalated.

As it prepared for take-off, Oliver quickly reached for his noise-cancelling headphones. Turning them on, he placed them over his head and adjusted the cans to effectively cover his ears.

Leaning back again in his seat, he gave a sigh of relief. Silence had been restored.

The first line from *Desiderata*, written by Max Ehrmann in the 1920's came to him: *'Go placidly amid the noise and haste and remember what peace there may be in silence.'*

There had admittedly been no mention of seaplanes in the prose poem and it was about far more than just silence, but Ollie, as his friends called him, still considered it appropriate. Ironically, it was his search for silence which necessitated him being aboard the amphibious aircraft. With retractable wheels, it could take off and land from airfields as well as water, making it the easiest way for him to transfer to his very own desert island.

Oliver Longbridge was still only 30 years of age but had already done a lot in life. He had taken over an extremely successful investment business 12 years ago, when his multi-millionaire father had died of a heart attack. Hard work and determination had, until recently, enabled him to build up a considerably large property portfolio from the London based office he had inherited.

He was 5'8" and good looking, but his overall appearance was deceptive. With shoulder length black hair, faded jeans and a half unbuttoned black shirt, he looked more like a 1970s rock star than a multi-millionaire businessman.

There was good reason for his change in attitude as to the priorities in life. Something extraordinary had happened on the day before his 25th birthday. It could only be described as an out-of-body experience. He had no knowledge at all about such phenomena at the time and had rarely spared a thought about the spiritual side of life. As for religion, he considered it was something which could wait until he was a pensioner in God's waiting room. Success in accumulating material wealth had until then taken precedence.

The completely unexpected psychic experience was hypnagogic, meaning it occurred in those transitional moments between wakefulness and sleep. He had been starting to doze off, when he became aware that he was entering a long dark tunnel. At the end of it, in the far distance, was a blindingly bright white light. Its intensity had initially forced him to shield his eyes from the rays, but gradually they adjusted.

About halfway between him and this light stood a strange, but non-threatening hooded figure, dressed entirely in black. Its right hand was making a beckoning gesture, its soothing voice repeatedly whispering, 'Come, come, come.'

Without the slightest trepidation he had started to walk towards the mysterious entity. Inexplicably, with each step he took he felt increasing tranquillity. Never in his entire life had he encountered such peacefulness and well-being.

Then he had stopped, not that he wanted to, for he was curious and inspired by what was happening, but something made him.

'No. I have to go back,' he had told the figure reluctantly, but knowingly.

As he slowly turned and retraced his steps away from the light, the vision of the tunnel began to slowly fade until it was no more.

He found himself back in bed, his eyes wide open, staring at the ceiling.

For nearly an hour he had lain there thinking about what had happened. Although excited, he was emotionally left with a sense of loss. It was as if he had walked away from his rightful place of existence. He desperately wanted to tell someone about it but was afraid most people would suspect it was simply his imagination, a dream or an hallucination.

Knowing it to be something of far greater significance, he had started looking for evidence. His research revealed hundreds of individuals who attested to something similar. For many it had been a near-death experience, although this was unlikely in his case. Even so, determined to discover the truth about what had happened, further delving unveiled numerous books and websites dedicated to the subject.

Ollie would never forget what happened that night. The brief but transformational glance into a world beyond had changed his life. Convinced of existence outside of the physical body, he contemplated the possibility of survival after death and even reincarnation. He craved the soothing peace and serenity, which he had been blessed with in the tunnel. His sole desire being to rediscover such spiritual bliss, he realised he could only succeed through dedicating the rest of his life to silence.

Under such circumstances it was an easy decision for him to walk away from the multiple distractions of his now pointless business life. There was no one to stop him from doing what he knew he must. His parents had divorced when he had still been a child and his mother tragically killed in a car crash, two days before she had been due to remarry. Ollie had no romantic ties either, having ended the relationship with a former girlfriend months ago. She was certainly no kindred spirit, considering his theories about the supernatural to be nothing more than mumbo jumbo. Their parting had been amicable, both being better off without the other.

He had spent all his spare time over the past five years learning about the paranormal, mysticism, spirituality and what was generally termed occult. Accepting the need for quiet reflection, contemplation and meditation, he planned his vital escape from the noise polluted modern world.

Closing his business, he sold off all his property investments and other major assets, leaving him with an enormous personal fortune, which amounted to many millions of pounds. With considerable help from Brad Lithtrop, the personal assistant he had the good sense to retain, he had searched for the most perfect place of solitude.

His first thought had been to perhaps take an extensive

retreat at a Roman Catholic monastery. A solemn vow of silence would be essential and welcome, but he dismissed the idea completely after looking into the Church's dogma. He was unable to sympathise with such a belief system and considered the hypocritical behaviour of some of their priests to be abhorrent.

Eventually came the exciting idea of acquiring his own uninhabited desert island, where he would be the sole occupant. With much enthusiasm he and Brad searched the websites of companies specialising in the sale of private islands, surprised at how many were available.

After many false leads and even more disappointments, he finally found the ideal. It was in Fiji, which is made up of over 300 islands, his chosen one being between the tropical Mamanuca volcanic archipelago and the soaring peaks of the more rugged Yasawa chain.

He bought it on a lease and by paying above the asking price was permitted to give it a name of his own, for the years he was to live there. It did not need much thinking about. He called it *Yanuyana Vakanomodi*.

Translated into English, this means *Quiet Island,* or even more appropriately, ***Island of Silence***.

2

Emma clicked *send* on her email.

That was one important message out of the way. Now Sarah Fernsby, her agent, would know she would be unavailable for work for at least a couple of months.

The young model took a sip of coffee. It was stone cold. She had until then completely forgotten about it, despite it being right next to her. Her mind had been on the wording of the email, crucial as it was for Sarah to understand how much she needed a holiday.

The world of commercial and glamour modelling could be tiring, especially for those in as much demand as Emma Eve. Her real surname was Saffery, but she had changed it at her agent's request. It had worked, for there had been plenty of job offers for nearly the last four years. This was the first time however, there had been such a long gap between bookings. She had no idea why and was not really bothered. More to the point, she was going to take advantage of the situation.

Her height of 5' 5", or 1.65 metres as it stated in her portfolio, had determined the sort of modelling she would be successful at. Unlike fashion models who were nearly always taller, she had to make sure it was her body which men and women lusted after, rather than any textile design she might be wearing.

Although only 25 years old she knew careers like hers had a limited shelf-life. The expiration date would depend on how long her desirable assets lasted. Fortunately, for now she was still extremely well blessed. Her face was stunning, with high cheekbones, mischievous hazel eyes, a pronounced jawline and sensual full pink lips. Her to-die-for natural blond hair cascaded in beachy waves over her shoulders and loin stirring sex appeal oozed from every part of her gorgeous curvy body.

Whilst she was often photographed in swimwear, or scanty lingerie which left little to the imagination, sometimes she was required to do nude poses. These would very often be artistically creative, or for a photographer who contributed to naturist magazines. There were also erotic photo shoots, which although still artistic had to be sexually suggestive. These she never refused and had become expert at, being perfectly at ease with her body.

Newspaper photos of 'Page 3' girls had practically stopped, but images of her partly dressed and undressed appeared in a whole range of magazines, advertisements, posters and calendars. A picture of her was even on the side of one of those novelty fun mugs, her bikini disappearing when hot water was poured in. She knew where to draw the line however and had always refused to do pornography. Taking things too far could ruin her successful career.

The only thing fake about her was her tan. She had never had the time to acquire a real one and this was just one of the reasons why she needed a holiday. It had to be somewhere far away, hot, sunny and exotic, preferably with some nice fun-loving young people for company.

Emma could afford such a vacation. As well as her own savings there was still the 'bank of Mum and Dad' to rely on. She had been born in London's Chelsea, to parents who were substantially well-off. Both still alive, her father was a dealer in modern and contemporary fine arts, along with continental and Oriental furniture, plus rare antiques. Her mother was in huge demand as a highly regarded interior designer, with more than enough mega-rich clients.

They had originally not been at all keen on her modelling career, but knew it made her happy and in time her success had made them proud. Seeing pictures, of what they still considered to be their little girl, so often in the media, had become fun for them. Although they were broad minded, her more risqué poses did sometimes make them gasp or blush.

As for boyfriends, Emma was disappointed to find most of them only seemed interested in one thing. Afterwards, they just wanted to brag to their mates about their prized conquest. Relationships never lasted long, which did sometimes concern her, but she was sure the right man would eventually turn up.

She typed *exotic holidays* into her browser and clicked. Up came page after page of travel companies and links to videos on YouTube and Facebook of places like the Maldives, the Galapagos Islands, Mauritius and Malaysia.

Studying several pages of search results, www.overCtravel. org caught her eye. It was probably the clever use of the 'C' abbreviation for 'sea' in the company's name which drew her attention to it.

She clicked on the link and a colourful homepage was displayed, showing a perfect sandy beach, lined with palm trees. 'Welcome to Over C Travel,' she read, 'home to the holiday you deserve in Fiji, the jewel of the South Pacific.'

It seemed they specialised in just one small but outstanding island, which was 'almost untouched by tourism, with lush green tropical rainforests, cascading waterfalls and beautiful white sandy beaches.' They promised there would not be any language barriers, as it was owned by an English family and was 'undoubtedly the most romantic desert island in the world, with just six luxurious bures.'

Emma was not sure what a bure was and so opened a new window on the browser and googled it, finding it to be a traditional wood and straw hut, rather like a cabin.

Returning to the Over C Travel site she found photographs of the interior. It looked luxurious and promised 'stunning uninterrupted views of the beach and crystal-clear sea, the coral reef being unparalleled for snorkelling.' This was something she had always wanted to try and made a mental note to take the snorkelling mask a friend had given her.

The all-inclusive package included everything she could possibly want. She would have her own outdoor shower, a jacuzzi, seashore fine dining and excellent twenty-four-hour personal service. Most appealing of all were the photos of their great all-night parties. She could hardly wait to join the fun, especially as the bar looked well stocked with bubbly!

Despite the usual ABTA and ATOL logos being displayed, the advice was to book her flights directly with the airlines, which they said would give her better options. From the glowing

5-star reviews displayed, which were encouragingly similar and recent, it seemed to be what all the previous holidaymakers had done.

She entered the 2019 arrival and departure dates she wanted for the resort and was thrilled to see they were still available for such a last-minute booking. The price was almost unbelievable. There was no single person supplement and even a 30% discount when paying by bank transfer directly to the company's account, rather than by credit card.

Alerted by a flashing message on screen that there were 98 other people looking at the same dates, she submitted her details quickly, determined not to miss out.

She was in luck, for her booking had been accepted and she was given the account details of a Mr. Acharya, the travel company's manging director, for transferring her payment. Confirmation, including the name and exact location of the island, would be sent to her by first class post. In the meantime, she should go ahead and book her flights to Australia and on to Nadi in Fiji, which she did straight away with an airline.

Full details from Over C Travel arrived just three days later. It was a simple one-page document, with no wordy conditions for her to have to wade through but it wished her a happy holiday. They suggested it would be one she would long remember. Signed by Mr. Acharya personally, it also gave the name of the Fijian island she was going to.

It never occurred to her to translate *Yanuyana Vakanomodi* into English. She was far too excited.

Having poured herself a Prosecco, her favourite drink, she danced around the room, singing along to the first track from the Jonas Brothers' *Happiness Begins* album.

It was a song called *Sucker*!

3

There was no door between the cockpit and cabin on the single-engined de Havilland Otter.

Benny leaned over, just enough to poke his head around the opening. 'We'll be landing very soon,' he shouted, knowing his sole passenger was not wearing the plane's wired headset.

Seeing him, Ollie removed his noise cancelling headphones. They were still turned on, but not plugged in. 'Sorry, but I missed what you said,' he hollered back.

'We're almost there,' Benny repeated in his New Zealand accent. 'Landing shortly. Have you got your seat belt on?'

Ollie nodded, pointing to it around his waist.

'The sea's smooth today but it can still be a bit bumpy,' Benny warned, 'so best keep your belt buckled.' He thought it wise not to mention it being more difficult for a pilot to judge altitude accurately when landing on glassy water, with no wind and a very reflective surface. 'Water makes a wonderful brake,' he informed his passenger instead, 'so we'll quickly have you at the jetty.'

First Charter Aviation (South Pacific) were quite a new company, based at Fiji's Nadi airport, but were already building a good reputation and had been highly recommended.

This was one of their smaller planes. Built in 1960, its old radical engine had been converted to a turbine and it was operated by just a single pilot. Ollie would be seeing Benny every couple of weeks when fresh provisions were flown to the island.

Talking to him earlier, it had turned out that he was the son of the company's owner. His father wanted him to take a management role at headquarters, but Benny had always had the flying bug. Reluctant to sit behind a desk, even the temptation of a huge salary increase had failed to ground him.

In his late twenties, clean shaven with neatly cut black hair, he looked very smart in his white uniform, complete with epaulette shoulder decorations and insignia. He had removed his hat, upon entering the cockpit, but the confident and contented smile on his face remained a permanent fixture.

Brad would be waiting for them to land, having just about overseen everything, including the construction of the floating jetty. It had been erected a few months earlier in 2018, along with a cabin for Ollie to live in and a few utility and storage buildings. Fresh water came from a natural coral filtered well and there was a small treatment plant for sewage. Solar power supplied the electricity and hot water.

It was just as well these facilities had not been built a couple of years earlier, for in 2016 cyclone Winston had struck. The Southern Hemisphere's most intense tropical cyclone on record, with winds of over 177 miles an hour, would probably have destroyed any man-made structure on the island. There had been a few minor storms since but nowhere near as bad. Even so, Brad had sensibly suggested Ollie got settled in to island life well before the cyclone season.

The seaplane's landing turned out to be surprisingly smooth, proving to Ollie what an excellent pilot Benny was.

In no time at all they were making their way along the jetty, clutching bags.

Brad Lithtrop was waving them a welcome from the shore. In his mid-fifties and wearing sunglasses, his baseball cap partially hid his greying hairline. Less successful were his floral shirt and cut-offs at disguising his overweight frame. He had worked for Ollie's father for years and there had never been any doubt about Ollie keeping him on. Stubbornness kept him smoking too much and despite his doctor's pleading, he refused to change his diet. Had he done so, his diabetes might have been better controlled.

As an employee though, he could turn his hand to just about anything, whether it be negotiating deals, wording contracts, or working on designs. Most importantly, he was reliable, thoroughly loyal and trustworthy.

He had the foresight to bring a small trolley with him down to the beach.

After a bear hug and the manly patting of shoulders, as if they were the greatest of buddies, he asked Ollie how the journey had been.

Without waiting for a reply, he huffed and puffed along the jetty to collect the rest of the luggage.

This was not the first time Benny had flown to the island of course. He had brought Brad over months ago to sort things out and again for him to get everything ready for Ollie's arrival.

He had also transported some of the construction workers back and forth between Nadi and the island too. It seemed strange to him that within an hour or so there would only be his latest passenger on the island.

Benny helped Brad pull the laden trolley across the beach and along the path, which led to the buildings. The older man was almost out of breath when they got there and even the young pilot's brow was dripping with perspiration.

Once everything had been carried into the cabin and storage huts, Ollie handed them each a beer.

'Not for me thanks,' Benny insisted, handing it back.

'It's fully chilled,' Brad assured him. 'It's been in the refrigerator for several days.'

'I'm on duty,' he reminded them, 'and I've got to fly the plane back to Nadi shortly.'

'A good point,' Ollie accepted. 'Sorry, I didn't think.'

Brad fetched him a glass of chilled water instead and turned to Ollie. 'Do you want me to show you around the facilities and explain how everything works? You've only seen pictures of the place up to now.'

Ollie thought it a good idea. 'You'd better give me some guidance on how to survive on the island. Once you fly back to Nadi with Benny, I'm going be all by myself.'

Brad gave his boss a look of concern. 'Are you absolutely sure it's what you want?'

Ollie jogged his memory. 'It's the very reason I bought the island remember, for peace, privacy and total seclusion.'

They started with the cabin, which was built as a traditional bure, but intentionally large enough for Ollie to be comfortable. Then followed a demonstration of how everything worked on

15

the technical side, especially the water well, sewage plant and solar energy controls.

It took nearly two hours for Brad to go through everything and by the time they had finished Benny was noticeably concerned about the time.

Ollie accompanied the two of them back down to the jetty and along it to the plane.

He shook Brad's hand. 'Thanks for everything you've done. I'll let you know if I need anything in an emergency. In the meantime, have fun, because your nice long paid holiday has officially just begun.'

'I guess the next time we'll meet up,' his assistant presumed, 'will be if you ever decide to take a break from the island.'

'Which could be a matter of years,' Ollie made clear, 'but we'll have to wait and see how I get on.'

Benny had apprehensions too. 'Are you really not at all worried about getting lonely all by yourself?'

If Ollie was, he hid it well. 'Not in the slightest. Anyway, you'll be flying in provisions for me every couple of weeks and we can catch up then. It'll give me something to look forward to.'

Brad's bags were loaded on to the plane, but as he began to climb inside, he turned his head. 'One last thing. Remember to keep the satellite phone on charge just in case you need anything.'

Ollie gave him a mock salute. 'I will, but don't expect to hear from me unless I'm in dire trouble. I know you talked me into having the telephone, but I'm sure I'm never going to use the thing.'

*　　*　　*

The engine spluttered to life and accelerated. Ollie watched as it left the jetty, moving into open water and take off.

As it disappeared into the distance, he made his way across the sand to the path.

Either he was going to love it here, or he had just made the biggest mistake of his life. He had intentionally kept quiet about any last-minute doubts he might have, following instead the advice of Confucius, the ancient Chinese philosopher: *'Silence is a true friend who never betrays.'*

4

Emma could hardly believe it. No sooner had she landed at Melbourne airport and switched her mobile over from flight mode, than a message came through from her agent.

'Squeezed in one more job,' the text read. 'Good money, but in Sydney, so book flight. Suggest stay there at Park Hyatt Hotel for 3 nights. Further info to follow. Sarah.'

She had added her usual two kisses.

Before Emma had time to utter the first appropriate expletive to come to mind, another text arrived.

'PS Don't forget. Change onward flight to Fiji's Nadi, so from Sydney rather than Melbourne.' There were no kisses this time, just a smiley emoji.

Emma felt extremely annoyed. Sarah might be smiling, but her own facial expression was decidedly a scowl. At least her passport and incoming passenger card check, followed by the immigration procedure in Terminal 2 were reasonably speedy. The bag claim on the other hand took far too long.

She was quite surprised when her bags finally appeared on the carousel. Being almost the last to make their appearance, she had by then fully convinced herself they had gone missing.

As she hauled them off the belt, she blamed them for keeping her waiting.

Although she was not carrying any prohibited goods, she quite expected one of the border force's dogs, in their little on-duty uniforms, to start sniffing around her. As it was, she was completely ignored and made her way through the exit to the taxi rank directly outside.

The journey to her hotel took about half an hour and the first thing she did was to alter her reservation. As she had booked a couple of nights at the Park Hyatt, Melbourne, it was reasonably easy to make it one night there and three in their Sydney equivalent. A very obliging middle-aged concierge also helped her change her flights.

Jetlagged and exhausted, she ordered a light chicken salad and a bottle of Prosecco from room service. She only managed a few small bites and one glass of wine, before crashing onto the bed.

Despite the possible misalignment of her internal body clock, she fell asleep immediately.

Had it not been for the wake-up call she would have missed her flight to Sydney.

As it was, after the taxi ride to the airport, checking in her luggage and clearing security, she boarded the plane with only minutes to spare.

With a flight time of just an hour and a half, better behaved luggage and the short transfer to Sydney's Park Hyatt, the whole journey was relatively painless.

The hotel was in an excellent location, between the Opera House and Sydney Harbour Bridge. The splendid view from her balcony was of the former, with its iconic gleaming white sail-shaped shells of a roof. According to the information sheet by the bed, a few locals still referred to it by its nickname of 'a bowl of oranges.' This was because the designer was said to have had a light bulb moment, when peeling the skin from the citrus fruit.

Having had hardly any time at all in her Melbourne hotel, she was able to at least enjoy the luxury of this one. The fittings, carpets and designer lighting could not be faulted. The personal butler was an opulence she was not used to, but best of all was the pampering she received in the hotel's spa.

After taking advantage of some wonderfully hedonistic beauty and body treatments, she relaxed away some of her jetlag in the steam room and sauna, before cooling in the pool. Whilst doing so, she excitedly thought about her forthcoming holiday in Fiji, looking forward to everything the travel firm had promised.

Back in her room she entered the complimentary wi-fi code into her smartphone. There was an email from her agent this time, rather than a text, giving brief details of the photoshoot and what she should take with her.

The call-time was scheduled for 11am the next morning, aboard a yacht in Sydney Harbour. She was instructed to take a taxi to the meeting point at King Street Wharf, Darling Harbour, which was near to Sydney's city centre. The creative director from the advertising agency would be looking out for her. It added that King Street Wharf was Sydney's best waterfront restaurant precinct, where she had been invited to dine after the shoot.

She quickly got everything ready for the morning. Not having expected to be working on holiday, she had left her full modelling makeup kit and dressing robe back home but had the basics. She also knew a makeup artist would be there. The message added that a bikini in her size would be provided if needed, suggesting it was more likely to be a nude photoshoot. Even so, from her suitcase she selected a few different undies and bras. For travelling there, she chose her denim jacket and jeans, a white blouse and a pair of black shoes.

With this sorted, she ate in the Dining Room, the Park Hyatt's rather obviously named but pleasant restaurant, which also overlooked the harbour. The food was good, but she was still too tired to really appreciate it.

Pleased to be back in bed, sleep again came easily.

As instructed, the hotel concierge had booked her taxi at a time to ensure she arrived at least fifteen minutes early at King Street Wharf. She had never been late for a photoshoot, as being so was unforgivable in her profession.

Emma was spotted straight away by the redhead awaiting her, who held the model's comp card in her hand. This mini portfolio-come-business-card had a close-up headshot on the front and some smaller photos on the back. Her statistics and agent contact details were also listed.

'Hi! You must be Emma,' the woman said. 'It's so good to finally meet you.'

As expected, the friendly routine of a hug, along with kisses on the cheeks followed.

'My name's Donna darling,' the Australian informed her. 'I'm the creative director. There's coffee onboard, but we can have a cup over there first if you prefer.' She pointed to the restaurant opposite.

Emma was trying to work out if *Darling* was Donna's surname or used as just a term of endearment. 'Yes, that would be nice,' she agreed.

They crossed the road and sat down at an empty table, which a waiter had ready for them.

After ordering, Donna removed her dark tortoise designer sunglasses, revealing a nice pair of honey brown eyes. It was a cloudy morning anyway. 'So, how was your journey?' she asked, partly for small talk, but also out of politeness.

'Fine thanks,' Emma told her. 'I was coming to Australia anyway.'

Donna seemed pleased for her. 'What fun! You'll love it here. There's so much to see and do. What have you got planned?'

It was obvious Emma had been misunderstood. 'I've nothing arranged at all, especially if you mean sightseeing. I'm only here today and tomorrow and then I fly on to Fiji.'

Donna misconstrued the purpose of her trip again. 'For another photoshoot?'

Emma put her right. 'Not at all. I'm off to a lush island resort, for a luxurious holiday.'

'Lucky you,' her new acquaintance enthused. 'I wish it were me going. It sounds fun. Still, at least we were able to book you for today's shoot on the way there. It's fortunate you were travelling via Sydney.'

Emma was tempted to reel off the story of her agent's greed for commission, which had disrupted her original travel plans, but thought it unprofessional to make such a disclosure.

'Tell me,' she asked instead, 'what's happening today? My agent only gave me brief instructions.'

Donna seemed surprised she had not been told what sort of shoot it was. 'It's mainly for a client's mag and poster campaign. They're delighted we managed to get you for it.'

She pointed to the boat which she had been standing next to when Emma first arrived. 'We're working aboard the Riviera sports yacht. It's going to be the classic Australian setting of Sydney Harbour, with the Opera House in the background.'

Emma thought it sounded exactly like the view from her hotel room, but perhaps from a different angle. 'How will I be posing?'

The reply she got was unexpected. 'You must promise not laugh when I tell you, for it might seem rather silly at first, but it's going to be a lot of fun. That much I can promise you.'

There was a prolonged pause. It reminded Emma of the annoying drawn-out wait they give audiences when announcing winners on the 'Strictly' or 'Britain's Got Talent' TV shows.

'So?' she was finally forced to ask.

'Well …' Donna seemed to be choosing her words rather carefully. 'You'll be nude, getting an all-over tan on a sunbed at the front of the yacht. Then, Dan, the good-looking male model, who plays your boyfriend, will come up behind you. Suddenly and without warning he'll …' She paused again.

'He'll do what?' Emma was getting anxious to know.

Donna giggled. 'He will pour a bucket of water over your head.'

Emma wondered if she had heard the creative director correctly. 'A bucket of water? Over my head? Why would he do that?'

'It's supposed to be a prank,' Donna maintained. 'A practical joke on his part. A bit of harmless love-play.'

Their coffees arrived. Emma could still not grasp the point of what was being described, but she took a sip before continuing. 'Sorry. I am trying to get this clear in my head. You mean the shots will be of me lying there, soaked to the skin, my hair dripping wet?'

'Absolutely,' Donna confirmed excitedly, 'with Dan standing over you, laughing his head off. The cleverest thing is the advertising slogan, which will be added in big bold lettering. You're going to adore it, for it's going to read: *Don't pour cold water on the one you love.*'

Emma forced a smile. It seemed rude not to. 'And what's the product?'

'A snazzy brand-new sports car,' Donna enthused. She knew explaining this would make more sense, as most car ads seem to steer clear of saying anything about the vehicle itself. 'The car's brand, model and logo will appear at the bottom of the picture,' she continued, 'but we are deliberately not using an image of the car. We are aiming instead to portray the sort of person we think will buy it. In this case it's Dan, the confident, stylish, well-off man with bags of pride. He's seen in this awesome location, with all his desirable things around him, such as the super yacht and —'

'A woman like me,' Emma cut in. 'Toys for the boys in other words.'

Donna looked rather uncomfortable. 'Perhaps, but it's precisely why we chose you, the desirable sexy young lady, who's up for fun as well as romance.'

Emma put her at ease. 'Don't worry, I'm not an ardent feminist and I don't have a problem with it, providing my agent has negotiated a good fee. The nudity isn't an issue either, but won't it limit which mags and poster sites can carry the campaign?'

'Not at all,' Donna anticipated. 'Shots will be taken at discreet angles, similar to the nude perfume ads I know you've done.'

Emma understood well enough. She had recently posed for a memorable black and white underwater shot for a Mauritius holiday resort's campaign. Although she was completely naked, it had been taken from the side, her nipples later discretely airbrushed out to make it acceptable for an upmarket travel magazine.

'Whilst suggesting total nudity,' Donna went on, 'no naughty bits will actually be shown.'

'Naughty bits?' Emma questioned mirthfully. 'There's nothing naughty about my bits. It's why I get so much work. They're highly appreciated and not just by the male gaze.'

Donna blushed. 'Our clients would certainly agree, from their reaction to the shots we showed them of you. We will probably end up using just a headshot, or down to the top of your boobs, but need to make sure there's no bikini in the way. It will give us more options.'

Emma cast a thought about her male co-model. 'What about Dan? Is he going to be nude too, for the same reason?

'I'm afraid not,' she apologised, as if Emma might really care. 'He'll be wearing a pair of fashionable beach shorts. If not, his dangly bits will be seen right behind your head. It's an ad for a car remember, not a porno film promotion.'

'Just as well,' Emma let her know. 'I never do porn.'

When they went onboard the yacht, Emma was introduced to her pretend boyfriend. It was good casting, as he epitomised everything Donna had said he was meant to. Aged in his early twenties, he was unquestionably handsome. Sharp featured, with short light brown hair, his tanned face boasted electric blue eyes and chiselled cheekbones. His athletic shoulders and arms topped a toned tanned torso.

Emma was more than impressed with this straight-from-the-gym hunk, clad in just miniscule black swim briefs.

Unfortunately, any fleeting dream she might have had of a possible after work encounter was dashed. The moment he spoke, his style of speech left no doubt at all about his sexual orientation.

Donna introduced her to the captain of the yacht, then to Pete, the middle-aged photographer, plus his assistant, who was clutching a diffuser. Emma was well used to this piece of equipment which was intended to soften the light from the sun and prevent harsh shadows. For the time being it might just as well have been packed away, for the sun had disappeared, leaving them all standing in a cloudy cool temperature.

The weather decided then to gift them some drizzle. Like a tribal ritual of some kind, everyone simultaneously held out their hands, palms up, to gauge whether it really was raining or not.

Accepting the inevitable, they hurried below deck to shelter.

At least Emma finally met Sandra, the makeup artist, as well as a young man called Noah, who was handing out coffees and snacks. Hearing his name, Emma asked him in fun if the boat was a downsized version of his Ark.

From the puzzled look he gave her by way of reply, she regretted mentioning it.

By the time Sandra had applied Emma's makeup and enhanced her fake tan with a waterproof body bronzer, the sun deemed to make another appearance.

Soon there was not a cloud in the sky and with the yacht already in position the scene was set on the front deck.

Emma sat upright on a sun lounger, with Dan behind her. A small tourist boat passed close by and several of its passengers, seeing her there with nothing on, clapped and cheered. Pleased at having far more of their attention than even the Opera House, Emma gave them a friendly wave and blew pretend kisses. At least it would give them something to talk about later she figured.

Donna briefed her two models on their pose, facial expressions and gestures.

Pete checked the three cameras, two of which were hanging from his neck, the other being on a tripod. He also moved around, working out the best angles to shoot from, without risking falling overboard.

It took no less than nine attempts to get everything right. Although Emma had no idea why, considering she was supposed to be wet, Donna insisted she was dried off between each one and the bucket refilled every time.

Emma was used to long and often tedious photoshoots, but never in all her career had so much water been poured over her.

There was relief all round when they finally got to the restaurant opposite the yacht to eat and drink.

The place was full, with a throbbing atmosphere and deafeningly loud music, just as Emma liked it. They raised their glasses of Prosecco to a successful campaign, shouting out the slogan, 'Don't pour cold water on the one you love.'

Emma decided it warranted another toast. Getting to her feet, she yelled even louder, 'And here's to my holiday in Fiji, where all I'm going to do is non-stop PARTY!'

5

Ollie woke up early. There was no reason to, for he had all the time in the world, but he wanted to see the sunrise.

It was warm already. In fact, it had remained so all night, so he just put on a pair of shorts and sandals and made his way along the path that led to the beach. As he did so he took several deep breaths, savouring the purity of the air. It was so fresh. All he could smell was nature at its best.

There were none of the nasty man-made fumes and pollutants which he had grown accustomed to in London.

Most noticeably absent was all the noise of the city. Only in his memory now could he hear the constant rumble of heavily congested traffic. In an endless rush hour, the cars were always bumper to bumper in gridlock, zooming far too fast when the lights changed, their brakes screeching to a halt as they switched again.

How he had hated the impatient and continuous frantic horns of road-raged drivers and the boom, boom, boom of blaring tuneless music from wound-down windows.

He certainly did not miss the whizz and roar of motorbikes, their would-be stunt riders determined to jump the lights, or the hammering of roadwork pneumatic drills.

Gone were the car and intruder alarms, beeping and buzzing, along with aeroplanes humming and droning overhead, their jet engines growling as they climbed and whining on descent.

Non-existent too was the banging, crashing and clattering from construction sites and the rowdy chants of raucous football fans, making their way to the match.

No longer thank God had he to put up with innocent, but exceedingly annoying babies, crying and squealing ear-piercingly, hungry for their mother's precious life-sustaining milk.

Here, in contrast, there was only silence, punctuated now and again by the pleasant sound of birdsong. In the distance he could make out the tranquil acoustics of gentle waves, caressing the soft and powdery white sand of the beach.

He hurried on and was just in time to witness the beauty of the sun as it rose from its slumber.

As the majestic solar disc appeared on the horizon, he was reminded of the Egyptian goddess Nuit, who was believed to swallow the sun in the evening and give birth to it at dawn. In the religion of *Thelema*, which he had taken an interest in, she was the *'Queen of Infinite Space,' 'Our Lady of the Stars'* and *'Lady of the Starry Heaven.'*

For him, this glorious sunrise, with its hues of orange and yellow, blended with natural hints of pink, heralded an exciting new beginning. It announced the glorious start of a serene and untroubled life. By blocking out all the noise of his old world, he hoped instead to hear that of the inner voice, which only speaks in silence.

*   *   *

With some reluctance he left the beach, to hurry back to the cabin.

Halfway he suddenly stopped. Why was he rushing? What was the haste? His stomach rumbled, wanting some breakfast, but it would have to be patient. From now on he intended to take his time.

Slowing his pace, he took in the flora around him. In particular, he loved the coconut palms. His tropical island could not be paradise without them.

Moving closely to the swollen base of one, he placed his hand against its slender, ringed light greyish-brown trunk, palm to palm, man to tree.

Looking up, he admired its glorious crown of giant green feather-shaped leaves. He could see the light-yellow female flowers and the more numerous but smaller male ones. Best of all he admired the clever way the tree curved to get more light, leaning towards the sea, where it could closely drop its seed, the milk-filled coconuts.

As he continued again along the path, he remembered that Brad had thoughtfully left him a small book about Fijian flora and fauna. He decided to use the rest of the day to explore his new uninhabited kingdom.

After giving into his hunger and fulfilling its needs, Ollie set off to stake out what he had spent so much money on. He made sure to take with him some sunscreen, along with water to quench his thirst and a beach towel to recline on.

The illustrations in the book made it reasonably easy to identify most of the flora which was growing around him.

He spotted several sorts of tropical pines, umbrella trees and the Indian Beech, with its aromatic flowers. There were some vividly coloured orchids and he came across the Mallotus Tiliifolius, with its hairy leaves and spiny fruit. Close by was the Tahitian Gardenia, an evergreen shrub with glossy green leaves and fragrant creamy white flowers.

All this lush tropical foliage, which covered parts of the island, did limit where he could walk, especially as he was wearing flip-flops. He made a mental note to possibly consider sturdier shoes the next time he explored.

The book listed no fewer than 76 land and sea birds, which were to be found on some of the islands and he considered himself fortunate to see a couple of very colourful parrots. There was also the Kula, the name derived from its green and red feathers, along with the darker and smaller honeyeaters.

Surprisingly, he came across a rather unwelcoming area of mangrove trees, which apparently protected that part of the coastline. The smelly, rotten egg-like odour and muddy, swampy conditions were enough to prevent him from venturing into the mini waterlogged forest.

In complete contrast, he was elated to discover two more beautiful white sand beaches. On the second of these he unrolled his towel, kicked off his flimsy sandals and sat down. Thinking it wise to apply some sunscreen, he smoothed the lotion over his face, arms and chest.

Although knowing he was the only person on the island, he still automatically glanced around to double check, before sliding off his beach shorts.

*   *   *

He had first discovered naturism on the beaches of Spain's Canary Islands, where complete nudity was common. Fuerteventura and parts of Lanzarote attracted a high number of devotees, but his favourite was Gran Canaria. He had stayed at all three naturist resorts there, namely the excellent Petite Hotel Natura and Artika Natura, along with the bungalows of Magnolias Natura.

He had also holidayed at a lovely naturist resort in Spain's sunny Andalucía, called Costa Natura. Although on the coast, with its own beach, it was similar in style to the iconic white mountain villages.

He would always remember the friendliness of the staff and guests and the wonderful time he had at all of these places. There were similar resorts which offered plenty of opportunities for an all-over tan in a growing number of countries throughout the world.

Sadly, this was not the case in Fiji, public nudity being heavily frowned upon and illegal. He considered this island to be an exception, however. After all, he was not in public. He was on his own island, all by himself, with no one at all to be offended.

After applying more lotion, he lay back in the sun and closed his eyes. By freeing his body of clothes, he found it liberated his mind and spirit. Any worries or concerns were quickly forgotten in the sheer joy of being at one with nature.

He scooped a little fine warm sand into each hand and then parting his fingers let it trickle slowly back onto the surface. As he did so, his ears could hardly miss the 'grrri-grrri, heech-heech' calls of the black-naped terns.

Only half opening his eyes, he watched in privileged

wonder as the long-winged, snow-white birds glided and dipped, picking their prey from just below the surface of the tranquil blue sea. They were noisy, but it was a sound he could accept.

His eyelids fell again, his mind swimming dreamily in peaceful tranquillity. All was as he had hoped and imagined it would be. Inner silence was attainable.

His spirit shone as bright as the sun.

Sleep must have crept upon him cunningly, for he was unaware of its presence, at least until he awoke.

He had no idea how prolonged his slumber had been. It might have been barely a minute, or more likely many, but was of no consequence. All he felt was happiness.

Slowly he got to his feet, then brushing the sand from them, slipped on his flip-flops. Gathering up his other things, but not bothering to dress, he began to make his way back. Fortunately, he had a good sense of direction, because it was not the same track as he had originally taken.

It proved to be a quicker route and although the beach was not as near to the cabin as the one with the seaplane jetty, it was easily reachable. With a third beach, which he had also discovered earlier, he was going to be spoilt for choice. They were all his, to enjoy as only he wanted.

Thinking it a nice idea to name them, he settled on *Tern Bay* for the one he was returning from, in honour of the birds he had watched. The choice of a suitable title for the nearest beach to the cabin was even easier. It had to be *Benny's Beach*, in recognition of the seaplane pilot, who would regularly be bringing him supplies. He could not remember precisely where the third beach was, so for now he called it *Distant Sands.*

Oliver slept well that night, after having cooked himself a nice fish dinner. He had admittedly cheated a little, the fish coming from the refrigerator rather than freshly from the sea. The idea of catching them alive by hook or net did not appeal. Their fortnightly arrival by air with the other provisions suited him much better.

It also gave him more time to meditate, which was something he intended to do often. Having once tried Transcendental Meditation, or TM for short, he much preferred to detach his mind from thoughts without the use of a repetitive mantra.

Ollie referred to the system he had developed instead as *Hypnotic Meditation.* It was a combination of self-hypnosis and meditation techniques, which included visualisation and breath control.

With his eyes closed, he would firstly concentrate on a separate part of his body at a time, starting with his feet and finishing with his head. Breathing deeply, he would tell himself to relax on each exhalation, then counting down from five to zero he entered a trance-like state. This was deepened by visualising an old spiral staircase, comprised of ten steps. As he floated down from the top to the bottom, mentally thinking the number of each step, the feeling of serenity would grow deeper and deeper. From there, with practice, it was only a short journey to stillness of the mind.

Francis Bacon, the philosopher and statesman once said: *'Silence is the sleep that nourishes wisdom.'* To Ollie, silence was becoming the sweetest sound of all.

6

Ollie quickly established a daily routine, always rising early to watch the sunrise from Benny's beach.

Sometimes he would meditate there, or wait until he was back at the cabin, but the practice was never missed. Treasuring these moments so much, he decided to add a midday meditation and another in the evening, after the sun had gone down.

It was the sound of a seaplane, accelerating for take-off, which rudely disturbed his middle of the day session at the cabin.

Having stilled his mind, he was annoyed at being cheated back to consciousness. He was also baffled, for he had not heard a plane arrive and it was days before Benny was due.

Cautiously, he slipped on a pair of shorts and headed for the landing jetty. He knew the plane would by now be well out of sight but needed to find out why it had landed in the first place.

He could hardly believe his eyes. Standing on the beach end of the short jetty was a stunningly attractive woman. She had long blond hair and wore a revealing short pink dress. Beside her were two bags, one a wheelie carry-on, the other an oversized suitcase.

Before he could say anything, she began to wave at him.

'Hello!' she called excitedly, 'I've arrived!'

Ollie was speechless. It was as if the young lady had been expecting him.

She seemed impatient. 'I've been waiting for you to take me and my luggage to the resort.'

He was even more lost for words.

She pointed to the trolley, which Brad had used when he was leaving with Benny. 'I can see your trailer over there.'

All he could do was stare at it, then at her bags and then at her again.

'Who are you?' he finally managed to ask.

'Emma Eve,' she told him. 'Reception will have my name down on today's list of arrivals.'

He gasped in disbelief. 'Arrivals? How many more are coming?'

She shrugged her satin smooth shoulders. 'I've no idea, but I was led to believe the resort can accommodate up to twelve. Some are probably here already.'

'There's not a single one,' he assured her.

Emma was miffed to hear this, as it suggested they were all couples. 'Am I the only unattached female?'

Ollie tried putting it another way. 'There is no one else here at all.'

'I must be the first then,' she guessed, trying to make sense of what he was saying. 'The rest will still be on their way.'

'On their way?' He thought she was talking nonsense. 'I think you had better explain what you're doing here.'

Emma supposed the person questioning her must be a new employee at the resort. If so, he was decidedly in need of some basic training in customer care. She made a mental note to mention it to the manager in due course. 'I'm here to soak up the sun, to enjoy the hospitality and most of all to party.'

The last word she said sent a shiver down Ollie's spine. Parties were the last thing he was having on his island.

He closed his eyes and took a few deep breaths to calm himself. 'How did you get here?'

'By plane from Nadi of course,' she thought obvious. 'It was much too far to swim.'

Her witticism was not appreciated. He had heard the plane leave anyway and so knew she had not come by boat. Why would Benny, or anyone else at First Charter Aviation, have brought her here? They were fully aware of this being his island, which he wanted solely for himself.

'What kind of plane was it?' he asked, hoping for some sort of clue.

'A small one,' Emma described.

He tried not to laugh at such a ludicrous statement. 'I hardly thought it would be an Airbus A380, the largest passenger plane on Earth.'

'No,' she recalled. 'It was definitely much smaller and could land on water.'

'Which is just as well,' he felt the need to point out, 'or you'd probably have drowned. Which company did it belong to?'

Emma knew this, for their name perfectly described her expectations of the resort. 'It was Paradise Pleasure Flights. They were a little crazy and kept making me laugh. First, they made out they had never heard of the island and then pretended to make several phone calls.' She sniggered, recalling something else they had said. 'They even told me the plane I'd be flying in was named after a furry rodent. There was no way I was going to fall for that.'

From this, Ollie could easily guess what the plane was. 'They were actually being serious. As it can take off and descend on land or sea, they called it a Beaver, after the semi aquatic animal which lives on the ground and in the water.'

She finally understood the connection but was getting restless. 'It's been nice talking, but can you take me to reception now?'

Ollie needed to get to the bottom of this. She appeared to be perfectly sane but absurdly thought she was at some island holiday resort. He had no idea why. 'I'm going to make this perfectly clear. There is no reception. There's only me and I own the island.'

A look of relief appeared on her face. 'Ah! I see. You own the resort. I'm so sorry, but I thought you were the porter.'

He could easily have been offended by such a preposterous suggestion, but it was the least of his concerns. 'Please, try and understand. This is a private island, which is solely for my own personal use. What were you expecting to find here?'

Emma knew exactly. It was everything the travel agent had described on their website. 'There's supposed to be six luxurious holiday accommodations for a start. They call them bures.'

'I am fully aware of what a bure is,' he made plain. 'It's the Fijian name for a traditional cabin, constructed of wood and straw.'

She rolled her eyes. 'As if I didn't know. I googled the word and I've even seen pictures of them.'

'You keep using the plural,' he had noticed, 'but there's only one bure, or cabin, here on the island.'

'Only one?' she queried, taken aback. 'It had better well overlook the beach and sea.'

He was about to disappoint her again. 'It doesn't.' He pointed to the path. 'It's down there and is surrounded by trees.'

Emma was getting worried. It was finally dawning on her that there was something seriously wrong. 'What about the all-inclusive amenities, the seashore dining, snorkelling and round the clock personal service?'

Ollie laughed aloud at hearing of these. 'You'll find nothing of the sort here. There's only me, my cabin and a few very basic facilities. I'm quite happy to show them to you. Why don't you come with me and we'll try and sort out what's gone wrong with your holiday arrangements?'

He headed for the path, gesturing for her to follow.

'What about my bags?' she asked apprehensively. 'We can't just leave them here. They might get stolen.'

'They'll be perfectly fine,' he promised. 'There's no one else on the island except for us. Judging by the size of your luggage, I doubt the birds are likely to fly off with them.' He certainly had no intention of lugging them up to the cabin, only to bring them down again for her imminent departure.

As he led the way he mentioned his name. 'I'm Oliver, for what it's worth, but people call me Ollie.' He noticed she was attempting to use her mobile. 'I do hope the call you're trying to make isn't important.'

She stopped walking. Holding the phone high in the air,

she slowly rotated 380 degrees. 'I don't seem to have a signal.'

'That's because there isn't one,' he clarified. 'You're on a small island, surrounded by the Pacific Ocean.'

Hearing this bothered her. 'What about roaming data?'

It was necessary for him to double her dismay. 'You can't get that either and I doubt you have any offline GPS apps installed.'

She gave him a blank look, having no idea what such apps were. 'It'll have to be wi-fi then. What's the code?'

'There isn't one,' he revealed, 'and to save you asking me why, it's because there is no wi-fi. Your so-called smartphone is completely useless here, at least when it comes to connecting to anything.'

Emma looked distraught. 'You mean I'm cut off completely from the outside world, from all my messages, social media and the rest?'

'I'm afraid so,' he broke the bad news. 'There's no broadband anywhere on the island.'

'How do you manage then?' she asked, feeling jinxed.

'Very well thank you,' he was delighted to let her know. 'I deliberately don't have internet access.' Although he had decided not to mention the satellite phone, he was fully intending to use it the moment he got the chance.

Emma was relieved when they came to the cabin. It looked nothing at all like the luxury accommodation which had been pictured by Over C Travel, but at least it was habitation of a sort.

Ollie pointed to the wooden bench outside the door. 'You sit there. I'll get us a drink in a moment, but first I need to quickly check something.'

Disappearing into one of the small huts, he hoped she would assume he had need of the toilet. It was actually where the electrics where housed and the satellite phone kept, his plan being to call Benny and get him to come and take her off the island as soon as possible.

Unfortunately, the phone turned out to be as dead as a doornail. He remembered Brad telling him it was necessary to be outside to connect via a satellite, but that was not the problem. The phone would not even turn on. As it appeared to be correctly attached to the power supply, he could only assume there was something wrong with it. He very rarely swore, but justified himself doing so now, albeit beneath his breath.

'So, what would you like to drink?' he asked her, emerging from the hut.

Emma fancied a nice cool glass of her favourite sparkling wine. It was what she had been expecting as a welcome drink when she first landed on the island. 'A Prosecco would be good.'

Ollie apologised. 'I'm sure it would, but I don't have any. How about a beer? There's Fiji Gold, or Vonu lager.'

Neither of the names meant anything to her, but at least it was alcohol. 'I really don't mind, as long as it's cold.'

He strolled towards the cabin. 'At last. Something I do have on the island.'

Returning a couple of minutes later, his hands clutched an open bottle of each. 'Take your pick.'

She chose the Gold, simply because it included the name Fiji. It tasted good, at least for a beer.

As she went to take a second sip, she noticed the look of expectant curiosity on his face. It was obviously time for her to explain how she came to be on the island.

Starting with a description of the website, she went through what had happened in quite some detail. 'Not for one minute did I suspect there might be a problem,' she tried to convince him.

Ollie took a long deep audible breath. This time it was not to compose himself, but in recognition of the dreadful mess she had got herself into.

'I don't want to sound patronising,' he assured her, 'but I do sympathise completely with the position you're in. There are some very nasty conmen around and you've been well and truly scammed. Here's how they got away with it. You said it was the name of the company which caught your eye, thinking *overCtravel.org* was a clever play on words. Perhaps so, but domains ending in '*.org*' are rarely used for online shopping, or holidays. They are more for non-profit making organisations, such as charities, or those which provide the public with free information. Nearly half of all for-profit businesses use '*.com*' in fact. Can you recall if the website address started with '*https://*' or not, as it indicates encryption is in place to protect your personal details? A padlock next to it should have confirmed this too, although scammers can buy or forge the symbol.'

She had not realised any of this was important at the time. 'I can't remember, but the website did display the ABTA and ATOL logos. I know the former stands for the Association of British Travel Agents and the other one is something to do with airlines.'

'It's the Air Travel Organiser's Licence,' he verified. 'They both cover different types of package holidays, but you booked the accommodation separately anyway. Seven out of ten people say they are more likely to use sites with well-known financial protection schemes like those, but it doesn't mean the site has a genuine right to show them. To be sure you would need to verify their membership. Did the website give the company's contact details, terms and conditions and privacy policy?'

Her embarrassment showed. 'It sounds rather silly now, but at the time I was quite pleased it didn't. It kept things simpler, without lots of wording for me to wade through. There were some excellent up to date reviews of the company and the resort though. Every single one said similar nice things.'

'Probably because they were all written by the same person,' he considered.

Such a thing had never occurred to her. 'Gosh! Do you think so?'

'It's most likely,' he believed. 'Didn't the eight-week luxury holiday being so cheap and without a single supplement make you suspicious?'

'Thinking about it now, I realise it should have,' she feared. 'The whole thing sounded wonderful. It was almost too good to be true.'

'Sadly, that's exactly what it has turned out to be,' he commiserated. 'Too good to be true.'

He had finished his beer. 'Fancy another one?'

Her thoughts were understandably elsewhere, so he went to fetch them anyway.

Whilst doing so, he had come up with something else he wanted to ask. 'What about their recommendation of booking the flights directly with an airline, rather than through their company?'

He handed her a bottle of Vonu lager, so she could try that one too.

Emma gestured a thank you, despite her gloom. 'They said it would give me more choice.'

'It was actually to avoid raising suspicion,' he hinted, 'which you would certainly have had, if you'd paid them for the plane tickets, which didn't then turn up.'

'I felt under so much pressure,' she recalled, 'with the site saying there were nearly a hundred other people looking at the same dates. I didn't want to lose the holiday.'

Ollie could understand. 'A surprising number of legitimate companies use the same sort of fear tactics to close a deal. Your biggest mistake of all was falling for the offer of a big discount if you paid by direct bank transfer. It was virtually the same as handing over cash, which has none of the safeguards credit cards provide. Your money would be almost impossible to trace, as you sent it directly to a Mr. Acharya, the company's so-called managing director. You were not to know, but it's a very common surname in India. Quite ironically, it's also a Sanskrit word meaning *teacher*.'

'Well, I've certainly learnt my lesson,' she conceded, her face blushing.

'Don't be too hard on yourself,' he insisted. 'Scammers like this are very cleaver. I'm surprised you got verification in the post, even if it was fake. In order to minimise attention to their fraudulent scheme, they're probably selling fake holidays to lots of different islands, rather than just one. I only hope no one else ends up here. Can you remember the name of the island they said you were going to?'

She passed him the letter of confirmation, which she had

been intending to hand to reception.

Being so brief, it only took a few seconds for him to read through it. 'I've no idea how they got hold of the name of the place. It's only been called this since I bought it. In English, *Yanuyana Vakanomodi* means *Island of Silence.*

Hearing this was just about the last straw for Emma. 'So much for all the noisy parties I was looking forward to then.'

Ollie made no comment. On this occasion he thought Euripides, the great Athenian poet and playwright, had the right idea: *'Silence is true wisdom's best reply.'*

7

When they had finished their drinks, Ollie showed Emma the inside of the cabin.

It was modestly furnished, but sufficient for his needs. Open planned, with no interior dividing walls, there was a small kitchen and dining area nearest to the door, a sofa and comfortable armchair on a matted area at the centre and, as she spotted immediately, just one bed at the far end.

Noticing the slightly concerned expression on her face, he reassured her. 'Don't worry. If we can't get you off the island by tonight you can sleep there. I'll use the hammock outside.'

Despite her disappointment at not being able to enjoy the holiday she had expected, she managed a smile. 'Let's hope it won't come to it. I don't want to put you to any trouble.'

They went outside again. She had probably spotted the hammock earlier, slung between two trees, but it had been of no consequence then. 'Are you going to be warm enough?'

He dismissed her concern. 'I'll be fine. The temperature's not going to fall much and it's unlikely to rain. There's always the sofa anyway. Let me show you the other world-class facilities on offer.'

She pointed to the hut he had been in earlier. 'Is it alright if I pop in there first? I'm dying for a wee.'

'I'd rather you didn't,' he teased.

'But I'm desperate,' she pleaded. 'I haven't been near a toilet since I left Nadi.'

'Perhaps not,' he explained, 'but you don't want to do it in there. It houses the electrics, which link up to the solar panels over there, along with a stand-by generator.'

He drew her attention to an even smaller outbuilding further along. 'The toilet's in there and it's connected to a small sewage treatment plant.'

'I'm only going to have a pee,' she stressed, heading off in that direction.

Her doing so gave him the opportunity to check the satellite phone more carefully.

It was still completely dead. He fiddled with the charging lead, hoping it might just be a loose connection, but without success. He unplugged it and pushed the on/off switch several times. Tapping it on the bench was a waste of time too.

Shaking his head in disbelief, he knew it meant he was stuck with his unexpected guest for several days.

He went outside, closing the door behind him.

'At least you have a washbasin,' she had discovered, shaking the water from her hands. She saw a towel drying on the line, which was strung between two trees. 'What about a shower?'

'Not just now thank you,' he wisecracked, 'I had one earlier.'

She realised he was pulling her leg. 'I was asking if you had one.'

'It's this way,' he revealed, leading her to some bushes.

In between them was a suspended shower head. 'My fresh water comes from a natural coral filtered well, but the shower's fed from a desalination plant.'

He turned on the tap.

She held the palm of her hand under the running water and waited a moment. 'Does it get any warmer?'

'It can be heated,' he confirmed, turning it off, 'but I don't usually bother. It's more refreshing at this temperature.'

She was more used to having hot water to wash in. 'If I'm still here in the morning I'll give it a go and let you know.'

With the satellite phone not working, Ollie realised she had no idea of the likely duration of her stay. He also felt she was rather taking things for granted. 'We're on a desert island in the middle of the Pacific Ocean don't forget. We are fortunate to have any water at all, other than seawater. There are so many places in the world where it's a scarcity to have any, fresh or desalinated.'

'Are you talking about anywhere in particular,' she asked inquisitively.

He tried to come up with somewhere to strengthen the point he was making. 'Let's take Namibia for example.'

She was aware of it being a country somewhere in Africa, but not its precise location.

'Where's that?'

With his forefinger, he drew an imaginary shape of the continent in the air. 'You've got South Africa down here and Namibia's above it, with Angola to its north, then Botswana and Zimbabwe to the east. Being so dry there, the Himba women never wash. They instead take a smoke bath every morning, squatting over hot coals and herbs.'

Emma pictured the scene. 'Ooh! Aren't the sparks a bit dodgy?'

'Most likely,' he agreed, 'but I'm sure they're careful to avoid them. Such a bath apparently opens the pores of the skin, cleansing and purifying it. Afterwards, they cover themselves in a red paste, made of butter, fat and red ochre, which protects them from biting insects and the sun.'

She was quite sure it was not a treatment which had been on offer at the spa in Sydney's Park Hyatt Hotel. If it was, she was pleased to have missed it. 'I bet it repels the men as well.'

'Not at all,' he affirmed. 'Sometimes it's scented with aromatic resin to make the women smell nice. They think the colour makes them look even more beautiful.'

'If that's the case,' she pretended, 'I'd better try and get hold of some.'

He was tempted to compliment her, by saying she was beautiful enough already, but thought she might question his motives.

Instead, he decided to tell her how long she was likely to be stuck on the island. 'The construction behind us is my main store, where all the provisions are kept. A pilot by the name of Benny flies in the things I need and I'm afraid there's no way of getting you off the island until he's next due.'

'And when's that likely to be?' she asked with slight concern.

'In several days' time,' he told her.

'Several days?' she questioned back. 'Can't you get hold of him before then?'

'I'm afraid not,' he admitted, shaking his head. 'I've got no way of contacting anyone.'

She combed her fingers through her hair, considering her

dilemma. Whilst the island was nothing at all like she had been expecting, Ollie seemed pleasant enough. He also appeared to be the type who would look after her, rather than do her any harm. It was the thought of being completely cut off from the outside world which perturbed her the most. 'Let's hope one of us doesn't have an accident or become ill.'

'We'll be fine,' he felt sure. 'Anyway, I've got a small basic first aid kit if it's any comfort.'

She tried to decide whether his last comment was a further attempt to humour her or not. 'What about food and drink? Is there enough for me as well?'

'Plenty,' he emphasised. He was discreetly only concerned about the possibility of her spoiling his daily routine of watching the sunrise, several meditations and silence. 'We had better get your cases from the beach.'

Emma had completely forgotten about them. 'Thanks for reminding me. I suppose I might as well try and make the best of it. I'll change into something else before dinner.'

'Wear what you feel most comfortable in,' he advised. 'Casual's the dress code here.'

For fear of alarming her unduly, he had already decided it was best for him to keep his shorts on for now. There was plenty of time for her to find out about his love of naturism.

With the cases collected and now at the cabin, Ollie cooked while she unpacked. Although she did not appear to have any reservation about changing her dress with him there, he politely kept his eyes averted.

'Inside or out,' he asked her. 'Where would you prefer to eat?'

'Outside would be nice,' she considered.'

'Great. I'll set the table.' As an afterthought he added, 'Red or white?'

She laughed. 'Are you discussing those beautiful women in Namibia again?'

'No,' he said with a grin. 'I was asking what sort of wine you preferred. I suggest white with the fish and red with the dessert.'

As they had dinner, she asked him why he had bought the island.

After telling her a little about his business background, he decided to share with her the real reason for his determined change of lifestyle.

She was fascinated to learn of his out-of-body experience and how it had changed his beliefs. As spirituality, occultism and religious thought were not things she was at all familiar with, she made him promise to tell her more about them during her few days on the island.

He in turn asked about her own background and career and was not really surprised by her reply. Although he did not say so, he could hardly see how a woman as beautiful as her could be anything but a model.

Emma kept quiet about the nude photoshoots she sometimes did. She feared someone who had admitted to once considering solitude in a Roman Catholic monastery might be too prudish for such a confession.

Thinking it best to move their conversation away from her type of work, she instead returned to the reason he had given for buying the island. 'Was it really necessary for you to go to such an extreme, to so much trouble and incredible expense, just to find silence?'

'Not entirely,' he admitted. 'There was a Swiss-American psychiatrist by the name of Elisabeth Kubler-Ross. She was a pioneer in near-death studies and wrote the international best seller, *On Death and Dying.*'

'You talk about her in the past tense,' Emma noticed.

'That's because she died in 2004,' he conveyed. 'One of the things she said was: *'There is no need to go to India or anywhere else to find peace. You will find that deep place of silence right in your room, your garden or even your bathtub.'* So many spiritual teachers have come to the same conclusion over the centuries and they're right. It is possible to find peace and silence anywhere, providing you search within and use the right techniques for sustaining it. I could have remained in London and found it there, but here I've the bonus of round the clock tranquillity.'

She could understand this much, but not why he had to have silence. 'It's the very thing I try to avoid. Silence can scare me. I've always been surrounded by noise and when it stops my mind tells me there's something wrong. I feel alone and anxious. It's like I imagine death will be.'

Ollie knew only too well that lots of people felt the same way as her. 'Having been bombarded by noise for so long, the only way for you to discover the joy and importance of silence is by working on your subconscious mind.' He tried to put it as simply as possible. 'I'm no expert on how the brain works, but there are basically three essential parts of the mind. The deepest is the unconscious, the bit which automatically controls all the vital functions of the body, such as our breathing, heart rate and so on. Then we have the subconscious mind, which is like a permanent library of all the experiences we've ever had, along with all our habits and beliefs. It's similar to a computer hard drive and being pre-programmed to ensure we follow specific routines, is tremendously powerful in controlling what we do. At the outer level is the conscious mind. This is the thinking, analysing, judging part, where our present awareness is. It stops any suggestion we don't like, or anything contrary to our present beliefs, from entering our subconscious mind. This internal filter can be bypassed however, by use of the hypnotic trance, allowing direct constructive suggestions to get through to the subconscious. Old perceptions can then be wiped away and replaced with positive transformation.'

'Such as allowing me to overcome my fear of silence?' Emma probed.

'Exactly.' He came to the gist of her problem. 'I think you've convinced your subconscious that you cannot do without continuous noise. You can overcome this by using what I call hypnotic meditation. Our subconscious is far more receptive to new information and positive messages when we're totally relaxed, so I combine self-hypnosis, or self-induced trance, with visualisation, affirmations and other meditation techniques.'

Whilst listening carefully to everything he was saying, Emma was also enjoying the food. The classic Fijian dish he had prepared comprised of fish known locally as mahi-mahi, simmered in lolo, being coconut milk. He had added sliced onions, chopped tomatoes and ginger, to further enhance the flavour.

'This meal is delicious,' she praised. 'Did you catch the fish yourself?'

He gave an honest reply. 'No, I don't do that sort of thing, but Benny will be bringing me more from Nadi in a few days' time.'

Hearing so made her feel better about taking his food. 'Lucky you. Going back to what you were saying about hypnosis, isn't it dangerous? I once saw a hypnotist at a nightclub controlling minds. He made people do all sorts of weird things.'

'Stage hypnosis is a form of entertainment,' Ollie stressed, 'and I'm sure the audience had a really good laugh. It's not the same thing as we've been discussing though. You'll have noticed the hypnotist had a lot of volunteers to choose from. Through careful elimination, he would have selected the ones who could go into trance most easily, through rapid induction techniques, which also lowered their inhibitions. Volunteers who do not respond as expected, often worry they might have a problem, or will be considered inadequate. Fearing they will be asked to leave the stage, they give the hypnotist their consent and do what he asks them to. The important thing to realise is that they are still able to refuse to do anything they're really uncomfortable with or which is against their will. They are still in control and can come out of the trance state at any time they want, just as they can in medical and psychological hypnosis. With self-hypnosis we are putting ourselves into a self-induced trance anyway, using a pre-recorded session, a recording of our own instructions, or mentally speaking to ourselves whilst in a very relaxed state.'

Noticing her glass was empty he poured her more wine, topping up his own too.

They clinked glasses, both toasting the other with a very

English, 'Cheers!'

Although he was keen to explain everything to her, he was concerned about making the conversation too heavy. 'We can chat about something a little lighter if you prefer.'

'No. Not at all,' she insisted. 'Everything's great and you're an interesting man. Is it true that only certain people can go into a trance?'

'It's actually a naturally occurring state,' he was keen for her to know. 'Sometimes we refer to it as daydreaming, especially when it occurs whilst we are doing mundane things, which can make our mind drift. We could be watching television, driving, or in my case shaving. It's something we experience most often in the short slot between wakefulness and sleep, either last thing at night, or first thing in the morning. Hypnosis is nothing new. It was used by the Ancient Egyptians, Hindus and Greeks, the latter at their Temple of Apollo for the Oracle of Delphi.'

'Another technique you mentioned was visualisation,' she seemed to remember.

He was pleased she had, as he was really enjoying their conversation. 'It can help get us into a hypnotic trance, by imagining we are somewhere relaxing, such as on a beautiful beach, like the one you arrived at earlier. We can deepen the trance by pretending we are descending a staircase or going down from floor to floor in a lift. We can also use it to program our minds with positive and empowering images. Visions and symbols are far more powerful than any words.'

'You also referred to something called affirmations,' she recalled.

'They are positive phrases or statements,' he imparted, 'which challenge negative thoughts. By choosing a simple affirmation and repeating it to yourself over and over at each session and even throughout the day, you replace the negative thoughts programmed into your subconscious with positive messages.'

Ordinarily, when Emma was eating with someone, there would be loud music playing, making it difficult to hear what the other person was saying. Here, the only background sound was the gentle wash of the sea in the distance. She closed her eyes and breathed in the atmosphere. When she was ready, she asked him about meditation and whether it was the same as mindfulness.

Ollie reached for his glass and took another sip of wine. 'There are similarities between the two and some meditation techniques can be used for the latter. For me, the real purpose of meditation is to calm the mind and find inner peace and wisdom, by going into the silence. Mindfulness is about being in the present, the here and now, fully aware of your thoughts, feelings, actions and how these affect others around you. In guided meditations you are talked through a series of visualisations. With mantra-based meditations you repeat a mantra over and again, either by chanting aloud, or just in your mind. By concentrating on your breathing, you can learn to control it and become aware of the silence between each breath inhalation and exhalation.'

As they had both finished their fish, he stood up and headed for the cabin with the plates.

'You're not leaving me I hope?' Emma asked playfully.

'I'm just getting the desert and a bottle of red. I'll be back in a moment, so you just relax.'

Such a suggestion was easy. She sat back in her chair and looked up at the perfect night sky, filled with millions of tiny glittering stars. This ever-inspiring heavenly sight stole every thought from her mind.

Although she was unaware, for just a moment she entered an inspired silence.

8

It was probably a combination of the wine and a perfect evening, but Emma slept well.

The sun was already up when she awoke next morning. There was no sign of Ollie in the cabin and so she checked outside. Not seeing him there either, she assumed he had left for the beach much earlier.

Back inside, she noticed a couple of neatly folded towels and some sun lotion on the sofa, which he must have left for her. He had also thoughtfully provided a pleasant-smelling shower gel and a 2-in-1 shampoo conditioner.

The water from the outside shower was cooler than she would have liked, but it was refreshing, just as he had suggested.

So too was the glass of coconut milk, which she helped herself to from the jug in the fridge. She poured a little over a couple of Weet-Bix, adding some chopped banana, as suggested by the illustration on the front of the box. Although the cereal was not the same brand as the Weetabix sold in the UK, it tasted just as good.

When it came to the decision over what to wear, she chose a fashionable, but very revealing costume she had posed for in a spa guide supplement. Made of a loosely woven grey material, it was almost see-through. With the thinnest of ties at the neck and just above the waist, it covered only the front of the body. Leaving the sides and the back, above the waist, completely exposed, the cheeky bikini bottom was also deliberately designed to show off the female form at its best. As she put it on, she did wonder if Ollie might disapprove, but decided to risk it.

Slipping her feet into a colourful pair of lightweight beach shoes and picking up a towel and the sun cream, she headed off to find him.

As she reached the beach, she spotted him straight away, sitting on the sand. His toned legs were stretched out before him, his hands resting on his knees.

Moving nearer, his eyes appeared to be closed. As she lowered her line of sight however, her own eyes bulged to their widest at what she saw. He was completely naked!

Glued to the spot, her mind raced in sheer surprise. She had no idea whether to quickly retrace her steps, or quietly sit down beside him.

Eventually choosing the latter, she realised he was meditating, but why had he taken off his shorts? She could only wait until he had finished and ask him.

Marking time, she started to apply sunscreen to her face, pleased to find it was a non-greasy formula. So engrossed was she in avoiding it getting into her eyes, that she almost jumped out of her skin when he unexpectedly spoke.

'Do you want me to do your back?' he offered.

'My back?' It took a moment for her to register what he was talking about. When she did, she handed him the lotion.

'Thank you.'

Moving behind her, he knelt and began to slowly smooth the liquid over her velvety skin. 'The ultraviolet rays are much stronger here than back in England,' he reminded her, 'so protection is essential. I'm hoping it'll soon be considered safe to use the SPF tablets they've started to market instead. With no reliable research on them yet, it's probably too risky at the moment. Would you agree?'

Any reply was rather slow to come. The sensual pleasure of his strong, but gentle masculine hands upon her longing-to-be-touched body was far too pleasurable. She was tempted to rip off her costume and ask him to rub the lotion all over her front as well.

Resisting such a desire, she asked instead about his meditation. 'Are you always naked when trying to quieten your mind?'

'It depends on where I am,' he quipped. 'Most definitely on a lovely island like this, but not if I'm waiting for a flight in a noisy airport or sitting on a plane.'

His reply amused her. 'From the short time I've known you,' she told him, 'I had no idea that you take your shorts off.'

'They'd get awfully dirty if I didn't,' he twisted her words.

She gave him a playful slap on the arm. 'You know I didn't mean that. I was asking if you prefer not having them on?'

'I wear clothes as little as possible,' he openly admitted. 'It's far healthier and natural without them and a lot more comfortable too. I only kept the shorts on yesterday out of respect, as I thought you might be offended by nudity.'

Hearing this was too much for Emma. She creased up in a fit of hysterical laughter.

Such a reaction bothered Ollie. 'What's so funny? My not liking clothes, or the sight of a naked body?'

His manly concern only added to her amusement and it took a couple of minutes before she could shake her head and utter, 'It's neither.'

Gradually managing to compose herself, she apologised. 'Oh dear. Sorry, but what you said was so funny. You asked me last night at dinner what I did for a living and I told you I was a model. So as not to shock you, or make you think less of me, I deliberately didn't mention a certain aspect of my work. The thing is, that whilst I am often photographed in skimpy beachwear like this, I quite often work nude.'

He regrettably managed to misinterpret her confession. 'Are you telling me you're a porn star?'

'No way!' she made plain. 'A lot of my photoshoots call for me to be suggestive and erotic, but they are always artistic. I'm also often featured in naturist type magazines.'

Realising his mistake, he tried to wriggle out of it. 'I wasn't intending to imply you did hardcore pornography. Even if you had done it wouldn't matter. I've got nothing against porn stars.'

'Neither have I,' she agreed, 'providing they're doing it willingly and haven't been forced into it. I've been asked to do explicit sexual acts lots of times but have always turned it down flat. It's just not me and it would limit the amount of legitimate work I get.'

He could completely understand her reasoning, but something else occurred to him. 'If you've modelled for naturist magazines, I might have seen you before without realising it. What was your most recent job?

'For something completely different,' she explained. 'It was on my way here, in Australia, to promote a new car. They're planning to use it in several countries, so my agent will have negotiated a good fee for me.'

He could not quite get his head around what she was describing. 'You had to be naked for a car advert?'

'They insisted,' she told him. 'I had to have buckets of water poured over me and as the photo was meant to suggest I was nude, it made sense for me to be so.'

'Why the water?' he asked, trying to picture the scene.

She lowered her voice, not that there was anyone else to overhear what she was about to say. 'Don't tell anyone I said this, but I actually thought the advertising slogan was rather silly.'

He waited with bated breath for her to tell him what it was.

She said it slowly. *'Don't pour cold water on the one you love.'*

Ollie repeated it aloud several times, trying the emphasis on different words, to see what worked best. 'Just think,' he concluded, 'someone was probably paid a massive amount of money to come up with that. Not a bad way to make a living.'

They sat in silence for a moment, Emma wondering how much the creative team earned from those nine words.

He was meanwhile contemplating how open-minded she must be, with her type of modelling. 'You must be perfectly comfortable, working naked in front of others.'

'Of course,' she acknowledged, 'otherwise I wouldn't do it.'

She glanced down at herself. 'Actually, it seems rather silly for me to be sitting here in this ridiculous costume when you've got nothing on. I've never considered myself to be a naturist, but I did hope to get a genuine all-over tan whilst on holiday.'

Without further comment she got up and untied the straps, allowing the flimsy material to fall away. Her beautifully formed breasts and smooth stomach completely uncovered, she slipped out of the miniscule bikini bottom and sat down again. 'That's better. Now we're both the same.' Noticing his discreet but admiring glances she added, 'My boobs are real by the way. No nasty silicone implants.'

Ollie felt his face redden at having been caught out by his natural male curiosity. Although her scanty swimwear had done nothing to hide her voluptuous curves, seeing them undraped brought to mind Venus, the unrivalled goddess of love, beauty, sex and desire.

He tried to not let his thoughts dwell on such things. 'What made you think I might have been shocked last night, had you told me about your nude modelling?'

Emma was busy applying sun lotion to the regions of her body only just exposed. 'You said you had once considered going on a long retreat to a Roman Catholic monastery.'

Sneakily taking another peep at the source of his masculinity, she was pleased he had not wasted it by locking himself away in such a place.

Ollie found himself mesmerised by the way she was massaging the cream into her jiggling breasts. Fearing the stimulating effect it might have on him, he looked elsewhere. 'I couldn't reconcile myself to the Catholic Church's beliefs and I've come across a far more interesting religious path since my out-of-body experience. We must find time to talk about it before you leave the island.'

Right now, she could think of far more enjoyable things

they could be doing together. He made fascinating company and she was beginning to wish she could stay much longer with him.

The temperature was rising, in more ways than one, but fortunately Ollie had brought a large bottle of mineral water with him. He passed it to Emma, encouraging her to drink.

'I think I might dip my toes in the water,' she decided. 'Are you going to join me?'

'Sorry,' he replied, declining her invitation, 'but the sea and I don't get on.'

She only took a few steps towards the water, before stopping. Turning her head back towards him, her face showed concern. 'I hope there's nothing nasty lurking in the shallows.'

'It depends entirely on what you mean by nasty,' he specified. 'On some Fijian coastlines for example, there's a thing they call fire coral. It's an organism which looks like ordinary coral, but swim too near and it will do it's best to sting you.'

Emma did not like the sound of it. 'Why would something on a reef do that?'

'To kill you of course,' he told her in a matter-of-fact way. 'Then it can eat you.'

He could tell she was not sure if he was joking or not, but he was actually serious. 'Then there's very poisonous sea snakes, jellyfish, viciously sharp-toothed moray eels, extremely venomous sea snails, which they call cone shells, as well as the death-dealing crown-of-thorns starfish.'

All this was beginning to really frighten her. 'Oh dear. I brought my snorkelling mask on holiday with me. I was going to try it out.'

'I would think very carefully first,' he warned her. 'I haven't even mentioned the sharks yet.'

Emma grimaced. 'Sharks?'

'Of course,' he emphasised. 'They love warm waters like this. You could find whitetip sharks, tiger sharks, bull sharks and perhaps even some great whites, but they're far more likely to find you first. Strangely, despite their danger, some Fijians actually consider them to be sacred.' He had read this in Brad's flora and fauna guide.

She scuttled further from the water edge. 'I don't care how venerated the things are. They're not having me for their lunch!'

Ollie jumped to his feet and grabbing both her hands, pretended to rescue her by pulling her towards him. 'Talking of lunch, if you'd like to accompany me to the cabin, I'll fix you a snack.'

Neither of them bothered to dress.

'By the way,' he cautioned, 'just so you know, nudity is illegal in Fiji. As there's only you and me on the island though, I don't see it as a problem.'

Emma was pleased to hear it. 'I feel good like this, even if there's no one paying to take photos of me.'

'Regrettably, I'm out of small change right now,' he kidded.

His wisecrack made her smile. 'Don't worry. My agent accepts cheques, PayPal and most major credit cards.'

'One only has to look at you,' he decided aloud, 'to know why so many people want you for a photoshoot. As William Blake, the poet, artist and visionary, rightly said: *'The nakedness of woman is the work of God.'*

9

Olli was annoyed with himself. He was allowing an attractive woman to steer him away from the very reason he had come to the island.

The pop music blaring from her phone, which she had downloaded before travelling, was irritating to say the least. He was tempted to shout to her through the open window, insisting she used earphones. Instead, he tried to ignore it and carried on preparing the banana, papaya and coconut for lunch.

He was disappointed by his own behaviour on the beach. His decision not to wear clothes came from a long-held conviction that it was perfectly natural. When Emma had stripped off her costume however, he had found it extremely difficult to keep his eyes off her. The sensual thoughts which had entered his head were perfectly healthy and normal, but as a committed naturist he needed to be able to control them.

Glancing at her through the window, he watched as she swung side to side in the hammock, contentedly nude and distractingly enchanting. He had cautioned her about the dangers which lurked in the sea, yet no one had pre-warned him about her. She was unquestionably gifted with as many seducing powers as the most voluptuous mermaid. Her beauty and sexiness could so easily lure him from his spiritual desire for tranquillity and silence, into an ocean of turbulent and resounding sound waves.

He remembered the words of Violet Firth, better known as the famed occultist Dion Fortune. *'The still, small voice is never heard in the thunder, or the whirlpool, but only in the silence.'*

Her Fraternity of Inner Light had owned a small chalet called Avalon, quite possibly in the grounds of a British naturist club. She might even have met Gerald Gardner there, the founder of Gardnerian Witchcraft, who had become an enthusiastic nudist after his doctor suggested it could benefit his health.

One day on a trip to Pompeii in Italy, Gardner had seen a fresco of naked Roman women. It was in a room called the Initiation Chamber at the Villa of Mysteries. Perhaps it was this which gave him the idea of introducing ritual nudity, known as being *Skyclad*, into his brand of witchcraft.

From the noisy music Ollie concluded, if he told Emma this, she would think he was referring to the British heavy metal band called Skyclad.

Taking the two bowls of fruit outside, he called her over to the table, before returning to the cabin for some spoons and beer.

Mercifully, by the time he got back she had turned the music off.

'This is great,' she exclaimed, sitting down. 'Irresistible!'

'I hope it's to your liking,' he checked.

'Oh yes,' she purred. 'I like it a lot.'

The way she was staring at him, her eyelashes fluttering,

rather than at the food, made him wonder if they were talking about the same thing. He thought it best to avoid anything which could be misconstrued, especially as he wanted to talk to her about the naturist lifestyle.

'You were telling me earlier,' he recalled, 'that although you take your clothes off for much of your work, you've never considered yourself to be a naturist?'

'I never have,' she reconfirmed, 'but now I'm beginning to think I could easily become one. What's the difference between a naturist and a nudist?'

Ollie opened the beers. 'I tend to think the terms are one and the same, being about people who enjoy going naked when possible. The word naturist was first used in 1778 by a Belgian, called Jean Baptiste Luc Planchon, to indicate a natural and healthy way of life. In those early days it was not just about nudity, but a philosophical lifestyle which included things like respect for nature, regular exercises for the mind and body, healthy eating and in some cases abstinence from tobacco and alcohol.'

'I've never smoked,' she disclosed, 'but I do enjoy a drink.'

'You're not the only one,' he concurred. 'It seems that most Europeans today tend to use the word naturist, but in America it's still often nudist. Things like this make going into precise definitions rather complicated. British Naturism, the national organisation, say on their website that naturism is going without clothes, perhaps just occasionally on a beach, in the garden, or more generally in everyday life. Some might only go nude whilst away on holiday, especially at suitable resorts, or designated beaches, but others seek every opportunity to get out of their clothes.'

Her eyes had a wicked look. 'I bet they do! They're only human after all.'

'Naturist organisations are keen to point out that naturism is not about sex,' he hoped she would see. 'A group of people preferring not to wear clothes does not mean they have any sexual intentions. That said, I do think their sexual health is probably better, as they'll be more comfortable with their bodies.'

Emma sat thinking about this for a moment, whilst trying to peel the label off her beer bottle, deciding it would most likely be the only souvenir of her time in Fiji. 'If you're right, I might already be a naturist without realising it, because I'm more than comfortable with my body.'

She took a bite of banana. 'Does all this delicious fruit grow on the island?'

He had no idea how abundant any of it was, having only been around the island once. 'This lot arrived by plane I'm afraid, flown in by Benny.'

Not wanting to become side-tracked, he got back to what they had been discussing. 'Historically, those who lived without clothes often had philosophical or doctrinal beliefs for doing so. A good example would be the Ancient Indian wise men who went naked. They were called *gymnosophists* by the Greeks. Extremely self-disciplined, with religious and spiritual convictions, they considered things like clothing and meat to be detrimental to the purity of thought. Nudity certainly played an important part in their philosophy of life.'

Emma had once been to India, on a photoshoot for a travel company, but her stay there had been too brief for any culture or sightseeing. 'Are there people still there who don't wear clothes?'

'Oh yes,' he was able to assure her. 'There are still thousands of naked holy men in India, mainly Naga sadhus, who are referred to as naked saints. They are strict devotees of the Hindu gods. You'll also find quite a few Jains, who are followers of an ancient Indian religion, which dates to about 500 B.C.'

Ollie had been talking so much that he had hardly touched his fruit. He savoured a couple of mouthfuls before going on with what he was saying. 'When it comes to talking about religion and nakedness, many Christians immediately think of the Bible's Adam and Eve. It's myth of course, supposedly symbolising the way humanity became conscious of good and evil. If you remember the story, Adam and Eve were both naked and perfectly happy in the Garden of Eden. Then along came a huge snake, which persuaded them to eat of an apple. The moment they did so, they became aware of their nudity. Horrified, they quickly covered their genitals with fig leaves.'

'I hope the fruit we're eating isn't going to make us do the same?' Emma joked. 'After all, Eve is my made-up modelling surname.'

'It won't,' he vouched, 'only apples and talking reptiles cause such a reaction.'

'Here's a new saying then,' she suggested. 'A banana a day keeps the fig leaves away!'

He pondered it. 'You've used an interesting mix of sexual symbolism there, but we can talk about it another time. As I was saying, fundamentalists and evangelicals, who take everything in the bible literally, think the Adam & Eve story is proof of nudity being wrong. The more enlightened on the other hand, believe covering their bodies in shame, which God had made to perfection, was the real sin.'

'I think he did a really good job in designing our bits and pieces,' Emma said with mock seriousness. 'Not many people know this, but he gave a penis to a man, rather than to a woman, to compensate for the male's lack of a brain!'

Ollie had heard the gag before, but it still made him chuckle. 'The ironic thing is that Christianity wasn't originally against nakedness. It was the Church which suppressed it, convinced of nudity having to mean sex and in turn eternal damnation. Their missionaries and the British colonists forced native cultures all over the world to conform to their misunderstandings and cover themselves up. For the actual origin of social nudity, we would have to go back millions of years to our first human ancestors. Rather more recently by comparison, there were examples of it in Ancient Egypt.'

'I've been to Egypt,' Emma told him excitedly. 'It was a photoshoot for a skin cream promotion.'

Ollie was impressed. 'I bet you weren't photographed there with nothing on.'

She shook her head. 'They dressed me in a long golden robe and headdress and sat me on a camel. It was rather an irritable one, which kept spitting at everyone.'

'I suppose you're going to tell me it had the hump,' he predicted.

'I wasn't actually,' she said convincingly, 'because it didn't have one.'

'Why not?' he asked, falling into her trap.

'Because …,' she said, with a smug look on her face, 'its name was Humphrey!

He let out a long sigh. 'I should have seen that coming. Getting back to what I was hopefully enlightening you with, they have discovered carved stone tablets in Egypt which date back to 1353 B.C. when Pharaoh Akhenaton and his Queen Nefertiti ruled. They prove social nudity was customary then, and perfectly acceptable for spiritual and health reasons.'

'What about the Ancient Greeks?' she mused. 'I've seen quite a few statues of them starkers.'

'There was a lot of nakedness then,' he agreed, 'especially amongst the men. It was partly for holistic reasons, but they also thought the human body was artistically beautiful and a delight to look at. Not only did they hope to please their gods by imitating them nude, but athletes trained for and competed in the Olympics, unhampered by clothing. The Greek philosopher, Socrates, had much earlier advocated nudity as a form of honesty.'

'What a clever man,' Emma japed. 'It must have made shoplifting a lot more difficult!'

Ollie was taking a liking to her sense of humour. 'The Romans enjoyed social nudity as well, especially in their magnificent bathhouses. There were the gladiators who fought without clothes, but then Emperor Theodosius made Nicene Christianity the Roman Empire's official religion and banned nakedness, declaring it a sin.'

'It keeps coming back to the Christians,' Emma felt. 'Naturism would probably be even more popular today if it wasn't for them.'

'There is a Christian naturist organisation,' Ollie informed her, 'but I'm not sure how many members they've got.' He noticed she had finished her fruit. 'Was it enough for you? I never eat much at lunchtime.'

'I'm fine thanks,' she let him know. 'Go on with what you're saying. If I am going to be a naturist, the more I know about it the better.'

He was pleased to be holding her interest. 'In the early 1900's a German movement emerged, known as Freikorperkultur, or FKK in short, which meant free body culture. They advocated a nudist approach to sports and communal living and since then, all sorts of individuals have embraced the lifestyle, although most in a less serious way. There have been people from just about every walk of life, including American presidents, English politicians, famous scientists, medics, poets, authors, painters, actors and pop stars. As the Italian sculptor and painter, Michelangelo, most wisely said: *'What spirit is so empty and blind, that it cannot recognize the fact that the foot is more noble than the shoe, and skin more beautiful than the garment with which it is clothed?'*"

'I can sympathise with such a statement completely,' Emma beamed, 'but then you'd expect me to, being a glamour model.'

Ollie was not so sure fashion models would be so likeminded. 'Naturists realise it's personality which matters, not what someone looks like. It's a great way to meet and socialise with people from all walks of life and even different nationalities on an equal basis. They tend to be very friendly too, all having a similar love for relaxing in a natural way. Conversations tend to start easily, because of their shared interests, such as which clubs and resorts they have visited and can recommend, beaches worth going to and most obviously the weather. They're only too aware of the benefits of the lifestyle.'

'When I've been on a nude photo assignment and it's really hot,' Emma thought it worthwhile mentioning, 'I've always considered myself the fortunate one. With the fully dressed people around me sweating buckets in the heat, some at least must have wished they could take their clothes off too and be like me. The few which didn't think so were probably the type who wear pyjamas or a nightie in bed. Doing so surely can't be good for them.'

He was pleased she was on the same wavelength as him. 'You can't sleep well when the body's overheated. The greatest joy for nearly all naturists, however, is the incredible feeling of freedom and liberation. Shedding the body of clothes releases and frees the mind. Naturism can be a spiritual experience, a celebration of the beautiful human body in all its diversity of body shapes, rather than what the media considers to be the perfect figure.'

Emma wondered if he might be knocking her choice of career. Plenty of people did, but she was well able to defend herself. 'We all know the saying: *'If you've got it flaunt it,'* and it's exactly what I do.'

'Why not?' He did not disapprove at all. 'I'm sure there are plenty of young women who would jump at your job, given half the chance. They won't all have the same figure as you though. As naturism clearly shows, people come in all sorts of sizes.'

'It's just as well,' she knew only too well. 'If we were all the same, I'd be out of a job!'

'Possibly,' he considered, 'but I'm sure you are also extremely photogenic. In a naturist setting it becomes clear that most people are fat or thin, with lumps and bumps, saggy bits and with the scars of lives well lived. Seeing this makes everyone more accepting and loving of their own bodies. They can let go of long-held hang ups and accept there's no part of the body which is shameful or dirty. This helps with a multitude of physical and psychological problems, reducing worries and stress levels. It also improves mental health and boosts self-esteem.'

Emma added something else to his list. 'As you pointed out about the Greeks and the early Olympics, clothing also restricts movement. Nudity is far more practical for swimming. Without costumes, new world records would probably be set.'

He finished his beer, hoping she would not try and prove the theory. 'There are many experts who believe being naked is better for the skin. It allows it to breathe, eliminating excess sweating, toxins, inflammation of skin follicles and it improves blood circulation. Fresh air and a nice cooling breeze are without doubt good for you, not to mention the huge benefit of getting natural Vitamin D from the sun. It detoxifies the skin and boosts your mood.'

'As you told me on the beach,' she recalled, 'it's important to be careful though, to use protective sun lotion and not overdo the sunbathing.'

'It's all common sense,' he proposed, 'just like the naturist etiquette of carrying a small towel to sit on.'

Hearing this, Emma leapt up, waving in the air the bright pink towel she had been using. 'You see? This proves I'm a proper nudist now and I love it. I don't think I'm ever going to dress again.'

Ollie was impressed with her new-found enthusiasm. Undressing as a model was one thing, but he was pleasantly surprised at how quickly she had taken to the freedom and enjoyment of social nudity.

10

Emma ensured she was awake early enough the following morning to join Ollie, as he made his way to the beach for sunrise.

Although he had slept inside on the sofa, he had meditated outside first for over an hour. She had meanwhile remained in the cabin, listening to more pre-downloaded music on her smartphone. Thoughtfully, she had kept the volume down.

'It would be preferable to watch the sun come up in silence,' he made clear as they reached the beach, 'and afterwards you can describe any emotions it might have stirred within you.'

'Fine by me,' she affirmed. 'I wasn't planning on giving it musical accompaniment anyway.'

He was pleased to hear it. 'As the Indian mystic, Osho, once said: '*Silence has a music of its own. It is not dead. It is very much alive. It is tremendously alive. In fact, nothing is more alive than silence.*''

They spread their towels on the sand and settled down beside each other.

Aware of Emma being quite restless, he gave her hand a reassuring squeeze. 'Take a couple of deep breaths,' he suggested.

'It will relax you.'

She smiled a thank you and directed her eyes back to the horizon, which had turned a yellowy orange.

Very slowly the radiant solar disc arose in all its splendour, its reassuring presence awakening the world from sleep. Stirring eager birdsong, a beam of light reflected its glory across the surface of the still dreamy blue sea. Steadily, the vivid source of creation transformed itself from energetic amber to purifying whiteness.

As always, it reminded Ollie of the Egyptian sky goddess Nuit. 'Did you enjoy the morning treat?' he asked her keenly.

'I've never bothered to observe sunrises so carefully before,' she wanted him to know, 'but I'm pleased I did this time. It was beautiful. I felt comforted by it, with thoughts about hope and of life overcoming death.'

He was pleased with her response. 'It's a good reaction. The rising sun is a symbol of rebirth, or reincarnation. Tell me, have you ever heard of Aleister Crowley?'

Her face showed no recognition.

'He was an extremely famous occultist and ceremonial magician,' Ollie explained, 'and the prophet of the religion known as Thelema, which I'm interested in. One of his rituals is called *Liber Resh*. It's used to greet the sun at sunrise, as well as at noon, sunset and midnight. At sunrise you address the sun-god, Ra, saying: *'Hail unto Thee who art Ra in Thy rising, even unto Thee who art Ra in Thy strength, who travellest over the Heavens in Thy bark at the Uprising of the Sun. Tahuti standeth in His splendour at the prow, and Ra-Hoor abideth at the helm. Hail unto Thee from the Abodes of Night!'*

'It might just be a coincidence,' she considered, 'but as the sun appeared, I was certain it was saying hello to me.'

'It was,' he affirmed, 'and to the whole of nature, humanity included. I could tell you quite a bit about Crowley and Thelema, but I doubt there will be time before you leave the island.'

Emma did not want to think about her departure. She had taken quite a liking to Ollie and the thought of saying goodbye to him upset her.

Glancing at his handsome face, she wondered if he had similar feelings towards her. He had certainly made no attempt at seduction, despite his admiring glances when she first removed her costume. She had been naked ever since, but his interest in her body seemed to have stopped. Either he was not interested, or his mind had been on other things.

He interrupted her thoughts. 'I need to do another meditation now. Feel free to either go back to the cabin or stay here. Which would you prefer?'

Her reply was a pleasant surprise. 'I'd really like to stay with you and try a short meditation myself. You did say you'd tell me more about the techniques you use.'

Ollie's eyes lit up at hearing this. 'You've really made my day and it would be a delight to.' He swivelled himself around to face her. 'First, we must get you into the right position. I usually sit when meditating, but as its your first time you might be better lying on your back.'

She seemed a little nervous, unsure of what to expect, but lay down on her towel. 'Shall I close my eyes?'

'It will help considerably,' he advised. 'We need to get you nice and relaxed. As I told you before, I use meditation to calm the mind, to find inner peace and wisdom.' He deliberately did not mention silence at this point, knowing how much she feared it. 'With your permission, I'd like to use a combination of simple relaxation exercises and hypnosis techniques.'

His attempt to convince her the evening before, that hypnosis could do her no harm, had obviously been successful.

'You told me it was safe,' she consented, 'and I believe you, so go ahead.'

'Remember, there's nothing scary about it,' he stressed. 'You can open your eyes and stop at any time. Ready to start then?'

She gave him a still slightly unsure nod.

'Now just try and relax,' he began. 'You'll notice I deliberately use the word *relax* quite a lot. You need to breathe using the diaphragm, which is the domed shaped tummy muscle at the base of the lungs. Put your right hand on your upper chest and the other on your stomach, just beneath your rib cage.'

Her left hand was not quite in the correct place, so he adjusted it. 'Better. Now take a deep breath in through your nose and you'll feel your stomach expand, as the diaphragm moves. As you breathe out through the mouth the reverse happens. Do you notice it?'

He could tell she was uncertain, so did not wait for a reply. 'Let us try it again, this time breathing in really deeply. Feel any movement there now?'

A slight nod accompanied by a smile indicated she did.

'Excellent. This is where all the rise and fall should be,' he tutored. 'If you're doing it correctly, the hand on your upper chest should remain perfectly still. You can put your hands back by your sides now.'

He waited for her to do so. 'Now, take a deep breath in through your nose, hold it for a moment and breathe out slowly through your mouth. It's a good idea to do it to a count, but today we'll start simply, by just getting a nice rhythm going. On each out breath think of the word *relax*.'

It was clear she was doing fine. 'Whilst continuing to breathe in and out like this, I want you to now concentrate on your feet. Just think of them in your mind's eye and imagine them relaxing. Any tension should fade away, so they become completely at rest. They are feeling heavy and are sinking down, through your towel and into the sand.'

Emma was impressed. Her feet felt exactly as he was describing.

'Do the same with your lower legs,' he urged, 'letting them relax completely, so they're heavy and sink down too. Remember, you are in complete control. Next, think about your knees, so they relax in the same way and then your upper legs and thighs.'

Slowly, he directed her concentration to each part of the body, a section at a time, up through the pelvis, to the stomach and chest, then to her shoulders and down her arms to her hands. Next, was her back and then her neck, face and finally the crown of the head.

Ollie paused for a short while.

Now she was nicely at ease he could move on to the next stage. 'I'm going to count down very slowly from five to zero. On each count you will feel more and more relaxed.'

Talking her through this had a tranquillizing effect. 'I want you to visualise something for me now. Use your imagination if necessary but see yourself standing inside an empty room. The four walls, floor and ceiling are painted black, but in one corner of the floor you spot some light, which is streaming up through an open trap door. See yourself walk over and peer down through the opening. You realise there's a spiral staircase, which leads down to the basement. It has a handrail on both sides. You can count the steps from where you are standing. There are ten of them in all, with number ten at the top and number one at the bottom.'

He gave her a few seconds to visualise it in her mind. 'Take hold of the rails, a hand each side of you, ready to descend the spiral staircase. As you do so, a step at a time, to the comforting sound of my voice, you will feel even more deeply relaxed. Start now, at step ten. Then move down to step nine, feeling even more relaxed. You are floating down to step eight, with not a care in the world. Now down to step seven, down, down, down, feeling beautifully relaxed. On to step six, deepening the placidness. Moving on to step five, which fills you with serenity. Now to step four, making you more relaxed than ever. Sink down to step three, relaxing to the sound of my voice. To step two. Deeper and deeper. Everything is so peaceful. Finally sink down to step one.'

The rhythm of breathing confirmed success. 'You are now more relaxed than ever,' he said convincingly. 'You feel wonderful. Slowly move off the spiral staircase and onto the floor of the basement, which we can call zero. It is covered in thick, soft sand, just like the beach. See yourself lie down and relax completely. Your eyelids are so heavy and you are almost, but not quite, drifting into sleep.

From the expression on her face, he could tell she was in her own little world. 'Thoughts will drift in and out of your mind,' he suggested. 'Although you are inside, you can still see the sky above you. Those fluffy white clouds are your thoughts. Watch them as they gently float on by. Do not try and stop them. Let them just float on as they wish, off into the distance, further and further away, disappearing. Now there are none.'

Although he had still not yet mentioned the word *silence*, he felt she was deep enough for him to do so safely now. 'Between each of our thoughts exists silence,' he whispered. 'When there are no thoughts there is only silence. You are enjoying and benefitting by being in this silence. Silence is good. Silence is beautiful. Only within silence can we find wisdom. It is in silence that truths are realised. Silence is the gateway to the spiritual you. Listen in the silence and when silence speaks, listen carefully.'

As Ollie well knew, it was essential for her to enjoy her first journey into the silence. Only by doing so could she overcome her fear of it in waking life and in time come to love it.

For a full twenty minutes he let her relish it. All the while he guarded over her, before offering her some affirmations. 'I want you to repeat in your mind the following proclamations, each one several times over. Being in the silence is enjoyable. Silence is good for me. I actively seek silence. Silence is my friend. I love silence.'

After allowing her to prime her subconscious with these positive and powerful affirmations, he gently brought her back. 'Soon it will be time for you to open your eyes but first I'm going to slowly count up from one to ten. With each count you will feel more and more awake. When you open your eyes at number ten you will feel wonderful and will fully know how much you have enjoyed and benefitted from being in the silence. One …two … three …four …slowly coming back …five …feeling more and more awake …six …seven …eight … almost back now …nine and ten. Open your eyes and give the world a great big smile!'

Emma sat up, stretching her arms and glanced around, her face beaming with happiness. 'That was so good. I want to do it again very soon, but for longer next time. Just a few minutes is not enough.'

Ollie gave her a grin. 'Your meditation was lengthier than you think.'

'Was it?' she asked in amazement.

'Very much so,' he wanted her to realise. 'Soon you'll be able to do all this without any help from me and whenever you like. All you need to do is learn the different techniques of hypnotic meditation. Right now, however, I think we should make our way back to the cabin and treat ourselves to some breakfast.'

He got to his feet, but she grabbed his arm. 'We can't go yet. You haven't done your own meditation.'

'It doesn't matter,' he assured her, 'I can do it later. My being able to help you was the priority and it made me extremely happy doing so.'

They shook the sand from their towels, folded them and headed for the path.

As they walked, he told her about Rumi, the 13th-century Persian poet and Sufi mystic. 'When teaching, he would talk of silence like this: *'Silence is an ocean. Speech is a river. When the ocean is searching for you, don't walk into the river. Listen to the ocean.'* I really hope this morning has given you something to work on.'

'It has,' she promised him.

'Ollie was delighted to hear her say so. 'Excellent. If any of Rumi's students were fearful, he would ask: *'Why are you so afraid of silence, silence is the root of everything. If you spiral into its void, a hundred voices will thunder messages you long to hear.'"*

'It's a shame I wasn't around in the 13th century, to hear it for myself,' she considered.

'How do you know you weren't?' Ollie questioned. 'Just because you haven't yet studied the subject of reincarnation, doesn't mean it's not a reality.'

Somehow, deep down inside she knew he was telling her the truth.

11

'Are you going to do your morning meditation now?' Emma asked as they finished breakfast.

'It's going to have to wait again,' Ollie told her. 'You've come all the way to Fiji and, apart from Nadi airport, all you've seen is my cabin and a beach. With so little time left before you leave, the least I can do is show you the rest of the island.'

Her face glowed with excitement. 'That would be so good. We could visit the other two beaches you told me about. What were they called? You did tell me, but I've forgotten.'

'I named the nearest one to Benny's beach Tern Bay. It seems to be the birds' favourite. I nominated the furthest one away Distant Sands. I'm sure I can find them both again if you like.'

'I'd love it,' she enthused, grabbing her towel. 'Let's go.'

Ollie took it a little slower. 'Have you put sun lotion on yet? You don't want to burn.'

She picked up the bottle and started to spread the cream over her skin.

He did the same. 'We'd better take some water with us and perhaps a couple of bananas, to keep us going. If we're only going to the beaches, flip-flops will be fine, but if you want to go into denser vegetation, we'll need tougher shoes and to put some clothes on.'

The last thing Emma wanted was to dress. She was enjoying the freedom of nakedness far too much. 'Let's stick to the beaches. I want you to tell me more about Fiji on the way.'

By taking along the illustrated book Brad had left for him, he was able to point out and name some of the trees and plants they passed. 'It says in here that the archipelago consists of over 330 islands, but only about 110 of them are inhabited.'

'I wonder if they've included this island in those figures?' she tried to figure.

He turned to the first page of the book. 'It was printed in 1985, which was 34 years ago, so not unless someone was living here before me.'

He went back to the page he had originally been on. 'Fiji is famous for its coral reef, of which there's over 4,000 square miles and home to at least 1,500 different species of sea life.'

'You've already scared me rotten about lots of nasty things in the water,' she reminded him.

'Not all the species would bite,' he theorized, 'any more than the friendly Fijian human population would.' He had an afterthought. 'Actually, they might well have done in the past, but we'll keep it for another time too.'

She had no idea what he was talking about.

Before she had time to ask, he was quoting from the book again. 'Over half of the country's citizens are indigenous to the group of Pacific islands known as Melanesia, or of a Melanesian and Polynesian mix. A sizeable percentage however are descended from the indentured Indian labourers. The British brought them to islands in the 19th century, to work in the sugar cane plantations.'

Hearing this made her inquisitive. 'So why don't any of them live on this island?'

He did not really know. 'I can only assume it's because there's nothing of natural value here. I wouldn't have been able to buy it, had it been inhabited.'

Just at that moment, a brightly coloured bird flew past them. It had a green body, with a red face and tail.

'That's a Parrotfinch,' he told her. 'They're common throughout Fiji and have an interesting mating ritual. Flying around high above the trees, they repeatedly call aloud to each other.'

'If men and women had to do that,' she bantered, 'there'd be a lot less mating!'

'There's a big difference.' he countered. 'We can't fly for a start.'

'No?' she quizzed back. 'What about aeroplanes and the infamous Mile High Club?'

He knew she was referring to the euphemism for people who have sex at high altitude during a flight. 'Naughty things such as that usually takes place in a really cramped toilet cubicle. If humans had flapping wings, they'd never squeeze in!'

They stopped for a moment to get their bearings. A natural path which led off to the right looked familiar to him. 'If I'm not mistaken, it will take us to Distant Sands.'

They set off again. 'What would you like to talk about now?' he asked.

'I'm perfectly happy to hear some more about Fiji,' she let

him know. 'It's probably going to be my only chance and you're an excellent guide.'

'Not me,' he put her right. 'I'm fortunate to have a good guidebook in my hand. I do know a little about Fijian politics though. I made myself familiar with the basics before coming here.'

She made a sour face. 'I only want to hear about them if they're more interesting than the UK's.'

'I'll keep it brief then,' he promised. 'We can skip over all the early history and just go back to 1987.'

'Which is still well before I was born,' she added.

'Who'd have thought it?' he asked cheekily.

Her hand gave his suntanned backside a playful wallop.

'Ouch! It hurt,' he pretended. 'I'd better get back to politics. They'll be less painful.'

'Not necessarily,' she decided, pretending to yawn.

He ignored the comment. 'As a parliamentary democracy, Fiji had an elected president, but successful military led coups overthrew the government. This resulted in Fiji's expulsion from the Commonwealth, whose roots you'll know go back to the British Empire. Fiji's present constitution was adopted in 2013, with an elected government, headed by the Prime Minister, the country being readmitted to the Commonwealth the following year.'

She faked another yawn, this one even more drawn out. 'Telling me about the President will do.'

'Alright,' he granted. 'Fiji's Head of State is elected by Parliament from nominations put forward by the Prime Minister and the Leader of the Opposition. The role of President is mainly honorary, but he holds certain reserve powers, which could be called upon in an emergency. He's also by status the Commander-in-Chief of Fiji's armed forces, which are in actual fact one of the world's smallest militaries.'

'I don't expect there's much need for them around here,' she supposed, 'certainly not on this island anyway. I'm the only invader and I came in peace.'

He played on her words. 'The more peace the better as far as I'm concerned!'

'Fair enough,' she accepted, 'you did after all call it the Island of Silence.'

'It's one of the reasons why I chose an island in this part of the world,' he explained. 'The Fijians believe there's eloquence in silence and so observe a dignified silence throughout most of their ceremonies, sometimes using it for dramatic effect.'

'I wish I could have seen some of their celebrations,' she pondered sadly, 'but I'm not going to get the chance.'

'It's most unlikely,' he agreed, 'but neither am I on this island. I do know a little about the Kava ceremony however. It's an important part of their traditional welcoming rituals. Kava, or *yaqona*, is a plant shrub from the pepper family, found on most of the Pacific islands. Its fresh or sun-dried roots and lower stems are pounded or grounded into a powder and then mixed with water. The traditional method is for it to be chewed by beautiful tribal women, or their children, as they believe it adds purity, before spitting it into a bowl. Their added saliva produces the strongest *grog*, as it's called.'

Emma screwed up her face. 'Yuck! It doesn't sound very hygienic,'

He thought likewise. 'That's why the English and French have tried to prohibit them doing it, but it doesn't necessarily mean they don't.'

'The final preparation must be quite strong alcohol,' she wrongly assumed.

'No,' he corrected, 'it's mildly intoxicating but is more of a sedating drug. I've never tried it, but it's supposed to numb the mouth. There are several variants of the beverage, but it's said to be relaxing, reducing anxiety, giving a renewed feeling of contentment and a better sense of humour. The effects can last for several hours and can also lead to more powerful and realistic dreams. Although it makes some people slightly disoriented and giddy, it's much gentler on the liver than alcohol. Perhaps it's the reason for becoming popular in some major cities around the world.'

'I bet it's not nearly as good as Prosecco,' Emma scoffed. 'I'm really missing my daily dose.'

He was not surprised. 'The Journal of Sexual Medicine reckons Prosecco heightens sexual desire. They say the drink's rich antioxidants trigger nitric oxide production in the blood, relaxing the artery walls and increasing sexual excitement.'

She gave him a saucy little smile. 'Not many people know this, but before Prosecco came along, the female version of Viagra consisted mainly of diamonds and cash!'

'I think we'd better get back to the subject of kava,' he laughed, 'which you mustn't confuse with *cava*, the Spanish version of champagne, which is spelt with a 'c'. People sit cross-legged on the ground for the Fijian Kava ceremony. The hardwood bowl it is mixed in has a string attached to the front, which can be rolled out to mark the beginning of the ceremony and curled back up to signify the end. Served in a coconut shell, the drinker must clap their hands three times and then swallow it down in one. The server proclaims *mac*a and everyone else claps their hands. The most important point is that with the exception of the *Matanivanua,* being the herald who directs the ceremony, everyone else has to remain silent throughout.'

He pointed ahead. 'Look, just beyond those palms, there's the beach!'

They ran towards it, Emma shouting hoots of excitement.

As their feet hit the sand, she danced a little jig and improvised a song: 'I'm falling in love with your island, so far from the cold Scottish highland!' Unfortunately, *highland* was the only word she could think of which rhymed with *island*.

Ollie hoped she was not getting too attached to it, with so little time before she had to leave. He kept the thought to himself, not wishing to spoil her day. 'It's certainly idyllic here. The sand is so white and soft.'

Unrolling her towel, she patted the fine grains beside her. 'Come and sit next to me. You don't need kava to be sociable.'

'I bet you wish we had Prosecco with us, rather than just water though,' he hinted.

Sitting down, he unscrewed the top of his plastic bottle and took a sip. 'You should drink some of yours too. It really is a lovely day. The temperature's exactly right and the sea is so still.'

'It's as if the waves are asleep,' she whispered. 'We mustn't wake them. What do you think they're dreaming of?'

'I'm not sure,' he said quietly back. 'Perhaps they are deep in meditation, or contemplating us, as we are them. Waves can be symbols of our human emotions or suggest things which might happen to us soon.'

'We must make a wish then,' she proposed, 'for something

we really want.'

Neither of them chose to reveal their secret desire.

She wiggled her feet in the sand, overturning a shell with her toe. 'I once dreamt I was on a desert island.'

'Well, there you are,' Ollie proffered. 'Dreams, just like wishes, can come true. I sometimes use my self-hypnosis before I go to sleep, to guide me into lucid dreaming.'

Emma was fascinated by another of his unexpected revelations. 'Tell me about them.'

'Lucid dreams are not the same as ordinary ones,' he described. 'In lucid dreams you become consciously aware that you are dreaming. As it is your own creation you can influence and control it. If you don't like what's happening in the dream, you can change it, so it takes another course, or simply end it. Lucid dreams are extremely good for exploring fantasies and desires, as physical laws don't apply. They're useful too in helping to solve any problems or dilemmas you might have. Similar awareness of you dreaming is important in the Hindu practice of *yoga nidra* and the Tibetan Buddhist's *dream yoga*. Along with astral projection, lucid dreaming is invaluable in spiritual and occult work, in eastern and western traditions.'

She gave a long sigh. 'I would give anything to enjoy such a dream.'

'You probably have already,' he was sure, 'many times, but without realising it. I showed you earlier how to combine self-hypnosis with meditation, so work on it. Lucid dreams come easier to those who meditate.'

She drank some of her water. 'I'm going to succeed,' she told him determinedly.

Ollie sincerely hoped she would but had understandable

doubts.

He stood and shook his towel. 'Now you've seen and sat on my Distant Sands beach, shall I continue my guided tour and show you Tern Bay?'

She gathered up her things. 'You lead and I'll follow.'

Ollie managed to re-find the second beach quite easily. Once they were on it, Emma did another of her little dances.

He half expected another desperate-to-rhyme song from her, but this time perhaps she could not come up with one. It made him happy nonetheless to see she had retained her youthful and inspiring excitement for life. It was an appealing trait which he hoped she would never lose.

'Welcome to Tern Bay,' he announced.

With a hand shielding her eyes from the sun, she eagerly followed the swift movement of the birds, as they circled, hovered and plunge-dived for prey. 'They're wonderful. You couldn't have given the beach a better name. What are they catching?'

'Mainly fish I should think and perhaps some squid. It must be good for them, for they live relatively long lives for birds, some more than thirty years.'

He pointed to one. 'You notice how big their eyes appear to be? It's deceptive. They are actually quite small, but they have a black ring around them, which makes them look larger. Although there's quite a number of the birds busy fishing now, you'd see even more of them if it was dusk or dawn. They're kept busy, with both parents needing to feed their chicks about every three hours.'

Emma imitated the guttural calls they were making.

'Heech-heech, grrri-grrri. What noisy little things!'

He could hardly disagree. 'That's the downside for me. It would be difficult to meditate on this beach.' He was reminded of his previous visit. 'Having said so, I did manage to fall asleep for a short while the last time I was here.'

She was not surprised. 'The temperature's ideal for dozing.'

'You came to Fiji at the best time of year,' he pointed out. 'It's usually between 26° and 31° centigrade in the daytime. The cooling breezes of the trade winds prevent it from getting unbearably hot. There's normally a wet season from November to April, with brief, heavy showers and sometimes cyclones between January and March. They're often too far south to present a huge danger, although there have been exceptions. Nature can really display its true strength then.'

'Is there no end to your talents?' she asked light-heartedly. 'You could have been a weatherman.' Her tummy rumbled, in protest of running on empty. 'Shall we have our bananas?'

He was much keener to return to the cabin for a beer. 'Let's head back. We can eat them on the way. Banana is *jaina* in the Fijian language by the way.'

'Thank you.'

'That's *vinaka,*' he informed her.

She looked puzzled. 'Vinegar?'

'No,' he corrected. '*Vinaka*. It's Fijian for *thank you*.'

'Ah! In that case, vinaka for showing me some more of your breath-taking island.'

She blew him a kiss. 'Another wonderful day in the sun without the need for clothes. I've loved it!'

Ollie was pleased. 'There's an old Yiddish proverb,' he told her. 'Would you like to hear it?'

Whilst some people might have found his frequent quotes annoying, she really enjoyed them and nodded enthusiastically.

' *'The truth can walk around naked; the lie has to be clothed.* "

12

The day Emma was dreading finally arrived. Benny was due to fly in from Nadi with the food and drink. When he departed, he would be taking her with him, away from the island.

She had hoped Ollie would change his mind and invite her to stay for a little longer, but it seemed not. He had offered to help her pack her things, but she told him she could manage.

He was instead on the beach, watching the sunrise, after which he would no doubt do his morning meditation.

There were tears in her eyes as she started folding clothes and putting them in the suitcase. She had so enjoyed her time with him, despite the discovery of being conned by the fake travel company. Eagerly adopting Ollie's lifestyle instead, she had become an ardent naturist, relishing every minute of her newly found body freedom.

As she packed her beach costume, which had been worn for less than an hour the first morning, she reflected on what was really causing her so much unhappiness.

She had not intended to fall in love with him, but it had happened, not that he seemed to be aware. He had been exceptionally nice to her but had failed to show any real affection or intimacy. She had secretly even questioned his sexual orientation, although his masculine mannerisms and mention of a previous girlfriend suggested he was heterosexual.

Emma could quite understand why he wanted to be alone. After all, it was the very reason he had sold up everything and bought the island. He had travelled halfway around the world in his determined search for solitude and silence. Had this not been his intention, then he would have surely brought someone else with him for company.

It was she herself who was the fly in the ointment, she needed to accept, for she had no place on his private retreat, even if fate had brought her to him.

Despite this, she and Ollie seemed to get on so well together and shared a similar sense of humour. Some of his rather unusual ideas appeared a little strange to start with, but the more they talked the more he fascinated her. His intelligence and encyclopaedic knowledge of things she had no previous notion of never failed to amaze her. His clever ability to come out with quotes had grown on her and were always apt to what they were discussing. He had also kindly offered to teach her more about his hypnotic meditation, the occultist Aleister Crowley and religion, but time had run out.

Ollie was undoubtedly her ideal man, being caring and protective. Extremely good looking, strong and alluring, she was filled with desire whenever their eyes met. Confident and uninhibited, his personality revealed a great depth of warmness and tenderness. Sadly, her longing to be cherished and for him to express reciprocal attraction towards her was now a rejected hope.

She packed the remainder of her clothes, the tiniest

consolation being that they were all unworn and so would not need washing.

Tears streamed down her face, as she sobbed her broken heart out.

Meanwhile, Ollie sat on the beach, staring out to sea. Although the sunrise had been as magnificent as ever, for once he had failed to enjoy its splendour. It was as if the sun and he had temporarily lost their fascination for each other.

As he thought about Emma, emptiness filled his heart. He had got used to her sitting by his side, as they watched creation's morning ascension together. Without her today he had felt only sorrow.

He recalled how despite his annoyance at finding a stranger on his island, he had taken an interest in her at first sight. He pictured her again as she had been then, the strikingly beautiful woman, standing on the beach end of the jetty. He could still visualise her in the low-cut short pink dress she had been wearing, her long messy blond hair dancing gently in the breeze.

The next morning she had slowly peeled off her costume, revealing her incredibly desirable figure. He had admiration for the way she had wisely used her natural assets to accomplish success in her chosen modelling career, free of concern over what some feminists might think.

Even more attractive was her natural, caring and kind personality, which had quickly shone through, along with a playful sense of humour and youthful enthusiasm for life.

Her self-assured eye contact proved she was comfortable in his company and her body language left little doubt she was keen on him. She would irresistibly flip back her hair and tilt her head when they were looking at each other, exposing her sensuous feminine neck. Just as captivating was her naturally seductive smile and the way she could put an amorous purr in her voice, which was hot enough to melt butter.

He was so confused. Part of him desperately wanted her in his life, to share and experience the things which mattered. She seemed really interested in what he had told her so far about spirituality and there was so much more he could teach her. He had been thrilled when she had asked him to show her how to meditate and she was beginning to overcome her long-held fear of silence.

There was one big dilemma, however. None of this had anything at all to do with the reason he had come out to Fiji. His sole aim had been to be alone, to explore and develop his own spirituality, through silence. If he asked Emma to stay with him, he would almost certainly be throwing all this away. He had already missed countless important meditation sessions and bitterly regretted it.

She was only a few years younger than him, but had come from a life filled with glamour, parties and loud music. It was more than likely she would quickly tire of him and such a remote existence in the middle of nowhere. He had to accept that their individual paths through life were so different. This relatively small remote desert island was no place for a woman of her temperament. Although she would not realise it, his insistence on her leaving was more than anything for her own good.

He made his way back up to the cabin.

When he got there, he saw her bags outside the door, ready to be taken down to the jetty.

'How was the sunrise?' she asked him, not really caring but trying to hide her emotions.

He was completely honest. 'Not at its best. There was something lacking. It was almost as if an inexperienced artist had painted it.'

His saying this gave her the chance to suggest he might have missed her. 'Do you think it was because I wasn't there with you?'

'Maybe,' he conceded, intentionally trying to sound non-committal.

The atmosphere was heavy and awkward, as they made the effort to eat breakfast. Neither of them felt hungry and just toyed with the food on their plates.

As they did so, he attempted to make conversation. 'What will you do when you get back to Nadi?'

She had given it little thought. 'I'm not sure. Perhaps I should phone my agent when the plane lands and see if she can set up some more modelling work in Australia.'

'If not,' he supposed, 'you'll go straight back to London.'

'I could,' she considered, 'and stay with my parents, as I often do when I'm working in the capital, or I could head straight back down to Brighton, where I've got a small flat.'

Ollie knew the city well, aware it was linked with Hove. 'You'll be able to go on the naturist beach near the Marina when it's warm enough. The Volk's tourist railway runs along the seafront to it, from just past Brighton's Palace Pier.'

'I've been on it,' she told him, 'but not to the beach, as I wasn't a naturist then. It's quite old.'

'If you're talking about the beach, it opened in 1980,' he had read somewhere, 'and claims to have been the first public naturist beach in the UK. Volk's on the other hand opened in 1883, making it the oldest electric railway in the world. There's also a more secluded, but unofficial naturist beach down the road from there in Portslade.'

'All the beaches around there are mostly covered in lumpy pebbles,' she pointed out. 'There's no soft white sand like I've been able to enjoy here.'

'True,' he had to admit, 'but Brighton's got lots of nightlife, with all its trendy clubs, pubs and wine bars.'

The hand gesture she gave was dismissive. 'I don't think any of them are going to have the same appeal as they did before I came here. They'll be far too noisy for my liking now.'

Ollie was left open-mouthed by what she had said. If she was being honest, her few days on the island seemed to have remarkably changed her way of thinking. What had happened to the Prosecco swigging party girl? He only hoped he had not ruined her life.

Knowing Benny would be arriving soon, he thought they had better make their way to the beach. 'I'm going to put your bags on the trolley,' he told her. 'You need to put some clothes on.'

It was certainly not something she wanted to do. 'I was going to wait until the very last minute,' she protested, 'and slip into something just before boarding the plane.'

'We both need to dress now,' he had already decided, 'before Benny spots us. I don't want to upset him, as he's my only contact with the outside world.'

*   *   *

He went inside the cabin and returned wearing his shorts. It felt rather strange, but knew it was necessary.

Emma slipped on the same short pink dress she had arrived in, confining her bra, panties and shoes initially to her flight bag.

Having second thoughts, she reluctantly took them out again and put them on. 'It's not fair, she grumbled. 'You men can walk around naked from the waist up, yet us women have to cover up. Even the outline of our nipples showing through our clothing can upset some people.'

Ollie totally sympathised with the point she was making but thought it the wrong time to start a discussion on the subject. Instead, he lifted her bags onto the trolley.

'You might want to use the toilet,' he recommended. 'It'll be your last chance before you get off the plane at Nadi airport.'

She took his advice, unable to stop herself from weeping again once she was out of his sight. She so wanted to beg him to let her stay but felt it would be unfair.

When she returned, Ollie immediately noticed how red and puffy her eyes were. To see her like this hurt him deeply, but he knew their parting was inevitable.

They did not speak at all on the way to the beach. He pulled the trolley and she pushed from behind.

As they got there, they heard the plane and saw it come into view. Circling around the island once, it touched down not far from the jetty.

Benny manoeuvred it closer and stopping the engine climbed out.

He waved to Ollie, but then a look of surprise appeared on his face, as he spotted a woman. 'You're not alone I see. Have you been taking in guests?'

'This is Emma,' Ollie told him as he got closer. 'She's been staying for few days. I won't go into detail about how she ended up here. It's a long story, but she was flown in by Paradise Pleasure.'

'I'm surprised they knew there was anyone living on the island, or what you'd called it,' Benny told him, 'but I suppose word soon gets around, even in this part of the world.'

He could see the cases on the trolley. 'Am I right in assuming she's leaving?'

'You've got it in one,' Ollie confirmed. 'If you can fly her to Nadi, she can sort herself out from there.'

'No problem at all,' the pilot assured them. 'Let's get all your food and other things unloaded and up to the cabin, then we can get Emma and her luggage onboard.'

Once everything was transferred, she explained to Benny about her intended holiday and how it had turned out to be non-existent.

'What a dreadful thing to happen.' he sympathised. 'Mind you, it was fortunate you ended up on an island with at least someone on it. I'm sure Ollie has looked after you.'

'He's been really nice,' she told him. 'In fact, I'm sorry to be leaving.'

She glanced over at Ollie, but he did not seem to have heard. 'Actually, I don't want to go at all,' she said in a much louder voice, 'but it seems the island is only big enough for one person.'

Ollie was too busy dealing with the frozen foods to take in any conversation.

Once they were safely stored, however, he brought out three chilled beers. 'Time for a quick drink Benny before you need to leave?'

'Not whilst I'm working,' came the reply. 'I've got three more flights today and I'm a bit pushed for time.'

Ollie had forgotten pilots do not drink on duty, even in the middle of the Pacific and instead gave him the list of things he would need delivered next time.

He went to hand Emma a bottle, but she declined too. It was probably the right decision, with there being no toilet on the small aircraft.

As she was finding it more and more difficult to hide her sorrow, it came as a relief when Benny said they had better get back to the plane.

With her cases safely loaded, Benny helped her aboard, making sure she knew how to fasten her seatbelt.

Only when the door was shut did she realise Ollie was not coming along the jetty to say goodbye. As they prepared for take-off, she could see him through the window standing on the beach. His hands were in his pockets and he looked as if he did not have a care in the world.

His presumed nonchalant attitude should have angered her, but her sadness was too great for that. She could only shed tears at the thought of never seeing him again.

Benny was totally unaware of her distress and as the plane accelerated, he moved it into deeper water.

Closing her eyes, she took a deep breath, ready to be

whisked away from the island and the man she had fallen in love with.

It suddenly became apparent that the plane was slowing down, rather than taking off.

She opened her eyes, wiping the tears with the back of her hand.

Looking through the window she spotted Ollie on the jetty. He was jumping up and down, waving his arms frantically in the air.

Benny had seen him too and realised something was wrong. Guiding the aircraft back, he stopped the engine.

Opening the door, he waited for an explanation.

Ollie's voice was choked. 'I'm sorry Benny, but there's been a change of plan. Emma's not leaving. I need her to stay with me, here on the island.'

The pilot turned to Emma inside. 'Did you hear what he said?' he checked. 'He's asking you to stay.'

Emma broke whatever the world speed record was for unbuckling a seat belt. She was on her feet and out through the door in just a couple of seconds.

In another she was in Ollie's arms.

Both were tearful, but now more from joy.

Benny needed no further explanation. What he was watching said it all. He offloaded her bags and squeezing past the embracing couple, put her luggage back on the trolley.

As Benny was about to board again, Ollie separated himself from Emma and shouted to him. 'I think you'd better deliver again next week and double up on all the orders, so there's plenty for us both. We'll also need additional sun lotion, aftersun and insect repellent.'

Benny gave him the thumbs up, but Ollie had one final request. 'This is particularly important. In future, please always add a couple of cases of the very best Prosecco!'

13

As Benny's plane disappeared into the distance, Ollie escorted Emma along the jetty to the beach.

The first thing she did was to slip out of her clothes. He did the same, both eager to continue their naturism.

'Hold me tight,' she whispered, desperately needing him close.

He took her in his arms and they stood hugging each other for a while.

'Thank goodness you changed your mind about me,' she sighed, 'but what made you, at the last moment?'

'I couldn't possibly let you go,' he needed her to know, 'for I would never have seen you again. I am so in love with you and want you as part of my life. It's why I couldn't say goodbye. I was trying hard to hide my distress, for a man should never let a woman see him cry.'

'Don't you believe it,' she enlightened him. 'A man sharing his emotions is endearing. It shows he trusts the person he loves with his heart. What about your plans though, your intention to live a life of silent meditation?'

'It's something I still want,' he admitted, 'but with you by my side.'

Emma was deeply touched. 'I'll try and give you all the space you need.'

'I'd prefer for us to work on this together,' he hoped she would agree, 'so we can both benefit by helping each other. It's the least I can do after upsetting you so much.'

'It wasn't entirely your fault,' she insisted. 'We should have both been more open about our feelings for each other.'

They kissed, no longer just as friends do, but as lovers.

As they took her cases back to the cabin, Ollie had an idea. 'Why don't we celebrate tonight? We could have dinner down on the beach, under the stars, with the water lapping at our feet.'

Emma pictured the scene. 'It sounds really romantic, but what about all those dangerous sea creatures you warned me about?'

'No worries,' he pledged. 'I'll be there to protect you. Anyway, it will be us doing the eating, not them.'

Emma was reassured and not just by what he said. Happiness was quickly making a return.

While she unpacked, he made himself busy with the trolley, moving the table and chairs to the beach, along with some coconut matting and cushions, in case they wanted to relax later. He transferred the crockery, cutlery, glasses, mineral water, wines and a bottle of Cognac in a large cardboard box.

'What would you like to eat tonight?' he asked her when he got back.

'Let's have something cold,' she urged. 'It'll be easier than trying to keep it warm.'

He thought it a good idea. 'How about chicken salad then? Although it's not very romantic.'

'It'll be fine,' she felt sure, 'especially with dressing.'

'Surely you don't want us to put clothes back on?' he doubted. 'You love naturism.'

'I was referring to the salad when I said *dressing*,' she clarified, 'not to us. I'll prepare it, whilst you cook the meat.'

'I'm pleased you're happy with the menu,' he let on, 'for the chicken's been defrosting since we got back, not that it takes long in this temperature.'

When everything was ready, Emma assumed they would be heading straight for the beach.

Ollie had another idea. 'Why don't we watch the sunset first?'

'We can do so down on Benny's beach, can't we?' she figured, 'like we do the sunrises?'

'Unfortunately not,' he explained. 'It faces east, which is fine for sunrises, but we need the west for sunsets.'

She immediately realised how ridiculous her suggestion must have sounded. 'Of course! I wasn't thinking properly.'

'An easy mistake,' he assured her, 'but not to worry. There's no beach directly west from here, but there's a rocky area and it's nearby, as the island's narrow this end. We'll just take a couple of cushions to sit on and some insect repellent.'

There was no path as such either in that direction, but it only took a few minutes for them to make their way between the trees.

He placed the cushions side by side on a flat rock, which made a quite comfortable improvised seat. 'Let's do a short meditation whilst we're waiting. It'll set the mood.'

They both closed their eyes. Emma could remember the technique he had showed her for stilling her mind, but tonight her thoughts were far too dominant. As she let one drift away, its place was immediately taken by another. The sea was distracting too, being slightly rougher and noisier on this side of the island. She tried to block out the sound but found it annoyingly impossible and so concentrated on her breathing instead.

After a few minutes she realised her breaths had become slower and deeper. If nothing else, she was at least nice and relaxed. It felt good.

'You can finish now if you like,' Ollie recommended, 'for the sun's going down.'

Opening her eyes, she gave them a rub, wondering how long she had been sitting there.

He could tell what she was thinking, merely by the bewildered look on her face. 'Time is irrelevant when you're meditating.'

They watched in reverence, as the incredible ball of fire seemed to be saying good night to them. It performed to perfection its famous illusion of sinking like an enormous orange into the horizon. Its brilliant rays stretched across the semi-transparent azure tropical sky, reflecting just as the sunrises did, on the surface of the water below.

The enchanting visual spectrum of extravagant and vibrant colours scattered and mixed crimson and scarlet reds, brilliant yellows, with soft hints of pink. Lilac and lavender purples joined in briefly too, but sadly nature's wonderous spectacle lasted for too short a time. It was enough however for the two watching to commit such a sunset to memory, just as Oscar-Claude Monet, the famous French impressionist, had to canvas.

Ollie broke the silence. 'Do you remember our witnessing the splendid sunrise the other morning?'

She nodded. 'Yes. You made it special, by encouraging me to watch it closely. You also told me about the sky goddess Nuit.'

He was pleased she had not forgotten. 'Then you might also recall my mentioning Aleister Crowley, the famous occultist. I quoted the dawn greeting to the sun from his Liber Resh ritual. There's a similar salutation for the evening, also using Ancient Egyptian symbolism. It goes like this: *'Hail unto Thee who art Tum in Thy setting, even unto Thee who art Tum in Thy joy, who travellest over the Heavens in Thy bark at the Down-going of the Sun. Tahuti standeth in His splendour at the prow, and Ra-Hoor abideth at the helm. Hail unto Thee from the Abodes of Day!'* Reciting this marks the end of daytime in an extremely personal and spiritual way. There's a similar hailing for noon and at midnight and it's customary to follow each of them with the sign of silence.'

He stood up to show her. 'With your left hand at your side, you place the tip of your right hand's index finger on your lower lip. Such a position is associated with the Graeco-Roman Harpocrates, the god of silence, who was adapted from the Egyptian child god Horus.'

'It looks like the same gesture people use when making a 'Sshh' sound, demanding quiet,' she supposed.

'It does,' he agreed. 'Although not everyone knows where the symbol originated, it has become universal. Raising the index finger of the right hand has long been used to get attention and then placing it on the closed lips gives it that obvious meaning.'

She pointed her finger to her mouth, but playfully pretended to chew. 'And this gesture is just as important because it means Emma wants to eat. Can we go to the beach now?'

'Of course,' he chuckled. 'I'm getting peckish too.'

They called at the cabin en route to collect the hamper of food, carrying it between them.

Once on the beach, Ollie dragged the table and then the chairs across the sand, positioning them so that they were just in shallow water.

He unpacked the crockery, cutlery, and food, before opening a bottle of red and another of white. 'Which would you prefer, red or white?'

She pointed to the white and so he poured them both a glass of Sauvignon Blanc. 'I think you'll like this one. It's from New Zealand, with the aromatic notes of grapefruit, tropical fruit and cut grass.'

Emma was impressed. 'You're quite the connoisseur.'

He chose to come clean. 'Although I've drunk it before, I was cheating, by referring to the notes on the label.'

Pulling out a chair for her to sit on, he lowered himself opposite. They clinked their glasses, before both taking a sip.

She licked her lips. 'Umm. Dry, crisp and drinkable, but I still prefer Prosecco,'

'Somehow I thought you might,' he had already anticipated, 'but you'll have to wait until next week, when Benny brings you some.'

She had overheard him asking the pilot to add her sparkling wine to the deliveries. 'It was very thoughtful of you, but in the meantime, this will do nicely thank you. I enjoyed the red we were drinking the other evening by the way, whatever it was.'

He could not remember either. 'It could have been the Cabernet Sauvignon, Shiraz, Syrah, or Malbec. What do you think?'

She shrugged her shoulders. 'It's no good asking me. I've no idea. In the absence of Prosecco, I'll just have to try them all and then I might be able to tell you.'

She shuffled her feet in the water, causing little ripples. The sea was pleasantly warm. 'It's just as well I didn't wear my heels.'

'They would have been a big mistake on the soft sand,' he agreed, 'not that I've noticed you wearing them at all, since you first arrived. Bare feet are much more practical and I am sure more comfortable. The same goes for clothes. Who needs them on such a balmy evening?'

Thanks to him, she really had become truly hooked on naturism. 'Not me, for sure. This is perfect. Just the two of us, dining like this by the water's edge.'

She had admittedly been glancing down at her feet every so often, to make sure none of her toes were missing. Determined not to spoil the occasion, she tried to rid her mind of sea snakes and other unpleasant things.

With just the light of the moon, Ollie realised he had forgotten something.

Leaping up, he delved into the box he had brought things in and produced a candle and matches. Having no candlestick, he lit it and then secured it to a small plate with molten drops of wax.

'How romantic,' Emma thought aloud.

They touched glasses again and began to eat. 'You really

seem to enjoy the sunrises and sunsets,' she considered. 'You've made me appreciate them too.'

'Whilst the sun is always there,' he expounded, 'it seems to have even greater significance in its rising and sinking, almost as if it's making a statement. Humans have always considered the sun to be a mighty god, or at least the outer emblem of some majestic deity. Witnessing how the sun gives light and life to the world, led them to realise how much the whole of existence depends upon it. Anxiety grew when the sun became less visible, such as in wintertime and they welcomed it with sheer joy and celebration when it reappeared in all its glory. Their adoration of the sun formed the basis of their religious beliefs, as did the worship of nature's generative powers, the symbols of creation.'

They were both enjoying their simple meal. All the while she was contemplating what he had said. 'You come out with the most amazing things. It's one of the reasons you fascinate me so. You're so confident and knowledgeable about what you say, but you also make me laugh, which I like. A lot of men only seem to enjoy talking about women and especially sex, with football, rugby, cricket and alcohol next in line. Some are obsessed too with online gaming, cars and bikes, all of which are of no interest to me.'

'What do women discuss with each other then?' Ollie hoped to find out.

She gave herself time to think, savouring her food and then taking a large sip of wine. 'We talk about all sorts of things, a lot of them decidedly female and functional. We discuss the subject of sex probably as much as men do. We also enjoy naughty gossip about who's doing it with whom and sometimes make comparisons about our boyfriends.' She gave him a sly wink, adding, 'and other toys. We're just as interested in general beauty, useful health tips, fashion, food and social media. There's always work to discuss and even the lack of equality. Travel plans are a must, as are our ideas for the future.'

'On the subject of holidays,' he reflected, 'and although I've said it several times before, it's such a shame yours went so terribly wrong. There you were, expecting a fun time with lots of partying and instead you've ended up on a desert island with me.'

'I have no regrets at all,' she vowed. 'If things had gone to plan, I'd never have met you. That would have been really sad.'

Reaching over, he took her hand in his. 'It's nice of you to say so. Although I have always believed we have the right to determine our own course in life, the way unexpected things sometimes happen does suggest destiny might well play a part. Had I not had the out-of-body experience a few years ago, which I told you about, it's most unlikely I'd be on this island now.'

Emma counted her blessings he was here when she had arrived. As she sipped her wine, she wondered how his life might have been. 'What do you think you'd have been doing if you hadn't come here?'

'I'd probably still be running my former business in London,' he reckoned, 'investing in more and more property and clocking up the millions. At the same time, I would have been getting increasingly stressed about it all. The thought frightens me.'

'You must have been incredibly successful in your career,' she had already worked out, 'to afford to buy an island like this.'

'I was,' he confided, 'but I was fortunate to be young. They say people worry about things a lot more as they get older. Eventually, I would have got unduly anxious about everything under the sun, like changes to interest rates, inflation and so on. I can imagine myself lying in bed at night, wide awake and unable to sleep, troubled about how my commercial properties might become vacant, because of changes to shopping trends, a major financial crash, or even an unexpected health crisis, such as a pandemic. I would fear natural disasters, perhaps through climate change, or another deadly world war. Most, if not all of these fears would hopefully never materialise, but I'd still likely end up with a heart attack, just like my father did.'

She wanted to reassure him of having made the right decision. 'I can understand completely why you got out when you did, seeking instead a life of spiritual calm on this lovely island.'

He made light of it. 'Precisely and what apprehensions do I have now? Only that Benny might forget to bring your Prosecco!'

'Your priorities are spot on,' she commended. 'Such a disaster would be unparalleled.'

They both laughed. He noticed she had almost finished her salad. 'Is that simple but healthy meal going to be enough for you?'

She gave him one of her suggestive looks. 'You often ask me if I've had sufficient, but I'm deliberately leaving room for the desert.'

'There isn't one I'm afraid,' he apologised, refilling her glass.

'I know there's not,' she purred suggestively, 'but I'm sure we can think of something. *'Variety is the spice of life'* as they say.' She felt quite pleased with herself, coming out with a quote, even if it was a rather overused one.

She pointed to the cushions and matting he had brought to the beach. 'I see there's something for us to relax on.'

'I thought it would be a good idea,' he had presupposed. 'Just in case you didn't want to sit with your feet in the water all evening, tempting the nasties.'

Taking the red wine with them they settled down, side by side, looking up at the stars. The moon cast a shadow between the palm trees and the only sound was that of the water gently toying with the sand.

'Although I lost my holiday,' Emma told him, 'I'm happier now than I've ever been.'

Ollie was pleased to hear her say so. Leaning over, he kissed her lightly on the lips.

'Make love to me,' she urged, 'please,' her arms pulling him even closer.

A crestfallen look appeared on his face. 'I want to, so much, but as I wasn't expecting anyone else to be on the island, I didn't bring any umm …protection.'

She gave him a flirty smile, her hand reaching into the small bag she had brought with her. 'I was expecting to be staying at a party resort remember, so I came prepared, just in case.'

He took the packet she handed him. 'How sensible of you.'

Gazing deeply but warmly into her eyes, he could clearly see the tender soul within.

She likewise studied him, their closeness capturing his

natural male scent. 'You smell nice.'

'You too,' he complimented back.

'I should hope so,' she confided. 'I'm wearing a really expensive perfume. It was one I did a TV commercial for.'

He breathed in deeply, savouring the fragrance. 'Oh yes. It's a turn on alright. I can detect hints of jasmine and orange blossom, but mostly tuberose, which is appropriately known as the carnal flower.'

'You sound like you're at a wine tasting,' she teased.

'Well, women and wine are similar,' he alleged.

She groaned. 'Old joke. You're going to tell me they both improve with age!'

'They probably do,' he supposed, 'but I was actually going to say that the best ones are scarce but well worth waiting for.'

She hoped he was referring to her. 'I'm no rare vintage red. Just a tasty Prosecco.'

'Which makes you young, fruity, bubbly and fun,' he praised. 'What more could I want?'

Their repartee was undeniably corny, but they were both enjoying it. 'I hope you're not finding my humour too dry,' he added.

She wrapped her arms around his neck. 'Of course not. You're fun to be with and you say the sweetest things.'

He kissed her again, this time even more urgently, her eager lips parting in response.

As she cradled his head in her hands, he tenderly stroked the smooth soft skin of her neck.

Ever so slowly, his palm glided down to one of her perfectly formed breasts, just as she had been secretly yearning it to. He kneaded it gently, his fingers playfully arousing the delicate nipple.

Her chest tingled as his hand slid across to her other bosom, treating it to the same delectable pampering. As he lowered his head, his crimson tongue took over the skilful caresses.

She trembled with desire, affectionally stroking his lean bronzed masculine back.

With deliberate slowness, which made her almost cry out in frenzied anticipation, his exploration crept even lower.

His hand lingered on her velvety stomach, before sinking to a shapely hip. He squeezed her craving inner thigh, his fingertips enticingly close to the centre of her femininity. There they seemed to wait.

The delay was almost unbearable for her.

As little by little they approached her shaven, petal-smooth womanly furnace, she gave a sigh of anticipated relief. Rewarded by the feather-light movement of his slender probing fingers, her breathing slowed and deepened, then turned to tiny uncontrollable gasps.

In response, her hand sought and grasped his phallus, squeezing and stroking, inviting it to possess her.

As he shifted his position, her welcoming thighs spread more.

She felt the swollen head of his throbbing maleness, as it hunted the entrance to her feminine mystery.

The moisture from her readiness helped him sink slowly inside, causing them both to exhale a breath of pleasure.

As they relished the joy of their two having become one, the mighty fusion of love and lust stirred them to movement.

They were in perfect unison, their expressive gasps and

groans growing louder, the faster their lovemaking raced.

The finishing line came quickly, but they crossed it together, reaching the ultimate peak of frantic passion. Uncontrollable fiery rapture engulfed them, plunging the two lovers into the true whereabouts of the place some call Heaven.

When awareness eventually returned, Ollie withdrew, carefully lifting himself over and onto his back.

Glancing at her, he could see her eyes were closed, but there was a rewarding look of contentment on her face. He wondered what she was thinking. Sometimes he could pick up her thoughts, but not this time. Perhaps he was not meant to.

Letting her enjoy the afterglow of their lovemaking a little longer, he then gave her a special kiss, as an outer expression of his indescribable happiness.

She opened her eyes and they sparkled at him. 'I've been waiting for you to be intimate like this for days. I'd almost given up hope.'

'Thank goodness I saw sense in time and asked you to stay here with me,' he said in relief. 'I've been wanting to make love to you ever since you arrived on the island.'

She was puzzled. 'Then why didn't you sooner.'

'If I had,' he thought it important for her to see, 'I would have been taking advantage of you and the situation you found yourself in. You would have probably thought I was just using you.'

She listened to his reasoning but doubted it would have been her reaction. 'I don't think so. Anyway, from the incredible pleasure you've just given me I would have enjoyed being used.'

'There's nothing wrong with lust,' Ollie insisted, 'but it's far better when combined with love. That's how it was this evening, attraction and affection, simply perfect.'

Emma smiled at him adoringly. Her tears of the past were forgotten. Her once aching heart brimmed with yearned-for happiness.

14

Ollie and Emma were back on the beach the next day at dawn. Settling down on the sand together, they awaited the sunrise.

When it came, the magical morning illusion was the most beautiful ever. Its sublime glory stole their breath, as they captured the precious moment as lovers, hand in hand. Like a shared dream, its visual poetry spoke to them in conjured colours and they understood every word.

As they prepared for their meditations, he whispered to her something once said by Paramahansa Yogananda, the Indian yogi guru: *"Through the portals of silence, the healing sun of wisdom and peace will shine upon you."*

Emma tried hard to still her mind, but the excitement of the night before persisted.

Whilst Ollie succeeded in calming his thoughts, she found herself re-running memories. In her mind's eye, she fondly pictured them watching the sunset together, as they had the night before, then dining on the beach, before finally making love in the moonlight.

His voice brought her back to the present. 'You have a happy, contented smile on your face.'

'It's because I was thinking of last night,' she disclosed.

'Any particular part?' he asked out of curiosity.

'All of it,' she told him. 'Every single minute, but particularly of us making love.'

'We are fortunate in having this enchanting island to ourselves,' he reminded her. 'It's totally private, with no one to offend. We are completely alone here, with only nature looking on.'

He pointed to the nearest palm. 'That fine looking tree is a symbol of fertility.'

She was unsure of what he meant. 'In what way?'

'The erect towering trunk signifies the phallus,' he expounded, 'being the male generative organ, whilst its fruit is suggestive of the female ovaries. There are separate male and female flowers, which are either on the same, or separate trees, depending on the species.'

Emma got up and walking over to it took a closer look. 'I've always thought palm trees were exotic, but now I find out they are erotic!'

Ollie wondered if her rhyming was intentional or not. 'The date palm was sacred in the Mesopotamian religions, as it represented human fertility. There's so much symbolism in the world, which sadly most people have no idea about.'

He gestured towards the sun, which had risen higher in the sky. 'The beautiful burning star for example, at the centre of our solar system, has always been the most natural expression of divinity.'

She came and sat down beside him again. 'I can see you're going to intrigue me with your insight into even more things I've never really thought about.'

He hoped so. 'As the creator and preserver of mankind, the

sun has been venerated as either the deity itself, or its outward emblem. Many considered the star to be male and the earth and moon to be female. Gaia, the Greek mother goddess, was worshipped in recognition of our own planet, whilst Osiris, the male Egyptian god, who was often depicted with a giant penis, was believed to have dwelt in the sun. Then there was Mithras, the great Persian deity, who was worshipped as the Saviour and Preserver. There are images of him slaying a bull and then dining on it, with Sol Invictus, the sun god.'

'I wasn't brought up in a religious way,' Emma mentioned. 'My parents never encouraged me to go to Sunday school or church.'

Which was as well, as far as Ollie was concerned. 'You were given the opportunity to explore your own ideas and make up your own mind about such things. So many children grow up blindly following whatever their parents' beliefs are, especially when they're brainwashed into thinking it's all true.'

'At least I know what God really said after he created Adam, the first man,' she claimed. 'Looking at what he had brought into existence, God cursed in dismay: *Oh my Me! I have to do better than this.* Then he tried again and triumphantly created a woman!'

Ollie chuckled. 'His second attempt was definitely a marked improvement.' He was pleased Emma was in such a jolly mood.

'I didn't mean to trivialise what you're talking about,' she assured him, 'and I haven't forgotten what you told me about Adam and Eve when we were discussing naturism. You must have put a lot of thought into whether God exists or not.'

What she was saying was true. He had indeed but wanted to

work their conversation round to the subject of sacred sexuality. It seemed the perfect time, whilst their lovemaking the previous night was still very much in her thoughts.

'I tend to believe a great and powerful creative force exists,' he told her, 'which is beyond our comprehension. I'm quite happy to refer to it as God, but it's certainly not the same sort of deity which most Christians preach about. Nearly all religions are based on fear, which is used as a means of control. Humanity has always created its own gods and goddesses, in recognition of nature's productive forces and sex is unquestionably the most powerful force of all. Without the sex instinct humanity would end. People have recognised the importance of sex since the earliest of times and this influenced how they depicted their gods and goddesses. It's how phallic worship started, being the adoration of nature's reproductive power, symbolised by the male and female sex organs.'

Emma glanced at his and then her own genitalia. 'I think all of the human body is beautiful. Every part of it.'

He could only agree, having been a naturist for some years. 'The earliest Egyptian and Hindu records refer to phallic worship, which pre-dates the Christian era by thousands of years. The Hindus traditionally call the female sexual organ the *yoni* and the male one the *lingam*. As you already know, the phallus is another name for the male penis, especially when erect, and so a phallic symbol is something which resembles or represents it. There were many Greek and Roman temples dedicated to the phallus, for it was regarded as the ancient emblem of the incarnate source of being.'

Emma found this amusing. 'Sorry, but I can't help seeing the funny side. I know a lot of men are obsessed with their penis and worry unduly about its size, but having it worshipped in temples is something else.'

'Maybe, but the ancient people really were serious about this,' he emphasised. 'The worshippers of Dionysus, who was the ancient Greek god of wine and fertility, headed their processions with a great big giant phallus. The same happened in the festivities of Bacchus, who was the Roman version of Dionysus. The Roman phallic god Priapus, the deity of procreation, was also always represented by a figure of this kind. Many sculptures, engraved stones, and coins still survive, showing him sometimes alone, but often as the central figure in suggestive sexual scenes. The Hindu lingam is still a religious emblem throughout India. As the divine symbol of Shiva, the Reproducer, it can be found in just about every temple dedicated to his worship.'

'I love learning about all these remarkable things,' she assured him. 'I might even qualify to be a contestant on *Mastermind*, television's general knowledge quiz show.'

'And what would your chosen subject be?' he wondered.

'It would be the phallus of course,' she decided, 'and all the gods it inspired. I'm ready for some breakfast, but you can tell me more about it on the way.'

They gathered their things together and headed for the path.

Ollie was pleased she was taking what seemed to be a genuine interest in what they were discussing. 'You'd be surprised how many phallic symbols there are,' he went on. 'The fish, the cockerel and the arrow are three prominent ones on weathervanes and the fig tree is suggestively appropriate too. Its trilobed leaf is symbolic of the male genitals and so has long been used to cover nude figures.'

'Except for naturists,' she pointed out.

Her saying this reminded him of a funny story. 'There's a joke about the fig leaf, which I'll tell you later. In the meantime, it's important to remember that the ancient people saw things differently to us, as their knowledge was rather limited. For example, they believed the rain which made the crops grow, contained within it the seed of life, the male sperm. Therefore, they thought the rain was the heavenly semen of the all-powerful creator God.'

'What a massive ejaculation a cloudburst of torrential rain must have taken!' she kidded.

'No doubt,' he granted, 'but they also seriously believed the thunder and howling wind, which sometimes accompanied the rain, was the voice of God. The average person today has no idea that the names of Zeus and Yahweh, or Jehovah, the principal gods of the Greeks and Hebrews, were derived from the Sumerian, meaning *juice and fecundity*, *spermatozoa* and *seed of life*.' Hence the belief of anointing things with semen, to dedicate them and make them holy. In a similar way, most Christians are unaware that both the Semitic and Greek words for Christ, the anointed, or smeared one, came from the Sumerian terms, MASh and ShEM, meaning semen, or resinous sap.'

'Would a banana be alright for you?' he asked her when they arrived back at the cabin. 'No sexual symbolism intended. We can have something more substantial for lunch.'

'It'll do nicely,' she agreed, 'and a black coffee please.'

He set to work making a pot from pre-ground beans.

'I've told you so far mainly about the gods and the male side of phallic worship,' he recapped. 'It's only right you hear a little about the goddesses and the female principle.'

She was like-minded. 'Equal rights and all that.'

'Unfortunately,' he revealed, 'when it came to nature's productive forces, humanity once considered the male contribution to be far more essential than the female. As the woman's role was passive and receptive, it was seen as purely functional. Eventually however, they realised that not only was the union of the two sexes necessary, but the female aspect was vitally important too. The female sexual organs became revered as symbols of nature's generative powers as well. The yoni, which is of Sanskrit origin, from *yauna*, meaning vulva, womb, place of birth, origin, water and so on, became esteemed. Just as the phallus was symbolised by the male gods, the yoni was signified by the goddesses. These included Astarte, Juno, Venus, Diana, Artemis, Aphrodite, Hera, Rhea, Cybele, Ceres, and others.'

'Who was the very first goddess then?' she probed.

He was not sure. 'It's difficult to say, but Inanna was certainly an early one. She was worshipped in Sumer, the site of the earliest known civilisation, possibly as early as 4,000 BC. As the goddess of love and war, she became later known to the Akkadians and Assyrians as the goddess Ishtar. The ancient people were mystified by women, finding it incredible that they could cause the male penis to become erect, sometimes just by their physical presence. This led in time to allegations that the female ability to arouse a man's passions was sorcery, contributing towards the Church's hostility to sexuality and their distrust of the fairer sex. The Catholic Church's Inquisition murdered so many innocent people, often accusing them of much misunderstood witchcraft.'

She had heard this before somewhere. 'How many people do you reckon the Inquisition was responsible for killing?'

His answer came as a shock. 'Some historians put the figure at millions. The Inquisition was partly abolished in the early 19th century, but not in the Papal States. It survived as part of the Roman Curia, the administrative department of the Holy See, through which the Catholic Church's affairs are conducted. It's now known as the Congregation for the Doctrine of the Faith.'

Seeing her shake her head in disbelief, he lightened the tone. 'But enough of all this gloom and doom. Let's take our coffee and fruit outside and enjoy the sunshine.'

They sat down at the table, both taking a sip of coffee. The taste and aroma were pleasing.

He scratched his head, trying to remember where he had got to. 'What was I saying?'

'You were telling me about the fascination for women's seductive powers,' she helped out.

'Ah yes. I was indeed. The word *fascinate* comes from the Latin *Fascinus*, who was a Roman god of masculine generative power,' he explained. 'His rites were celebrated by Vestal Virgins and his symbol was the winged phallus. His followers wore smaller depictions of such a penis around their necks for protection.'

Emma giggled at hearing this, coffee escaping her lips and running down her chin. She wiped it away. 'I wonder what reaction I would get from men if I were to wear a willy around my neck?'

'Probably the wrong one,' he thought likely. 'There have

been times as well when the female sexual organs have been seen as the real symbol of sacredness. The vulva has long been considered a sacred symbol by the Hindu worshippers of Shakti, the supreme feminine creative deity, as it has in Indian Kaula and Tantra practices. Elsewhere, the conch shell is an emblem of the female organ and it's still worn in some parts of the world as a good luck charm and protective amulet. The custom of hanging a horseshoe above a door, the 'U' shape being another symbol of the female vulva, is likewise supposed to bring good luck and keep evil out. The fish too was sacred to goddesses of a sexual nature, its mouth being vulva shaped. Going back to the fig tree, its feminine significance is in its fruit, as it bears a resemblance to the shape of the female uterus. Eating the fruit was thought to promote fertility.'

His mention of the fig reminded her of something he had said earlier. 'You promised to tell me a joke about a fig leaf.'

'Alright then,' he obliged. 'You might have heard it before, but it should still amuse you. A guy was going to a fancy-dress party, so he phoned a costume shop and asked to be sent a fig leaf. When it arrived, he stripped off and tried it on, but it was too small, for he was very well endowed. After phoning the shop again and explaining the problem, a larger one arrived, but it still didn't cover everything. He phoned for another and it came with a note which read: *'This is the largest we have. If it's still not big enough, we suggest you paint your overlong penis black, stick it in your ear and go to the party as a petrol pump!'*

Emma creased up with laughter, so much that it took a couple of minutes for her to fully control her hysterics. Finally, she managed to say, 'He wouldn't have needed a fig leaf in the first place if he'd been a naturist.'

Ollie agreed. 'And it would have given a whole new twist to nude body painting!'

15

Two days later, Emma was still laughing on and off.

Ollie was amazed she had found the joke so amusing. 'It wasn't all that funny, surely?'

'I just keep thinking about the man arriving at the fancy dress party,' she pictured, 'his huge willy stuck in his ear, telling people he's come as a petrol pump. I then start imagining what their reaction would have been.'

'Shock probably,' he supposed, as they made their way to the beach, in readiness for the sunrise. 'Perhaps a few facts about animals might take your mind off the human penis. An elephant's penis can be more than three feet long, allowing him to rest on his erection, almost like a fifth leg. A whale's penis could even be about ten feet long, when out of its urogenital slit. A pig's penis is shaped like a corkscrew. Male snakes have two penises but only use one at a time. Male alligators have a constant erection which lasts their entire lives. The banana slug has a penis which grows out of pores on the top of its head. If it gets stuck inside the female, she will eat it. Likewise, the female black widow spider and praying mantis consumes the whole male in copulation.'

'None of what you're telling me is helping at all,' she

sniggered, 'and think yourself lucky I'm not a black widow spider!'

Their light-hearted fun came to a sudden halt as they reached the beach.

'What on earth is that?' he questioned, pointing to further along the sand.

They peered at the shape before them with trepidation. 'It could be a small beached whale, a shark or a dolphin,' he guessed.

'Crikey!' she exclaimed, wanting a better look.

His right arm shot out in front of her, forming a barrier. 'Don't get too close. If it's still alive it could be dangerous, particularly the tail.'

They stood stock still, looking for any movement from the creature, but the dawn light restricted their vision.

'You stay here,' he determined, 'but I need to be nearer.'

'Do be careful,' she entreated.

'I fully intend to be,' he assured her.

Moving a step at a time, he stopped only a short distance from it, his eyes constantly alert for any motion. 'It's a dolphin and I think it's dead.'

Emma had always liked dolphins. 'Oh no,' she uttered. 'Are you sure?' Despite having never seen one before, except in television documentaries, she thought they were rather special animals.

He held his nose. 'It must be lifeless, from the stench it's giving off. There's not much smell to them at all when they're alive, as there's no skin glands.'

He walked around it. 'I'm guessing it must have been dead

when it was washed up, although I can't see any outer signs of injury.'

He bent down, looking closely.

'No! Don't touch it!' she shrieked.

'I wasn't going to,' he made perfectly clear. 'Dead animals can carry disease.'

'Do you think it was ill and died from an infection or something,' she speculated.

'I haven't a clue,' he admitted, shrugging his shoulders. 'Dolphins have predators of course, such as large sharks and orcas, or killer whales as they're otherwise known. They enjoy the dolphins' high fat content. It's why for protection, dolphins usually swim around in pods.'

For a moment she thought he was having her on. 'Pods? Do you mean as in pea pods, or the type used with spacecraft?'

'Neither,' he established. 'A pod is the name given to a group of dolphins travelling together. They can fend off sharks, but their biggest killers are humans. Dolphins are a protected species, but that doesn't stop them from getting caught in fishing nets or colliding with boat propellers. Human pollution can also be fatal for them, as they can choke on some of the things which end up in the sea.'

He pointed to the horizon. 'Look, the sun's coming up.'

Emma had grown to love the sunrises, but it was the dolphin which still had her attention. 'What are we going to do with it?'

'Take it back to the cabin and barbecue it of course. We've got some parsley sauce.'

Although he managed to keep a straight face, seeing the look of disgust on her face he quickly added, 'Only joking!

We must leave it untouched, exactly as it is. It will probably get washed out to sea again. If not, the other wildlife will take care of it. Little goes to waste. In some countries the authorities ask for things like this to be reported, but I don't know if it applies in Fiji or not. It never crossed my mind to ask Brad what I should do if ever a dead dolphin turned up on the beach.'

Emma sensed a degree of sarcasm but proposed something practical. 'We could tell Benny when he arrives with my Prosecco in a few days.'

Ollie was tempted to suggest her white wine might go well with cooked dolphin but thought better of it. 'A good idea,' he agreed instead, 'and Benny can pass on the information to someone if it's necessary. Anyway, shall we go back to the cabin now? It might be better to do our meditation there today.'

She was relieved. 'Absolutely. I don't fancy sitting on the beach with a big dead fish for company.'

'Charming,' he pretended, 'you calling me that.'

'I meant the dolphin, you fool,' she pointed out, playfully kicking some sand at him.

As they made their way back, she told him how she had always liked dolphins.

'They do dolphin sighting tours and snorkelling trips from some of the islands out here,' he informed her, 'but unfortunately I don't even have a boat. They are certainly fascinating animals. I'm not sure what type of dolphin it is, but there's about forty different species. The most common is the Bottlenose and there's also the wonderful Spinner, which can jump as high as ten feet out of the water whilst twirling. They can dive an incredible thousand feet and swim up to 20 miles an hour.'

Emma was impressed yet again by the amount he knew. 'I bet there's even more you can tell me about them?'

'It's only from what I've read in books and learnt from documentaries,' he acknowledged. 'Did you know they never chew their food and have two stomachs? One is for storing food and the other for digestion.'

She had never heard of such a thing. 'How long do they live for?'

'Providing they are more fortunate than the unlucky one washed up on the beach, some can have a lifespan of up to fifty years, although the average is more like seventeen. Not only are they friendly, but highly intelligent too. Albert Einstein, the physicist who developed the theory of relativity, reckoned dolphins are smarter than humans as they play more. We can chat about them some more over breakfast if you like.'

As Ollie set the table, Emma prepared and brought out two bowls of Weet-Bix cereal, a jug of coconut milk and chopped bananas, along with their coffee.

They sat down and he continued their conversation. 'In Greek mythology the dolphin represented resurrection, rebirth and renewal, for it was believed their spirit escorted the spirits of the dead to the afterlife. Through helping humans survive shark attacks and rescuing them from drowning, they became known as a symbol of protection, sailors considering their presence to be a good omen. There's a lovely ancient story about Dionysus, the Greek god I told you about. He was set upon by pirates, who attempted to kidnap him for a ransom. Being a god however, they found it impossible to tie him up. He instead transformed their oars into vicious snakes and himself into a snarling lion. One by one he savaged them, turning the ones who survived into dolphins. As a punishment, he made them help humanity forever.'

'They got off lightly if you ask me,' she reasoned.

'It's only a story,' he reminisced. 'It would probably be considered fake news nowadays. Dolphins having been thought of as large fish by many, they later became a symbol for the mythical Jesus, especially in the form of a dolphin twisted around an anchor. It was supposed to represent Christ's allegorical crucifixion upon the cross. Pictures of dolphins began to appear on religious paintings, sculptures and jewellery. In many cultures, dolphins are supposed to bring good luck and have symbolised things like happiness, humour, playfulness, virtue, teamwork, and courtesy. Their peaceful nature and intelligence demonstrate emotion, which is related to the water element, combined with intellect, a quality of the air element.'

'It's intriguing,' she thought, 'not only about dolphins, but especially your belief that Christ's crucifixion was allegorical?'

'It was purely symbolic,' he controversially claimed, 'as I've hinted at before. It was made up to convey a hidden teaching, as was the entire story of Jesus. The portrayal of the conception and birth of Christ is almost identical to that of Zarathustra, whom I've also mentioned. The rest of Jesus's life seems to have been based on the Hindu sun-god Krishna, who was worshipped at the time of Alexander the Great, 330 years before the so-called Christ. Krishna had likewise been crucified between two thieves and rose again on the third day, before ascending into heaven. The Buddha, Zoroaster, Osiris, Mithras, Horus, Bacchus, Tammuz, Attis, Quetzalcoatl and countless other gods also rose on the third day. As for the cross, it's of sexual origin and has for thousands of years been the sign of a man-god.'

Hearing insights like this made Emma feel extremely fortunate. 'I love all this secret knowledge you're passing on to me,' she exclaimed, 'especially on things like spirituality and sexuality.'

'It's a fascinating subject,' he agreed. 'Carl Jung, the Swiss psychiatrist and psychoanalyst said: *'Sexuality and spirituality are pairs of opposites which need each other.'* The two really are inseparable. When we were discussing the ancient gods and goddesses and phallic worship, I explained how the early religions celebrated sex and even used it as a form of worship. The Christian Church on the other hand made people feel guilty and sinful about sex, mainly as a means of control.'

'Well, it hasn't succeeded with me,' she said defiantly.

'And don't I know it!' he added tongue in cheek. 'There are so many health benefits from a good sex life. It can make us feel younger and happier, slow down the aging process, relieve pain and lower blood pressure. Sex is good for our mental health and can boost immunity. It reduces the chances of diabetes and heart disease, along with risks of breast and prostate cancer. As orgasm releases prolactin, the hormone which makes us feel more relaxed and sleepier, it's a far better remedy for insomnia than any sleeping tablet.'

Emma could recall him describing the health benefits of naturism, the day after she first arrived on the island. 'Perhaps,' she urged, 'naturism and sex should both be prescribed on the National Health Service.'

'Another of your good ideas,' he accepted, 'although preferably not at the same time. It would play havoc with volleyball games, not to mention body painting sessions!'

This amused her. 'It's not fair. You've deliberately got me thinking about the man at the fancy dress party again, disguised as a petrol pump.'

'Although it's a funny story,' he put into perspective, 'it wouldn't work in real life. Men just don't have enough of a hosepipe. The world's longest recorded penis belongs to a man called Jonah Falcon from New York. When aroused, they say it measures thirteen and a half inches. There's a Mexican, named Roberto Esquivel Cabrera who, by attaching weights to his appendage, stretched it to nineteen inches.'

She screwed up her face. 'Perhaps he intended to go fishing. Are there any more interesting facts you've memorised about sexual matters?'

'Of course,' he replied. 'Sex is a basic human need and plays an important part in most people's lives. As Remy de Gourmont, the French symbolist and writer said: *Chastity is the most unnatural of all the sexual perversions.*' Wilhelm Reich, a pupil of Sigmund Freud, claimed the lack of satisfying sex could inhibit the life force, or *orgone*, as he called it. According to statistics, sexual intercourse is taking place globally 100 million times a day. This is not surprising, for 97% of us have sexual fantasies and 10% of our dreams include sex. Some men and women can be aroused even by the aroma of wines, which have a similar effect to human pheromones, the chemical scents which can heighten sexual response.'

'You just wait until my Prosecco arrives!' she promised him.

He pretended to ignore the invitation. 'Some think sex is good for losing weight, but it only burns up about five calories a minute, which is admittedly four more than sitting watching the television. Women are fortunate, for the female orgasm lasts three times as long as men. Finally, what do you think came first, the wheel or sex toys?'

Emma was confident she knew the answer. 'The wheel of course. It has to be.'

'No,' he stumped her. 'The wheel was only invented about 3,500 B.C. but ancient art exists from at least 30,000 years ago, depicting people pleasuring themselves and others with dildos.'

'Talking of which,' she fooled, 'as the banana said to the vibrator, '*I don't know why you're shaking so much. It's me she's going to eat.*"

'You should be writing corny jokes for adult Christmas crackers,' he advised.

'Not me,' she regretted. 'Where do you think I got that one from?'

Ollie had enjoyed their light-hearted conversation but needed to be more serious. 'It's time for us to cast aside such amusing thoughts and do our meditations.'

They cleared the things from the table and went inside the cabin. 'You can sit comfortably on the bed,' he proposed, 'and I'll use the sofa.'

'You know I find it difficult to try and still my mind,' she jogged his memory. 'Now you've made it even more challenging, with all that talk of sex.'

'Quietening the mind is not easy,' he accepted, 'specially to start with. As Swami Sivananda, the Hindu spiritual teacher, explained to his followers: '*Meditation is painful in the beginning, but it bestows immortal bliss and supreme joy in the end.*' You need to be patient.'

He had a good idea. 'Perhaps you should try something different today.'

Taking a candle and holder from the kitchen area, he lit it and placed it on the small table beside the bed.

'Instead of closing your eyes,' he mentored, 'just concentrate on the flame. Try to keep focussed on it, observing it closely and thinking about nothing else.'

Emma was slightly confused. 'But why the flame of a candle?'

He shared a line with her from the *Bhagavad Gita,* the famous Hindu scripture: "*When meditation is mastered, the mind is unwavering, like the flame of a lamp in a windless place.*"

16

Excitement! The day had finally arrived when Benny was due to deliver the supplies, including Emma's precious Prosecco. She could hardly wait.

Although she had grown to adore Ollie and his captivating conversations, she thought it would be nice for once to have a chat with someone else. She loved their lifestyle here on the island, but being completely cut off from civilisation, had no idea at all what was happening in the world. It was only Ollie's compelling knowledge of all things weird and wonderful, which had helped her cope with there being no wi-fi or mobile data.

It was amazing she had survived without access to social media. Her friends must have thought she had disappeared from the face of the Earth. Sarah, her agent, at least knew she was on an eight-week holiday somewhere in Fiji, but even she must have expected a message of some sort by now.

Fearing Ollie might mistakenly think she was tiring of being here with only him, she decided not to appear too enthusiastic about the plane's imminent arrival.

To Ollie, the arrival of Benny and his cargo was going to disturb his routine and although necessary, would be an inconvenience.

Helping to pile the provisions onto the trolley, haul them up to the cabin and store them away would be a chore, especially in the midday heat.

Even though Benny was a pleasant enough man, they had little in common, which meant any conversation would be fairly trivial. At least he had thought ahead and prepared the list of what they would need the next time around.

Ollie had, as he reminded himself yet again, come to the desert island for isolation, the Pacific Ocean making an intentional barrier between himself and the outside world. The unexpected arrival of Emma had completely changed things, from his original objective of living alone in solitude and silence. Worthwhile compromise was only necessary because he had fallen helplessly in love with her.

Fearful she might think he was tiring of human company, if he started whinging about Benny's visit, he thought it best to do the opposite and appear exuberant.

'We had better take the trolley down to the beach with us,' he suggested, as they set off to see the sunrise. 'It will be there ready then, for when our best friend Benny gets here.'

'I'd forgotten it was today,' Emma feigned, hoping he would believe her.

Ollie was taken aback. 'Really? You've been talking about the arrival of your Prosecco all week.'

'I know,' she admitted nonchalantly, 'but it's going to upset our day. I could so much better spend the time working on my meditation.'

Ollie could hardly believe what he was hearing. 'I thought you'd be as excited as I am about chatting to our favourite pilot in just a few hours.' His words were admittedly hypocritical, considering his earlier thoughts, but he did his best to sound sincere. 'You seem more concerned about quietening your mind than getting your favourite bubbly.'

She faked a look of disappointment. 'You should be pleased with my way of thinking.'

'I'm delighted you have your priorities right,' he encouraged, 'but I'm not sure about your reasoning. Meditation is of course far more important than fizzy wine, but I've never believed we gain spiritual points by unnecessarily depriving ourselves of pleasure. We are on this planet to learn through experience and progress spiritually, but there is nothing wrong with enjoyment and happiness.'

He looked along the beach when they reached it. 'At least we can be thankful the dead dolphin was washed away and hasn't returned. We can concentrate on the sunrise, do our meditation and then have breakfast before Benny lands.'

They settled down on their towels and awaited the arrival of the glorious sun. Although they watched it every morning, the experience was always slightly different.

As if knowing they had a busy day ahead, it did not linger. Very soon the Earth's nearest star crept into view. Rising majestically from below the horizon, it poured forth its dazzling display of petal-soft pink and pastel orange hues. It filled the morning sky with joy, reflecting as usual its precious colours proudly onto the surface of the serene and silent sea. Golden rays, like the comforting arms of nature, stretched towards them. The hands of their Father the Sun reached out and gently blessed their bronzed naked skin.

*   *   *

Ollie could tell Emma was daydreaming, just by looking. Although her eyes were open, the sunrise had captivated her, easing her into a trance-like state. He let her rest there for a while, only speaking when he sensed he should. *"Keep your face to the sunshine,"* he whispered, *"and you cannot see the shadows. It's what the sunflowers do."*

She turned her head, smiling. 'What lovely words. Did you make them up?'

'No,' he regretted, 'but I wish I had. Quite a few people have written something along those lines about optimism over the years, including Walt Whitman, the American poet and Helen Keller, a deaf-blind social activist.'

'I would like to think they were her words,' Emma decided. 'She must have been able to appreciate the true beauty of nature, even without the precious gifts of sight and sound.'

Ollie hoped so too. 'What an inspiring thought to start our meditations.'

When they were later sitting outside the cabin having breakfast, Emma suddenly leapt up and rushed inside.

She emerged a couple of minutes later, waving a compact camera in her hand. 'I had completely forgotten about this. I should have taken some photos.'

'You could have used your mobile phone,' he pointed out. 'You don't need roaming data or wi-fi for pictures.'

'But the camera's far better quality,' she alleged.

'I'm sure you're right,' he figured, 'but neither the camera nor mobile can store pictorial memories to the perfection of your mind. There, they will last forever, unless you willingly delete or record over them.'

She pointed the camera in his direction. 'I'm unlikely to ever forget you, but I'm still going to take a picture.'

'If you must,' he consented, 'although you'd make a far prettier shot. You're the glamour model remember, not me.'

She had an idea. 'I didn't bring a selfie stick with me, but if we rest the camera on something and use the timer, we could do some of the two of us together.'

'I'm not really a fan of selfies,' he admitted.

She looked bemused. 'Why not? They're fun.'

'It's egocentric,' he insisted, 'people taking pictures of themselves. It seems they can no longer take photographs of iconic things, without plonking themselves in the foreground. No longer are they content to have a nice picture of the Great Pyramid of Giza in Egypt, the Taj Mahal in India, or the Great Wall of China. Now it has to be a close-up photo of themselves, with the new wonders of the world relegated insignificantly to the background.

Emma detected she had touched a raw nerve and so instead just took a shot of the cabin. It looked decidedly uninteresting on the camera's LCD screen, especially in comparison to any of the great historical monuments and structures he had mentioned.

'We'd better head back to the beach,' Ollie thought necessary, 'as Benny will be here soon. I can hardly wait.'

She turned to leave. 'I'll bring the camera, just in case.'

'Aren't you forgetting something else?' he questioned.

Nothing came to mind. 'There's only the breakfast things and we can clear them away later.'

'I didn't mean those.' As a clue, he very noticeably ran his eyes up and down her body.

She still did not get it.

'You seem to have forgotten we are both naked,' he made plain.

'Of course we are,' she acknowledged, 'but why does that matter? Benny won't mind, will he?'

'He'd be delighted to see you like that, with nothing on,' Ollie was sure. 'He would think he was fantasising, but you've got to remember nudity is officially illegal in Fiji. It only needs him to inadvertently say something about our naturist lifestyle to one of his mates back at the airport and it could spoil everything. I'm just going to put on a pair of swimming shorts while he's here.'

Fortunately, what he said made sense to her. 'I get the message, but it's rather a nuisance. I'd better slip into a bikini then.'

'A good idea,' he agreed, 'but preferably one which is not quite as revealing as the costume you wore to the beach your first morning here.' He could remember it well, or at least what there was of it, being nearly all see-through. The designer had certainly succeeded in creating an extremely sexy garment. 'It'll only be for a short while and then we can be naturists again.'

It seemed Emma had suddenly elected herself as naturism's greatest advocate. 'Swimwear is the most ridiculous clothing ever invented,' she remonstrated. 'The only thing it's any good for is glamour modelling, when full nudity isn't possible. If ever I go swimming again, I'm going to be naked, just as nature meant me to be. No more tight, scratchy, itchy, tickly, irritating, awkward, soggy, cold, uncomfortable, annoying costume for me!'

Having made her point, she stormed off to the cabin, her mind searching for even more adjectives to describe her newly found dislike of swimwear.

Ollie thought a round of applause was appropriate.

She emerged a couple of minutes later wearing a revealing lime green tie-front bikini top and matching briefs.

'Will this do?' she asked him. 'I wore it for a shoot a few weeks ago.'

He thought she looked gorgeous. 'It's great. What product were they promoting?'

'A freestanding dishwasher,' she recalled.

He wondered if he had heard her correctly. 'If you had said a washing machine, I could have just about seen the logic, but a dishwasher?'

'It was a slimline one,' she described. 'I think I was chosen for my looks.'

'Ah! I see their marketing ploy now,' he fathomed. 'If the dishwasher looked anything like you do in that bikini, every husband in the world would persuade their wife they need one.'

She gave him a twirl. 'Do you think so?'

He stepped into his shorts. 'I know so. A little bit of cloth can be sexier than nothing at all, but then it's designed to be.'

Their timing was spot on. Just as their feet hit the sand the seaplane came into view.

As it landed on the water and moved towards the jetty, they gave a welcoming wave.

'Been sunbathing?' Benny asked as he popped his head through the door, spotting their attire.

'No time,' Ollie told him. 'We've been too busy discussing dishwashers.'

With Emma's assistance he pulled the trolley closer to the jetty, then helped the young pilot offload the provisions.

'How have things been on the island then?' Benny checked.

'Very good thanks,' Ollie confirmed, 'and the weather's been great. Emma has settled in and she is really good company. How's First Charter Aviation doing?'

'As busy as ever,' came the reply, as he went back inside the plane for more cargo.

Out came boxes of fresh fruit, vegetables, Weet-Bix, sparkling mineral water, beer and other essentials.

Emma was on the lookout for her Prosecco and was relieved when he emerged with boxes of bottles.

As she helped put them on the trolley, she took a closer look. There were red and white still wines, plus plenty of Ollie's beloved Cognac, but none of her bubbly. 'Haven't you forgotten something?' she asked the pilot.

Benny had a think. 'I don't think so. I've deliberately left the frozen fish and meat to last, so it won't be sitting around in the sun too long. There is more than enough for the two of you until I'm back again. I brought the suntan and aftersun lotions, plus the insect repellent you asked for. I'll just get the frozen things and then we can move it all up to the cabin.'

He brought the remaining items out, which were packed in ice. 'Right. That's the lot then.'

Emma's cheerful look had by now transformed to one of disappointment.

Ollie noticed immediately. 'Didn't you hear me ask for a

couple of cases of Prosecco?'

Benny pretended not to understand. 'Prosecco?'

'It's a sparkling wine,' Emma enlightened him.

'Named after the village of Prosecco,' Ollie qualified, 'now a suburb of Trieste in Italy.'

Benny shook his head convincingly. 'Sorry, but I don't fly that far in the seaplane. I'd have to keep stopping for fuel.'

Realising Benny was fooling with Emma, Ollie played along. 'I was rather hoping one of the supermarkets in Nadi might stock it.'

'I'll check with the office on my radio,' he replied, walking back to the plane.

He came out carrying a box. Placing it on the trolley, he brought out a second one. Printed on the side of them in big bold black lettering was the name *Prosecco*.

The pilot feigned surprise. 'I don't know how these got on the seaplane. I hope they're not illicit cargo.'

It was only at this point Emma realised he had been playing games with her. 'You rotten thing!' she shouted. 'You've been having me on.'

Benny said he was sorry. 'I couldn't resist. I know how much you ladies love this sparkling fizz.'

'And I can tell you why,' she replied, getting even. 'You don't have to be Italian, to be fluent in Prosecco!'

Benny and Ollie looked at each other and groaned, at what was actually quite a witty remark.

When they had stored everything safely away, they rested for a while. Ollie and Emma had a beer and Benny a cola.

The pilot was inquisitive. 'Being on this island, in the middle of nowhere, don't you sometimes wonder what's happening out there in the big wide world?'

'Not in the slightest,' Ollie said dismissively. 'I came here to get away from everything. Unless it concerns the island, which is unlikely, it's irrelevant as far as I'm concerned.'

Even Emma was slightly surprised by such a reaction. 'But surely, you must be curious about how the rest of the world is doing without you?'

'Not really,' he made clear. 'My not being out there isn't making any difference at all. It will be the same when I die. A few people might say nice things about me for a while, but then I'll quickly be forgotten.'

Benny was bemused at how their conversation had suddenly got around to the subject of death but added his own viewpoint. 'I think it's natural for people to hope they'll be remembered when they pass on.'

'If that's the case,' Ollie advocated, 'they had better make sure to follow the advice of Benjamin Franklin. He was after all one of America's Founding Fathers: *'If you would not be forgotten, as soon as you are dead and rotten, either write things worth reading, or do things worth writing.'*

Their briefest of conversations about dying reminded him of something he was meant to tell Benny. 'I almost forgot to tell you about the dolphin.'

Emma elaborated. 'We found it the other morning. It was washed up on the beach and it was dead.'

Benny showed concern. 'Are you sure?'

'If it was only pretending to be lifeless,' Ollie humoured him, 'I'm going to nominate it for an Oscar!'

Benny snickered. 'Very funny, but why didn't I spot it when

we were unloading?'

'Because it's not there anymore,' Emma explained. 'It was washed out to sea again. I should have taken a photo of it, but it never occurred.'

'If you had done,' Ollie was quick off the mark to add, 'it would have been a selfie. You would have been standing right in front of it, with your arms outstretched and a great big smile on your face.' He did an impression. 'Like this!'

She ignored his sarcasm.

'We were careful not to touch it,' Ollie testified more seriously, 'but I took a fairly close look and there were no outward signs of injury.'

'There could be several explanations for its death,' Benny suspected.

'That's exactly what Ollie said,' Emma clearly recalled, 'and he knows quite a lot about dolphins.'

'I'll log it in my report when I get back to the airport,' the pilot promised.

Ollie thanked him but had an afterthought. 'I only hope the island won't be invaded by hundreds of investigative reporters, all in search of a story about a mysterious dead dolphin.'

'It's highly unlikely,' Benny was sure. 'Dead dolphins are quickly forgotten.'

'Precisely, just like humans are,' Ollie reminded him in mirthful triumph.

'Not necessarily,' Emma proposed in equal jest. 'For all we know, the dolphin might have followed Franklin's advice and done something worth writing about.'

'Such as what?' Benny queried.

Her reply was the first thing which came to mind. 'Maybe

the dolphin had learnt to speak Welsh.'

Ollie shook his head decisively. 'Not a chance. Only whales can do that!'

17

No sooner had Ollie and Emma waved Benny off from the beach, his seaplane disappearing into the distance, than she practically tore off her bikini.

'This is so much better,' she cooed. 'Now I'm comfortable again.'

Ollie was surprised at her haste. 'I know you're a glamour model and are used to sometimes working nude, but you've taken to naturism as if you're making up for lost time.'

'Thanks to you,' she acknowledged. 'I feel so much happier in just my skin. I feel free, just as I did when I was a youngster. I could run around and play innocently without clothes, but then I grew up and was made to wear them, at least until I became a model. With just the two of us on this gorgeous island, I don't intend to dress until Benny's next visit.'

He stepped out of his shorts. 'Me too and just think of all the washing we're avoiding.'

They made their way back up to the cabin. 'I'd like to have dinner earlier tonight,' she mentioned. 'I'm quite peckish.'

He gave her a knowing smile. 'I suspect you really want to make a start on your Prosecco, which I'm chilling for you.'

She could hardly deny it. 'Perhaps I could have a glass whilst we are getting the food ready. You can have one too if you like.'

He declined the offer. 'It's very nice of you, but the bottles of bubbly are for you to enjoy. I'll stick to my usual Cognac. I know it's considered an after-dinner drink, but it makes a great aperitif with soda.'

Although there was plenty of choice now over what to eat, they settled on a simple salad, as they often did. Getting it ready, Ollie opened a bottle of Emma's Prosecco with a flourish.

She cheered at the familiar loud pop the cork made as it shot from the top.

'I don't know if it's the same with this sparkling wine as it is for Champagne,' he admitted, pouring her a glass, 'but apparently a couple of dozen people are killed by Champagne corks every year, mostly at weddings.'

She took a sip and licked her lips. 'Yummy. It's got to be worth the risk, for something tasting so good and it's cheaper than Champagne. I hope your Cognac's nice too.'

'It's my favourite drink,' he reminded her, as he decanted a generous measure, 'so it's always a treat.'

'You love your Cognac so much,' she teased him, 'you'd die happy if you were ever to drown in it.'

He did not exactly relish the thought. 'At least I would be in good spirits!'

Once the food was ready, they took it outside.

He topped up her bubbly and poured himself a glass of cabernet sauvignon.

'You've deprived yourself of silence today,' she reminded him, as they started to eat. 'You did a short meditation on the

157

beach this morning, but I know you like to do more.'

He was of the same opinion. 'I really must try and stick to my intended routine.'

'I'll do my best to make sure you do,' she planned, 'but for now, you must tell me more about the importance of silence.'

'It's what real meditation is about,' he emphasised, 'and I've revealed some of the techniques which can be used to achieve it. There is another form of silence which should also be considered, however. It's the art of knowing when to keep silent, rather than needing to speak.'

She looked aghast. 'Oh dear. You're suggesting I talk too much.'

He brushed her leg with his under the table. 'Not at all. I really enjoy our conversations. I'm referring to certain situations when silence can say far more than words. Can you see what I mean?'

She knew exactly. Saying nothing, she simply tilted her head slightly, gazed straight into his eyes and gave him her most flirtatious look.

It worked, for if he had been wearing a shirt, such body language would have made him hot under the collar. He wiped his brow instead. 'It's true. The most dangerous animal in the world really is a silent smiling woman.'

She gave him her impression of a slinky female panther, complete with a seductive purr and pawing gestures. 'We glamour models use it all the time to captivate our prey.'

'It's irresistible,' he admitted, 'but then you always are, without even trying. I was actually reflecting on the type of person who has to talk all the time, the sort who never knows when to keep their mouth shut. There's an old Spanish proverb which goes: *'Only open your mouth if what you are going to say is more beautiful than the silence."*

'Most appropriate words,' she decided, 'and I bet you have more up your invisible sleeve.'

He took a sip of wine and thought for moment. 'Well, Pythagoras, the Greek philosopher, once said: *'A fool is known by his speech and a wise man by his silence.'* Likewise, the writer, George Eliot, wrote: *'Blessed is the man who, having nothing to say, abstains from giving us wordy evidence of the fact."*

'There you go,' she maintained. 'You've given me something else to think about.'

'The important part is knowing whether it's appropriate or not to speak,' he determined. 'Silence during a discussion is perceived in different ways around the world. It's considered polite by Asians to pause before answering a question, as it suggests it has been given careful thought before replying. In the West, on the other hand, silences tend to only last a second or two. Any longer and it can be interpreted to mean the person is unable to answer and this can cause awkwardness and embarrassment. It's a shame really, because you don't have to be talking to be engaged in a conversation. You can be thinking and listening carefully, rather than just eagerly awaiting a gap, so as to jump in and have your say. Used correctly, silence can be a powerful tool for displaying empathy, or saying no without having to resort to harsh words. Then there's what's known as the pregnant pause, which can indicate something important is going to be said. Successful comedians use it as a timing technique, which is known as a beat, often to accentuate the most important part of a funny story, such as the punch line.'

* * *

Noticing that Emma's glass was empty, he topped it up with Prosecco, before filling his own with red.

She thanked him. 'What about staying silent when you think it's best not to say anything at all?'

'A good point,' he endorsed. 'There are many situations when saying nothing is even better than resorting to a white lie, to avoid upsetting or hurting someone.'

'What about matters you don't want to discuss at all,' she questioned, 'such as things which are private or confidential?'

'Silence is definitely called for in those circumstances,' he advised. 'Have you ever heard of what's referred to as the Four Powers of the Sphinx?'

She knew of the ancient monument, which is near to the Great Pyramid, in Giza, Egypt. 'I actually posed by it for a photoshoot once,' she told him proudly.

'Whilst on a camel,' he could easily bet.

'Of course,' she told him. 'Where would advertising be without camels?'

He saw her point. 'They're also far cheaper to run than any car, journeying through the desert on just a drop of water. Getting back to what I was saying, the Four Powers of the Sphinx were first talked about by Eliphas Levi, a French occultist. According to him, the powers are to know, to will, to dare and to be silent. These qualities are essential for magicians.'

'Even when they're doing card tricks?' she wondered.

It was obvious he needed to spell out the type of magicians he was talking about. 'I mean occult magicians who do real rituals, rather than stage conjurers who pull fake bunnies out of hats. The silence in this case refers to both inner and outer silence. Aleister Crowley wrote about the Four Powers of the

Sphinx too. He also believed he was Eliphas Levi in his previous life. In Diary of a Drug Fiend, which was one of Crowley's occult novels, he wrote: *'Having to talk destroys the symphony of silence,'* and that brings us back nicely to where we started this fascinating conversation. If ever you think I'm talking too much by the way,' he insisted, 'you must tell me.'

'We could hardly sit here and not have a conversation over dinner,' she pointed out.

'Why not?' he asked in all seriousness. 'As Ralph Waldo Emerson, the American essayist put it: *'Two friends are two people who are comfortable sharing silence together.'*

'He was obviously thinking about us,' she liked to believe, 'especially when we're lying closely in each other's arms.'

'If he was,' Ollie reasoned, 'he must have been gazing into a crystal ball, for he died back in 1882.'

Emma upended her glass, to show it was empty. 'Is there any Prosecco left, or have I drunk it all?'

He examined the bottle. The black coloured glass made it difficult to see, especially in the dim light. Holding it to his ear, he gave it a shake. 'There's still a drop, but I'm not sure about a full glass.'

'You'd better pour it then,' she opted. 'There's no point in letting it go flat overnight. Anyway, it's making me feel nice and relaxed.'

'I'll polish off the red then,' he thought fair. 'Have you had enough to eat?'

She nodded contentedly at his usual after meal question and gave him another of her irresistible smiles. 'I thought we might have an early night. Not that I'm tired.'

What she really meant by this was perfectly clear to him. 'Unfortunately, I forgot to ask Benny to bring some more condoms.'

She giggled. 'It's not a problem. I was expecting to be staying in a party resort for several weeks remember, so I have plenty. You must think badly of me.'

'Not at all,' he said, to her relief, 'but it does explain why you needed to bring such a massive suitcase!'

Gathering up the plates, they took their drinks inside.

'I love being a naturist,' she told him for the umpteenth time. 'The only thing I have to take off before bed is my makeup.'

Ollie poured his Cognac nightcap. 'You don't even wear that most days anymore.'

'You've noticed!' she gasped. 'I probably look hideous without it.'

He laughed so much that he spilled a little of his brandy. 'You don't need cosmetics. You're the most beautiful woman I've ever seen.'

'If so,' she worried, 'why do they make me wear makeup when I'm modelling?'

'Because they're probably trying to create a specific look,' he imagined. 'I'm told some women feel more confident wearing makeup and can use it to help express themselves, but you're unique and as pretty as a picture without it.'

She sought reassurance he was being completely honest with her. 'You're not just saying this to make me feel good?'

'You're the last person on Earth who needs telling how attractive they are,' he tried to make her see. 'You're absolutely gorgeous.'

Still not quite satisfied at his reply, she put it another way. 'But what if I wasn't? Would you still love me?'

'You know I would,' he vowed. 'I actually think it's great you don't have to be a prisoner to a mask. Anyway, those less fortunate than you should remember that real beauty has nothing to do with a person's physical appearance. As someone once said: *'Beauty is not about the fairest skin, it's about the purest heart.'* The only sort of people who could possibly be described as hideous are those who are self-centred, deliberately cruel, mean, nasty and ungrateful to others. Even they deserve our help and compassion.'

He was not sure how they had quite got onto such a subject. 'What were we talking about, before this?'

'It started by my saying how much I liked being a naturist,' she reminded him, stretching out on the bed.

'Ah yes,' he recalled. 'There are a lot more advantages than just saving time undressing. Although naturism is not about sex, it's perfectly natural for us to enjoy the latter. As I'm sure I mentioned before, being free of tight clothing in bed promotes vaginal health and boosts male fertility. As bare skin touches bare skin, it stimulates the release of oxytocin, the hormone which promotes feelings of love, attachment, social bonding and well-being.'

'In that case you'd better come and give me a cuddle,' she urged.

'What about my brandy?' he quibbled. 'I haven't finished it yet.'

'I know you'll find it hard to believe,' she promised him, 'but I taste even better.'

*   *   *

The temptation was too much. He put down his glass and joined her.

Getting close, he pressed his lips to hers.

She closed her yearning eyes, responding with igniting passion which almost took his breath away.

Studying the expectant look on her stunningly attractive face, he could not fathom how she could possibly ever doubt her looks. His deft male fingers delicately brushed a few stray strands of blond hair from her smooth unlined forehead.

Aching with longing, she grasped his masculine arms, pulling him closer, urgently needing to feel the heat of his skin against hers.

As she did so, she imagined the hormones, which he had said would be released.

He lowered his willing mouth to her regal neck, anointing it with pecks of love.

As she slackened her clutching grip, anticipating the delights to come, he was able to reach a delicious breast. Expertly, he massaged it in a circular motion, teasing the already excited nipple with his nimble tongue.

Her impatient hands ran up and down his back in desire, as he eagerly savoured the other one.

Tantalisingly, his tongue snaked further downwards, making a wet trail over her quivering flat tummy. Reaching the delicate softness of her inviting womanhood, it started to explore the already moist craving folds.

Tingling with pleasure, but fearing he was about to send her over the edge, she urged him up. Her eager fingers able to reach and encircle his already tumescent source of masculinity, stroked slowly up and down, as it throbbed to full rigidity.

Rolling on the necessary sheath, he lay above her, his strong elbows taking his weight.

Guiding his jutting hardness to its pink womanly haven, she inhaled sharply as he entered her.

Initially, their lovemaking was measured, with precise hip movements, but intensifying passion unleashed faster and more frantic thrusts.

Soon, his manly grunts and her female burning sighs turned to deep-throated groans and wailing shrieks of delight.

With pounding pulses and gasping breaths, flushed faces and delightfully sweaty skin, they reached the point of no return.

Backs arched, teeth gritted, facial muscles clenched, her trembling fingers dug into the flesh of his taut posterior.

As he thrust one final time, they simultaneously reached the pinnacle of human sexual pleasure. Each howled the other's name aloud, as spasm after spasm of shuddering orgasmic ecstasy imploded within them.

They lay joined in oblivion for several minutes.

Both basking in the afterglow of ultimate intimacy, their shared daydream was yet another example of being in the hypnotic state.

When their eyes eventually blinked open, each was greeted by the other's radiant smile of gratitude.

He hugged her tenderly and then kissed her yet again.

Only then did she speak. 'How do I compare to a glass of Cognac then?'

'Not bad at all,' he judged. 'You are unbelievably silky and smooth. A delight to savour. How do I rate against Prosecco?'

'I hate to admit it,' she told him, 'but you just won. Prosecco does a lot for me, but it can't make my toes curl like you do. I never want to leave this bed.'

'It's such a shame,' he called to mind, 'because we're up early in the morning to see the sunrise.'

She had not really forgotten. 'I'm sure it would have dawned on me by then.'

He ignored her deliberate pun and rewarded her with a kiss on the forehead.

Finally, he gave her something to dwell on as she drifted off to sleep. It was by Robert Loveman, the American poet: *"The dawn is a wild, fair woman, / With sunrise in her hair; / Look where she stands, with pleading hands, / To lure me there."*

18

Emma looked a little washed out the next morning when Ollie awoke her. As she had drunk a full bottle of Prosecco the night before, he feared she might be suffering from a headache.

'Sorry,' he apologised. 'I didn't really want to disturb you, but we'll miss the sunrise if we don't make a move fairly soon. Are you feeling alright?'

She sat up, yawned and stretched her arms. 'Give me a moment to properly wake up and I'll tell you.' She took the coffee he had made for her, blowing into the mug out of habit to cool it. 'How did you sleep?'

'Fine,' he answered, 'and so I should have. I mentioned the hormone oxytocin last night, but there are others too which are released during orgasm and with melatonin, which regulates the body-clock, they're great for relaxation and sleepiness.'

'So, lovemaking is good for us in more ways than one then,' she happily accepted.

'Definitely,' he was sure. 'My one regret is the necessity to use condoms. I know they're important for protection, but nature intended the male and female fluids to mix. Semen contains mood changing hormones, which when absorbed through the vagina can be beneficial.'

Her curiosity was aroused. 'In what way?'

'It can lessen depression for a start,' he qualified.

'But I don't suffer from it,' she was quick to point out.

'Well, there you are then,' he affirmed, 'proof enough that it works. Semen also embodies at least thirty proteins, along with vitamins, minerals and other healthy things. Likewise, a man can get his free prescription of lactobacillus, which is a kind of healthy probiotic bacteria, orally from a woman. It's important for me to add my strong belief that the sexual fluids are sacred, as indeed is sexuality itself.'

'Perhaps this is why the Catholic Church still preach against the use of contraception,' she suggested.

'They tell their congregation it interferes with the creation of life and to an extent they're correct,' he agreed. 'The real problem is the incompatibility between religious belief and science. When it comes to risks like HIV and AIDS for example, the Church's refusal to rethink their teachings has been responsible for the loss of so many lives. There's the possibility their stance on this might slowly be changing, but it's going to take time. Anyway, finish your coffee and we'll go and see the splendour of nature at its finest.'

Emma playfully pointed to her own naked body. 'You're looking at it already!'

How could he disagree? 'I most certainly am, but on this occasion, I was actually referring to the sunrise.'

There was something Emma felt she needed to clarify, as they made their way to the beach. 'When you said you regretted having to use a condom, were you suggesting we should stop?'

'Not at all,' he put her right. 'I was simply expressing a point of view and the key to what I meant was in the word *regret*. It would be different if we were in a long-term relationship.'

She sighed. 'I'd like us to be, but I suppose it depends on how long you let me stay on your island.'

'It's not solely up to me,' he reminded her. 'You've got a modelling career to get back to at some point, not to mention your parents and friends.'

She dismissed his concern. 'I'm in no hurry to go anywhere. As my planned holiday to Fiji was for two months, I've still got plenty of time.'

They spread their towels on the sand as they always did and sat staring out to sea.

She could see just by looking at his face that his thoughts were elsewhere. 'What are you thinking about?'

'I was simply remembering how I was here on the island all by myself, until you came along. It seems so long ago now.'

She stroked his arm sympathetically. 'I'm sorry if I spoiled it for you.'

'That's the thing,' he said pleasingly. 'You didn't. You simply changed my way of thinking, just as the Catholic Church should do about certain beliefs.'

They watched in wonder and reverence, as the horizon glowed a florid orange.

Intensifying, the majestic reassuring solar disc rose slowly in all its grandeur, casting its impressive beams of life directly upon them.

'I've mentioned the Thelemic goddess Nuit to you already,' he remarked. 'There's also an ancient Roman goddess of the dawn, who announces the arrival of the sun. Her name is Aurora, but she was known to the Greeks as Eos. She is mainly referred to in the sexual poetry of the time. Her abode is the sky, her symbols the chariot, the precious spice saffron and the cicada.'

'Why the cicada?' Emma pondered. 'They're those bugs which make a shrill droning sound.'

Ollie told her the delightful story about Aurora. 'One of her dear lovers was Tithonus, a prince of Troy, but being mortal meant he would one day grow old and eventually die. Wanting him to make love to her for eternity, she asked Jupiter, the king of the gods, or Zeus in the Greek version, to make him immortal. Her wish was granted and they lived happily together. Unfortunately, she had forgotten to also ask for him to be granted eternal youth. Without this gift, he gradually became older and older. No longer able to make love to her, his frail body continued to waste away. Eventually, only his voice remained, but it still sang of his love for her. Taking pity, Aurora turned him into a cicada, the insect thereby becoming a symbol of immortality.'

Emma loved the tales like this that he sometimes recited to her. 'I'm so lucky to be here on the island with you.'

He was fortunate to have her. 'I don't know who it was, but someone once made a promise to all those who sought love: *'Someday, you will find the one who will watch every sunrise with you, until the sunset of your life.'* With such heartening and reassuring words, we can start our morning meditation.'

They both closed their eyes and concentrating on their breathing, tried to let their thoughts drift away. This was still difficult for Emma, but then she still had so little experience. Ollie was more fortunate and easily transcending the thought process entered the serene and blissful state of pure inner silence.

Despite his usual ability to ignore distractions, on this occasion he became aware of Emma's voice. It sounded anxious.

His eyelids were heavy, but they flickered open. 'You seem to have a problem.'

She had not wanted to disturb him but had just realised something. 'I'm so sorry, but I've lost my ring.'

His eyes searched her fingers for the piece of jewellery she was presumably referring to. 'Perhaps you didn't put it on this morning. If so, it should be back at the cabin.'

She tried to think. 'I was definitely wearing it last night. It clinked now and again against my Prosecco glass.'

His mind went back to when they had later made love, but he drew a blank on whether she was wearing it then or not. 'If it's come off your finger it could be anywhere. It might be on the cabin floor, in the toilet, or on the path. We can only hope it's not lost in the sand, or goodness knows where else. Was it valuable?'

She was clearly upset. 'It must have been. It was gold and set with a ruby stone. I was told it came from somewhere in Afghanistan.'

'How did you get hold of it?' he was curious to know.

Tears were forming in her eyes, which she wiped away. 'My grandmother left it to me when she died. My grandfather had bought it for her. It's supposed to be lucky and to protect the wearer from misfortune. If only it were still on my finger, then it wouldn't have got lost.'

Although he could not quite follow her logic, he decided it would only confuse things by questioning it.

'I've got to find the ring,' she resolved, 'for sentimental reasons if nothing else.'

Crawling on her knees, she began to search the surface of the sand around where she had been sitting.

Ollie checked without success that it was not on her beach towel. 'It's like looking for a needle in a haystack. Do you realise how many millions of sand grains there are on this beach?'

She had no idea. 'It's not the biggest beach in the world.'

'Which is just as well,' he maintained. 'A mathematician once calculated there to be roughly seven hundred trillion cubic meters of beach on Earth, which would equate to about five sextillion grains of sand. I propose we have a quick look here and then go back to the cabin in case it's there. If it's not, then we'll come back and make a closer search.'

'Alright,' she agreed, 'but do you think there's any chance we'll find it?'

'It's not going to be easy,' he feared, 'although the red ruby stone should stand out more than had it been a colourless diamond.'

They spent a further half an hour checking the beach in the end, before heading for the cabin, scouring the path along the way.

Needing to use the toilet, he took the opportunity to check the floor and around the washbasin.

Emma meanwhile started inside the cabin, first looking in the most obvious place, being the small table by the bed. Not finding it there brought more tears.

When Ollie walked in and saw how sad she was, his heart went out to her. He took her in his arms, offering comfort. 'Try not to worry. We'll do everything we can to find it.'

'I know you'll do your best,' she sobbed. 'I'm being silly, making all this fuss over a ring, but I can't help it. You must be starving. With all this searching, we haven't had anything to eat yet today.'

He picked up a couple of bananas, unpeeling one for her. 'These will keep us going for a while and if the ring doesn't turn up, at least we can say our search hasn't been fruitless!'

She managed a tiny smile. 'Cheer me up with one of your clever sayings.'

'A tough challenge,' he admitted, trying to think. 'Ah yes. I have something appropriate. It was by Helen Hunt Jackson, an American 19th century writer: *All lost things are in the angels' keeping.*"

'I'd like to believe it's true,' she hoped, 'that an angel is looking after my ring and will guide us to it.'

Having given up in the cabin and the area outside, they started off back to the beach, heads down searching the path.

The sun played tricks with their eyes every so often, as it shone on any reflective surface. Their hearts would soar in hope, only to discover it was a shiny stone, a small piece of sea-weathered frosted glass, or even a tiny insect.

This made things even more difficult when they reached the beach, for the sun was now overhead and it reflected on almost every grain of sand. In desperation, they were soon crawling on their hands and knees again.

As they ran the palms of their hands over the surface, Ollie shook his head in regret. 'I wish I'd had the foresight to bring a metal detector to the island, but I never thought I'd need it.

Some are specially designed to find gold jewellery.'

Without such an aid, all they managed to uncover were a couple of highly coloured angler's fishing floats, a small section of what Ollie assumed was whale spine, a non-human tooth and more pieces of green and white sea glass. Even more unexpected was a piece of Lego toy building block and a yellow plastic duck, which had a bright red beak. It was a mystery as to how such things like this came to be washed up on an island in the middle of the Pacific. Even so, Emma thought the duck was quite cute and decided to keep it.

'We've got to face it,' she said with despondency, 'there's not a chance in hell of us finding the ring.'

'You're right about that,' Ollie concurred, 'for hell as a place doesn't exist. It was created, just like the devil, as a threat against those who don't follow the Church's religious teachings.'

'The same must apply to heaven then,' she assumed.

'Of course,' he insisted, positive he had told her this before. 'Right now, I need to meditate.'

Having spoiled his morning session earlier she could understand but thought he could have spared just a few minutes more to search. 'It's not going to find the ring,' she lamented.

'Wait and see,' was all he said.

Resuming their usual seated postures, they both closed their eyes.

Emma could not really see the point but was prepared to try anything. There was too much going on in her mind to quieten it and so she focused on trying to remember the last time she had seen the ring on her finger.

Ollie meanwhile had used his hypnotic trance inductions

to quickly enter the silence. Although he had not mentioned it, his intention was to call upon his Holy Guardian Angel for help.

Having first learned of such an entity from studying the writings of Aleister Crowley, he had worked hard ever since to try and contact it. Gradually, he had developed a sense of knowing whenever he was in the mysterious entity's presence. His hope now was that his angel might reveal where the ring was and so with love in his heart, he tried to communicate.

It was as if the entity had been awaiting him. Although Ollie did not hear anything, the angel's presence was undeniable. He knew it was there, listening to his every thought.

Mentally, he conveyed the depth of his love for Emma and how it saddened him to see her so unhappy. He pictured the ring as clearly as he could, fully aware that images are far stronger symbols than mere words.

Patiently, he awaited a response. He would have been filled with joy had he heard the angel's voice. This was not to be, for his ability to communicate at such a depth was not yet developed enough.

Instead, an image of the beach slowly appeared in his mind. Although his eyes remained closed, he could see everything as clearly as if they had been open. His inner sight was directed to where the beach joined the path to the cabin. There it lingered, at the very spot.

His attention was being drawn to a small green bush at the side of the path. The reason for this became obvious. He realised he was being shown precisely where he would find the ring.

As the image slowly faded, he thanked his Holy Guardian

Angel and drifted back into the silence.

When he opened his eyes, the first thing he spotted was Emma crawling around on the sand, still searching. 'Did anything come to you in your meditation?' he asked her.

She sighed and shook her head. 'Nothing at all. How about you?'

Although he did not want to raise her hopes, he felt quietly confident. 'We'll find out in a moment.'

He beckoned her to follow him along the beach to the path.

She hurried to keep up. 'You seem to know exactly where you're going.'

'I do,' he replied, his surety growing by the moment.

At the side of the path was the bush, exactly as it had been shown to him in the vision. He bent over, lowering his head to peer underneath it, but it was impossible to see anything.

Crouching down, and inserting his hand in the tiny space, he gently ran it along the sandy soil. There were what felt like tiny pebbles and pieces of shell, but then he felt something more promising. He grasped it carefully in his fingertips and stood up.

'Hold out your hand,' he urged, 'palm up.'

As she did so, he opened his fingers.

Emma gasped, her eyes marvelling, as the ring fell into her hand. She could hardly believe what she was looking at. 'My ring! My precious ring! You've found it, but how?'

'I had some help,' he rightfully acknowledged, 'from my Holy Guardian Angel.'

She did not understand. 'Your holy what?'

'After I had entered the silence in my meditation,' he

described, 'I contacted my Holy Guardian Angel and asked for guidance. I was shown in a vision exactly where your ring would be.'

She was utterly amazed. 'I had no idea you even had an angel.'

'Everyone has one,' he promised her, 'including you. They just need to know it, believe it and find a way of making contact.'

Although this was difficult enough for her to take in, something else occurred to her. 'If it was so simple, why didn't you contact the angel right from the start? It would have saved us so much time.'

'You can't treat your angel like some lost property bureau,' he explained. 'It's holy remember. It's important to first do everything you can to solve problems yourself. If we were automatically given all the answers our problem-solving skills would become redundant and they're an important part of our learning process. We searched long and hard for your ring and only when we had all but given up, did I feel I had earned the right to ask my angel for its assistance. There is one tiny thing which still baffles me. How did your ring come to be under the bush in the first place?'

Emma raised her shoulders to shrug, having no idea, but then it dawned on her. 'When we came down the path this morning, I seem to vaguely remember running my fingers through the leaves of the bush. I've done it before, as the foliage feels nice and soft. My ring must have slipped from my finger then.'

Ollie was delighted, not only because Emma had been reunited with her ring, but also for him to have received such guidance from the entity. He felt more determined than ever to strengthen the bond with his angel.

Emma was equally enthralled with everything which had happened. 'My ring really was in the angels' keeping. You've got to tell me everything you know about them,' she implored.

'I will,' he gave assurance, 'and also more about Aleister Crowley, for the Holy Guardian Angel plays an important part in Thelema. First though, we must celebrate finding your ring.'

'A great idea,' she agreed, 'and if we hurry back to the cabin you can choose how to.'

'Don't worry,' he was sure. 'It'll only take a Prosecco!'

19

Ollie continued to work on his meditation techniques, using them to make an even closer link with his Holy Guardian Angel. At the same time, he encouraged Emma to practise going into the silence too, confident that she would eventually find success.

It was a couple of days later when he took the opportunity to tell her more about Crowley. They had been down to the beach at dawn as usual for the sunrise, done their morning meditations and then had breakfast outside the cabin.

Deciding to spend the rest of the day on Benny's beach, they had gone back there, with towels and plenty of suntan lotion, plus a couple of cool bags, which were full of snacks and chilled beer.

'This is as good a time as any for you to learn about Aleister Crowley,' he proposed, as they lay on the sand staring up at the cloudless blue sky. 'The gutter press described him as *the wickedest man in the world* and claimed he was an evil black magician. Had they more intelligence and the ability to understand his teachings, they might have realised how wrong they were about him. Crowley said it was the most foolish statement ever made about him. He despised black magic and found it difficult to believe in the existence of people debased and idiotic enough to be involved with it.'

'It sounds as if the reporters were trying to create sensationalised stories to shock their readers,' she suspected.

'Such unjustified negativity towards him continues in the media to this day,' Ollie disclosed, 'but it has certainly kept his name alive. He's considered by many people to have been the most influential occultist ever and was voted the 73rd greatest Briton of all time in a 2002 BBC poll.'

'When did you first become interested in him?' she asked.

'It was after I had the out-of-body experience,' he explained. 'As I started looking into things which were classed as mystical and occult, Crowley's name kept coming up. I began to read about him online and bought copies of some of the incredible books he had written. It quickly became obvious why he's so highly thought of and considered a prophet, by those who follow Thelema.'

Emma was keen to find out more about the man Ollie was describing, but even more urgently had a thirst. 'I reckon it must be time for a beer.'

He never wore a watch, especially being a naturist, preferring no tan lines. He glanced instead at the position of the sun in the sky. 'You're spot on, for it's exactly beer o'clock.'

Taking a couple of bottles from the cool bag, he opened them.

'Aleister was a prolific writer,' he continued. 'He was extremely well-travelled, a notable mountaineer, a poet and a chess master, a British secret agent and a member of the Order of the Golden Dawn, the famous 19th-century magical society. In time, he went on to establish his own magical and mystical system, known as the A∴A∴ and became head of Ordo Templi Orientis, the worldwide occult fraternity. They still flourish, as does the Thelemic religion's Ecclesia Gnostica Catholica, or Gnostic Catholic Church. It has its own rites but importantly celebrates Crowley's Gnostic Mass. At the heart of all this is *The Book of the Law*, Thelema's most sacred text. It was dictated to Crowley by an entity called Aiwass, whom he later identified as his own Holy Guardian Angel.'

'From the praise you give him,' she suspected, 'you must surely have read the book.'

'Of course,' he enthused, 'many times. I have a copy back at the cabin. It lays down a simple code of conduct with its central tenet: *'Do what thou wilt shall be the whole of the Law.'* So many people misinterpret this, thinking it means you can do whatever you want. In fact, it urges people to discover, follow and fulfil their true nature, or course in life, which is known as their True Will.'

Emma thought it sounded fascinating. 'Why don't you read some of it to me after dinner tonight.'

Ollie was delighted. 'I would love to,' he told her keenly.

They applied more lotion and sunbathed until it was time for some lunch.

Traditionally, Fijians often enjoy fresh fish soup in the middle of the day, or sometimes Rourou soup, which is made by stewing dalo leaves in coconut milk, with cassava, a boiled woody shrub. Ollie and Emma however, had brought something more to their taste to the beach, being a selection of cheeses followed by fruit.

Although she had not finished her beer, he opened another one for her.

'You know I can't drink it quickly,' she reminded him. 'It gives me hiccups.'

'Just as anything carbonated can,' he claimed, 'even your precious Prosecco.'

'But that's worth hiccupping over,' she considered.

'And so is beer,' he justified. 'Look what Kaiser Wilhelm, the last German Emperor and King of Prussia said about it: *'Give me a woman who loves beer and I will conquer the world.'*

'Give me a man who loves Prosecco,' she echoed defiantly, 'and I will conquer his island.'

'If that's the case,' he told her decisively, 'I'm definitely going nowhere near your bubbly.'

She knew he was not keen on it anyway, so asked about the food instead. 'What cheeses are we having?'

Taking them from the cool bag, he pointed to them one at a time. 'There's brie, camembert, Stilton and feta, all made from local ingredients, by a gourmet cheese company on the mainland. They supply to Nadi and it comes here courtesy of Benny.'

She cut a slice of bread, spread some camembert on it and took a bite. 'It's good but tell me something. Does Benny actually do the shopping himself?'

Ollie opted for the brie. 'No. He's far too busy being a pilot. All the food and drinks are sourced in Nadi by a service company, mainly from a supermarket and a few smaller suppliers. They drop it off at the airport and Benny takes over from there.

Such efficient arrangements impressed her. 'It seems to be extremely well organised.'

'Thanks to Brad,' he asserted. 'He's extremely efficient and that's the reason I kept him on.'

This surprised her. If he had mentioned it before, it must have slipped her memory. 'He's still working for you?'

'I still pay him if that's what you mean,' he admitted, 'but I can afford to. He's back in England, on extended paid leave, just in case something needs dealing with. His most important instruction is never to disturb me.'

Emma had been eyeing up the Stilton and helped herself. She seemed to recall Ollie saying he had sold up all his business interests to purchase the island. 'I'm not prying, but it sounds as if you still had some money left, after forking out millions no doubt to buy this place?'

'I'm far from broke if that's what you mean,' he admitted. 'Although I'm intending to stay here for some time, who knows how things will work out? I made sure there are plenty of funds to cover any emergencies, not to mention all the ongoing expenses. I came here for peace and silence, not to worry about finance. As Rae Foley said: *'I always feel sorry for people who think more about a rainy day ahead than sunshine today.'*

She found the Stilton even tastier than the brie. 'By keeping Brad on, you get to enjoy the sunshine, whilst he deals with the rain. Who's Rae Foley by the way?'

'An author,' he told her, 'whose real name was Elinor Denniston. She wrote over forty mystery novels, under the Rae Foley pseudonym and other books under other made-up names. She died in 1978.'

Emma thought this sounded rather confusing. 'They must

have wondered what name to bury or cremate her under.'

'I don't think she'd have cared in the slightest,' he reckoned, 'especially as one of her books was called *No Tears for the Dead*.'

They both reached for the feta cheese at the same time, but he gestured for her to go first.

'Do you want to be buried or cremated,' she delved, 'when it's your time to go?'

Although he preferred to concentrate on the present, rather than his eventual demise, he could not deny it was something he had thought about from time to time. 'As I've made plain before, I've believed in reincarnation ever since my out-of-body experience. As far as the disposal of my remains go however, I would prefer dust to dust, over ashes to ashes. It should not really matter, but I have always had a great respect for the element of fire. It's responsible for so many good things, such as cooking our food, keeping us warm and so on, but there's a darker side too. Its ability to destroy is incredible. The elements of earth, air and water are just as capable, when you think of things like earthquakes, hurricanes and tsunamis, but to me fire is the most ferocious. As the body is the temple of the soul, I would rather give it the dignity of being buried in the ground, rather than it being placed in a furnace. Cremations can also produce fairly high levels of CO_2, which is not good for the planet.'

Sophie took a sip of her beer. 'Thoughts like this give me the creeps I'm afraid, but I do at least find your belief in reincarnation comforting.'

This was a doctrine he accepted without the slightest doubt. 'It makes total sense to me. We are here to learn, experience and grow spiritually. I don't think it can be done properly in just one lifetime. It can take many. Again, this is where finding our True Will comes in, making sure we achieve what we need to in each life. Our Holy Guardian Angel can guide us. When we die, so too does the personality, but the soul can never be destroyed and so it continues its journey. Just before I came to the island, I came across a podcast by the author of an historical occult novel called: 'From Manhood to Godhead: The Many Lives of Jean Vassar.' Apparently, there's a huge amount of interesting information and evidence of reincarnation in the book. Although it's a novel, it tells the true story of some of history's most famous occultists.'

Emma thought reading it would give her more insight into what they were talking about. 'Who is it by?'

He could not remember. 'It's slipped my mind, but I'm sure it must be available on Amazon. It also talks about the Plane of Rest, where our soul goes between lives.'

'Perhaps we should ask Benny to get us a copy,' she suggested. 'Something else has occurred to me too. With all the interesting ideas and quotes you come out with you should write a book as well.'

He reached for his beer. 'Perhaps one day I will. I had a go at poetry when I was a child. I wasn't particularly good at it, but then I was only young.'

'I'd love to hear a sample,' she urged.

Ollie thought back to one which had a direct bearing on what they had been talking about. 'It's only short, but it might amuse you. I called it *Mummy* and it went like this:

'Mummy,' the little boy said,
'What's it like to be dead?'
'I don't know,' said Mrs Stead
'And I won't know until I'm dead.'
The 31-bus travelled by,
The boy pushed his mother and said 'Goodbye.'
The wheels ran right over her pretty face,
The boy stepped forward one small pace,
'Mummy, what's it like to die?'
All was silent, there was no reply."

20

That evening, whilst Ollie was preparing dinner, Emma came back from laying the table outside.

'There's a slightly chilly breeze come up,' she told him. 'I'm not sure if it's warm enough to eat out there.'

He turned down the heat on the fish dish he was cooking and went to see.

She was right. The wind felt unseasonably cool against his bare skin.

Rubbing his shoulders, he went indoors. 'If we are going to have dinner alfresco, we'll need to put some clothes on.'

Emma looked aghast. 'We can't possibly dress. We're naturists and haven't worn anything since Benny left.'

'So it might be,' he rationalised, 'but even the most ardent nudists usually put something on if it turns cold. It's not as if they're made to take solemn vows, promising to remain undressed 24 hours a day, whatever the weather.'

'If they were in a naturist resort,' she humoured him, 'and slipped into something, a sign would have to be displayed at the entrance, saying: *'Clothed until further notice!'*

He enjoyed her witticism. 'People don't all feel the temperature to the same degree and so it's left to the individual to decide whether they need to dress or not. It's similar surely to when you're on a nude modelling shoot. You would be the one to determine if you wanted to slip into a dressing robe when there was a break.'

'In the past I usually did,' she thought back, 'but I probably won't in the future, now you've introduced me to naturism. I vote we eat here, inside the cabin, where it's nice and warm.'

It was fine by him. 'With the lights on, it will also be easier to read some verses from The Book of the Law.'

She disappeared through the door, returning with the plates and cutlery. 'A change of plan maybe, but I'm still having my Prosecco.'

'Of course,' he agreed. 'Get the glasses and I'll open a bottle for you. I'm going to stick to red as usual, once I finish my brandy.'

Whilst they were eating, he decided to first tell her a little more about the Holy Guardian Angel. 'To put this as simply as possible, there are two parts to human beings. There's the Lower Self, which is our basic animal-like, Earth-living personality. Then there is what is referred to as the Higher Self. It's a term used by many religions to describe our evolved, eternal and divine self. It's the real us, which exists beyond the physical body. Quite a few people consider the Higher Self and the Holy Guardian Angel to be the same thing. Over time, Aleister Crowley came to realize the Holy Guardian Angel is in fact a separate and individual entity. He also emphasized the importance of us contacting it.'

'You explain what I have to do,' she urged, 'and I'll give it go.'

'It's not quite that easy,' he forewarned her. 'It usually takes a huge amount of time and effort. There are certain magical rituals which can be of help, but they can be difficult to work and almost impossible without a lot of prior experience. I tried it another way. Using my hypnotic meditation techniques, I was gradually able to develop a link with my angel. The starting point is to be able to successfully go into the silence.'

'Which was your very reason for coming to the island,' she recalled, not that he needed reminding. 'Presumably, you wanted to develop the techniques which worked for you. It must have been a success, judging by the help you were given in finding my lost ring.'

He was eager to make sure she did not get the wrong idea. 'In contacting your Holy Guardian Angel, you'll find something immensely more important than that, although I know it was of huge sentimental value to you. If you can discover your True Will, you have a much better chance of growing spiritually. There is the prospect however, of your Holy Guardian Angel suddenly coming to your assistance, without any prior contact, such as in a moment of dire crisis or disaster.'

She had a thought. 'Is there the possibility of the figure you saw in the tunnel, during your out-of-body experience, being your angel?'

Ollie had obviously considered this over the years. 'I'm not sure, but I would like to think so. Anyway, let's move on now to The Book of the Law.'

'Finish your fish first,' she insisted, 'and give me a refill of Prosecco.'

He had been so busy talking that he had not noticed her glass was empty.

*   *   *

When they had completed the meal, he cleared the dishes and they moved to the sofa with their drinks.

Making herself comfortable, she lay back, her legs resting across his.

He took a sip of wine and bent down, picking up the small scarlet coloured book. The front cover lettering and Egyptian style design were in gold.

'It's important for you to make the time to read it for yourself,' he advised her, 'but tonight I am just going to give you a taster.'

'If it's as good as the fish you served,' she anticipated, 'I'm in for a treat.'

'This is far better,' he promised. 'The book is in three short chapters and as I told you on the beach, they were dictated to Aleister Crowley in 1904 by Aiwass, his Holy Guardian Angel. In the first chapter we hear from Nuit, symbolised by the Egyptian sky goddess, who is Lady of the Starry Heaven."

She had not forgotten.

'In this context she represents space,' he specified, 'the total possibilities of every kind. I'm just going to pick out a few verses, most of which you should find extremely beautiful.'

He opened the book. 'In just the third verse it is proclaimed: *'Every man and every woman is a star.'*

Emma was not quite sure what was meant by this. 'Is it referring to one of those shiny objects in the night sky, a leading actor, a famous pop singer, or what?'

Ollie laughed. 'Not quite and neither is it the name of a new TV talent show. I would rather give you Aleister Crowley's interpretation, as he was far more qualified to give guidance. To him, it meant we are all free, independent, shining gloriously, each one a radiant world, unique and necessary.'

Flicking through the pages, he chose another verse: *'Do what thou wilt shall be the whole of the Law.'*

'You've already quoted this to me on more than one occasion,' she reminded him. 'You explained it was about doing our True Will, rather than doing anything we wanted.'

He was pleased she had retained the explanation. 'It's also the phrase which followers of Thelema use as a greeting, the other responding with: *'Love is the law, love under will.'* This stresses the importance of keeping our highest ideal pure, making sure nothing can stop us, or turn us aside from our True Will. All is Love, with a capitol *'L'* along with peace, harmony, beauty and joy. There is a deeper meaning, but I'll keep it for another time.'

Emma needed more Prosecco, so he topped her up again, surprised at how quickly she was getting through it.

Whilst she took a sip, he moved forward a few lines and read some more: *'Come forth, o children, under the stars, & take your fill of love! I am above you and in you. My ecstasy is in yours. My joy is to see your joy.'*

His finger skimmed down the pages, as there was a particular verse which he knew she would like. *'Be goodly therefore: dress ye all in fine apparel; eat rich foods and drink sweet wines and wines that foam! Also, take your fill and will of love as ye will, when, where and with whom ye will! But always unto me.'*

He had deliberately emphasised *wines that foam* and it had not gone unnoticed.

'A reference to my favourite drink,' she hoped.

'More likely to Champagne, but your bubbly can foam almost as well.' Crowley's understanding of the verse was that every act must be a ritual, an act of worship, a sacrament to what Nuit symbolises.'

He moved on: '*I give unimaginable joys on earth: certainty, not faith, while in life, upon death; peace unutterable, rest, ecstasy; nor do I demand aught in sacrifice.*'

Without warning, he handed her the book.

She was not sure why. 'I thought you were going to be doing the reading.'

He drank some of his red wine. 'I was, but you're doing all the drinking and I can't keep up with you.'

Refilling his glass, he pointed with his finger to a particular verse. 'Aleister included this in his Gnostic Mass and so it's rather apt for you to read it.'

Having never set eyes on the text before, Emma was a little unsure of how she would do. She was also feeling a little lightheaded from the amount of wine she had drunk but gave it a try anyway: "*But to love me is better than all things: if under the night-stars in the desert thou presently burnest mine incense before me, invoking me with a pure heart, and the Serpent flame therein, thou shalt come a little to lie in my bosom. For one kiss wilt thou then be willing to give all; but whoso gives one particle of dust shall lose all in that hour. Ye shall gather goods and store of women and spices; ye shall wear rich jewels; ye shall exceed the nations of the earth in splendour & pride; but always in the love of me, and so shall ye come to my joy. I charge you earnestly to come before me in a single robe, and covered with a rich headdress. I love you! I yearn to you! Pale or purple, veiled or voluptuous, I who am all pleasure and purple, and drunkenness of the innermost sense, desire you. Put on the wings, and arouse the coiled splendour within you: come unto me!"*

He quickly indicated for her to continue reading from a line or two down. *"Sing the rapturous love-song unto me! Burn to me perfumes! Wear to me jewels! Drink to me, for I love you! I love you! I am the blue-lidded daughter of Sunset; I am the naked brilliance of the voluptuous night-sky. To me! To me!"*

'You read very well,' he complimented her. 'We've only recited a few extracts from the first chapter, but I hope it's stirred your interest in it, for it's an incredibly important book.'

'It's fascinating,' she added, 'and I promise I'm going to read it all the way through, but not tonight. I intend to polish off the last drop of Prosecco and then indulge in a glass of your Cognac if I may.'

'You're most welcome,' Ollie offered. 'Aleister Crowley liked brandy too. He also used to enjoy absinthe, the anise flavoured spirit, known as the Green Goddess.'

'If gods and goddesses really exist,' Emma was keen to know, 'what do you think would be their favourite drink?'

He pondered her question for a moment. 'According to mythology, it would have been *Soma*. They believed drinking it gained their immortality and so it's been considered divine ever since.'

'In that case,' she proposed, 'we should add it to Benny's next shopping list.'

Ollie was not so sure. 'He'd be risking his pilot's license if he tried to bring us some.'

She wondered why. 'Is there something about Soma I've yet

to know.'

'Oh yes,' he thought it best to tell her. 'Claims to its actual content differ, but many consider it to be a hallucinogenic, comprised of poppy, the ephedra plant and cannabis.'

'In which case,' Emma recommended, 'they should give some of it to all those noisy sea birds on the island.'

'Why would they want to do that?' Ollie asked, thinking she was serious.

Emma started to giggle. 'Because it might just leave no tern unstoned!'

21

Emma awoke with a hangover the next morning. Even so, she arose early and accompanied Ollie to the beach for the sunrise.

Their meditations which followed had lasted longer than usual. Hers had not come to much, but she had not wanted to disturb his silence.

Eventually, after opening his eyes and smiling at her, they made their way back to the cabin for breakfast.

The idea of food was not particularly appealing to her, but he did his best to convince her that she would feel better with something in her stomach.

Despite his sound advice, it took some determination for her to swallow even a mouthful of Weet-Bix and chopped banana.

'I'm sorry you're not feeling so good,' he sympathised. 'It was probably having a large Cognac after all your Prosecco last night.'

'Do you think so?' she questioned. 'I didn't have a hangover at all until I woke up this morning.'

'You just weren't aware of it whilst you were asleep,' he indicated. 'It's the carbon dioxide in sparkling wine which absorbs the alcohol into the blood stream quicker. There are also toxic chemicals known as congeners in dark drinks like Cognac and whiskey, which can make hangovers worse. You'll feel better as the day goes on.'

In order to keep their conversation going, he decided to say a few more words about the importance of going into silence. 'As Aleister Crowley emphasized, the ultimate idea of meditation is to still the mind. A useful starting point is: *'to still the consciousness of all the functions of the body.'* Have you ever heard of a man called Raphael Hurst?

The name did not ring a bell. 'Not that I'm aware of.'

'You're not alone,' he perceived, 'for neither have most people. He was a British author of several notable spiritual books, but he used the better-known pen name of Paul Brunton. His bestseller was entitled *A Search in Secret India*, and it was translated into more than twenty languages. In *The Secret Path*, another of his books, he taught that physical stillness is the first step to mental stillness. He recommended going to the same quiet place every day, occupying the same chair or bed and in the same position. His preference was to be sitting up, rather than lying down, to avoid falling asleep. The body learns through repetition and a regular routine like this to: *'respond automatically until it becomes non-resistant to the invading influence of the soul,'* as he put it.'

'This explains why you think it's so important to try and stick to your own daily pattern,' she recognised.

He indicated she was correct. 'Several ancient cultures, including the Greeks, believed everything was made up of four elements. Although modern science does not accept them as being the basis of the physical world, they are still important, especially in the Western mystery tradition. These elements can easily be related to the process of going into the silence. We need to relax the body, which is associated with the Earth element; take control of our emotions, which are linked to the Water element; empty our mind of thoughts, which are related to the Air element; and pacify the energy, with its connections to the Fire element. As Crowley put it when writing about yoga: *'Sit still. Stop thinking. Shut up. Get out.'* There's also a fifth element by the way, known as aether, or spirit, which alchemists termed the Quintessence, but I'll leave that for now, so as not to confuse you.'

Although Emma had been listening, her suffering still showed, so Ollie thought it best to change the subject. 'What do you fancy for dinner tonight?'

Unexpectedly, especially for someone suffering from all the symptoms of a hangover, she chose to give him an amorous look. 'You!' was all she said.

He chuckled, fully aware of the suggestive implication of her reply, but gave it instead a rather unpleasant culinary meaning. 'I might well have ended up on your plate out here in bygone days, for the Fijian Islands were once known as the Cannibal Isles?'

She stared at him open-eyed. 'You have to be joking!'

'Absolutely not,' he assured her. 'I don't think you really had it in mind to devour me, but Fiji does have a history of cannibalism. The eating of human flesh here goes back at least 2,500 years. It was steeped in mysterious ritual, with mesmerising drumming and eery chanting. Actually, my use of the word *steeped* is a rather appropriate pun, its meaning in cookery terms being to soak in hot water, or marinade.'

She got the picture. 'What on earth made them want to eat other human beings?'

'It probably wasn't a nutritional choice,' he supposed, 'but more for tribal or spiritual reasons. It no doubt gave them a sense of power and revenge, along with the mistaken belief of being a way to gain their enemy's knowledge.'

'Was it just one or two people they ate?' she asked aghast, 'or a lot of victims?'

'It wasn't as if the cannibals were going into restaurants and ordering the waitresses for a starter and the waiters as the main course,' he made fun, 'but there were a substantial number. The most prolific and hungriest cannibal, according to the Guinness Book of Records, was a Fijian Chief by the name of Ratu Udre Udre, who lived in northern Viti Levu, which is Fiji's largest island. He is believed to have eaten nearly a thousand people during his lifetime.'

To say she looked flabbergasted would be an understatement. 'How can they be sure it was so many?'

'The chief had kept a small stone as a record for each person he consumed,' Ollie detailed. 'Although there were 872 stones on his grave, there were quite a few gaps where some had been removed. One of his sons further confirmed his father had shared none of the corpses with anyone else but had eaten them all himself.'

By now, it was hardly surprising Emma was feeling even less hungry than she had been earlier. 'It's turning my stomach just hearing about such a disgusting thing,' she admitted. 'When did this cannibalism finally end?'

'Christian missionaries arrived in the 1830's,' he was able to tell her, 'and were appalled by what they witnessed. The last recorded act of cannibalism in Fiji was in 1867. The Reverend Thomas Baker, who was originally from England's East Sussex, was a Wesleyan missionary working for the Australian Methodist church. He was murdered in a village in central Viti Levu and then cut up, cooked and eaten, along with a traditional vegetable side dish.'

'I'm pleased you mentioned the side dish,' Emma mocked, 'or I would have worried the cannibals weren't getting their recommended five-a-day fruit and vegetables.'

'Talking of which,' Ollie was reminded, 'although Charles Darwin, the naturalist, geologist and biologist, suggested the normal food of man is vegetables, he wondered how some of the exotic animals he studied might taste. To find out, he decided to eat several of them, including iguanas, armadillos and the rhea. The last one is a large flightless bird, named after the Titan goddess of fertility and motherhood.'

'You're not going to tell me he was a cannibal too?' she dreaded.

'Darwin was alive at the same time,' he worked out, 'but there's no suggestion at all to my knowledge of him ever trying human flesh. Although the Reverend Baker is believed to be the only white missionary to be devoured by cannibals, six Fijian student teachers suffered the same fate the same day.'

She could hardly believe anyone could be so cruel. 'What justification could they have had for doing such a thing.'

'Having Christianity forced down their throats was probably enough,' he half-joked. 'More seriously, some think it was because the clergyman insulted the chief by taking back a comb from his hair, which would have been considered taboo. Others think it was more likely he got caught up in tribal feuding.'

Although such true events were well and truly giving her the heebie-jeebies, there was one thing she was curious about. 'Did they eat every single bit of him?'

'The only things which remained were his boots,' Ollie elaborated. 'They are still on show in a museum in Sava, along with the bowl in which he was served. Gradually, Christianity replaced the worship of the old gods in Fiji and today it's mainly a Christian country. Local farmers, whose crops were failing, thought they had been cursed by their ancestors' sins. In 2003 they asked for forgiveness and as a penance gave up smoking, drinking kava and having sex for a month. Today they make money by selling replicas in the souvenir shops of wooden cannibal forks and cannibal dolls made from coconut shells.'

'Hearing this has well and truly put me off my breakfast,' she let him know. 'It's hard to believe they even ate the missionary's feet.'

'We had better stick to something else for dinner tonight then,' he teased.

'Definitely,' she agreed, 'and it had better not be sole!'

22

'What would you like to do with the rest of the day?' Ollie asked, as they sat outside the cabin having lunch.

'It would be nice to do something different for once,' she urged, having managed to eat a little bit more than at breakfast. 'We go to Benny's beach almost every day and you've already shown me Distant Sands and Tern Bay. I've yet to visit the mangroves.'

'I've only been there once,' he said unenthusiastically. 'It's in a smallish, sheltered area of the coastline. According to Brad's book, the trees I briefly saw were probably black mangroves, which have tangles of elbow roots sticking up out of the mud. I didn't fancy venturing into the interior, but there are no doubt red mangroves growing nearer to the water's edge. They have prop roots to support them in the even softer mud, the submerged ones providing a nursery habitat for fish. There are probably other species of mangrove too, but the whole muddy area is part-flooded, mosquito-infested and full of bacteria and decay. The smell itself was enough to put me off, for it stinks like rotten eggs.'

She held her nose between her thumb and forefinger wryly. 'Poo! If it's as bad as you describe, I'm happy to leave going there for now.'

'I'm probably being a little unfair,' he had to admit, 'as mangroves do have a positive side. The trees grow where most other timbers couldn't survive and help fight climate change, as they absorb more carbon from the air than forests. They are also thought to reduce ocean acidification, which helps prevent the harmful bleaching of coral.'

'I would like to see them for myself some time,' she decided, 'but the beach sounds far more appealing for today. What if we head back to Tern Bay this afternoon and check out the birds again?'

He started clearing the things from the table. 'It's fine by me. I'll just put these inside and we can make a move.'

Packing their towels, suntan lotion and bottled water into a couple of bags, they made their way to the beach. As they walked, Emma asked about the fauna on the island. 'I know there are lots of birds, but where are all the other animals?'

'The only mammal you'll find here is the fruit bat,' he explained, 'and possibly creatures such as snakes and geckos. There are also iguana on some islands I'm told, but they are rare.'

'With all these trees,' she imagined, 'you'd think there would be lots of cheeky monkeys swinging from them.'

He sighed with genuine regret. 'I only wish there were. The nearest would be a bat known as the Fijian monkey-faced flying fox, but they are critically endangered. They only live in a small rainforest region on the island of Tavenui, on a single mountain, above 1,000 meters. They are quite furry but have wings rather than tails.'

'Not all monkeys have tails either,' she informed him. 'Chimpanzees don't for a start.'

'But chimps aren't monkeys,' he corrected. 'They are great apes, along with gorillas, orangutans and bonobos. Gibbons and the closely related siamangs don't have tails either, but they are lesser apes. Whilst most monkeys have tails, there are exceptions, such as the Barbary macaque, which is native to the Atlas Mountains of Algeria and Morocco. Those on the Rock of Gibraltar are the only wild monkey population in Europe.'

She was most impressed by his understanding of these animals. 'Only now I discover you're an expert primatologist!'

'I would love to be,' he conceded, 'but my knowledge of them is limited. Still, I have always had a great love, fascination and respect for monkeys and apes. It must go back to when I was given a soft-toy chimpanzee, named Jacko, at the age of five. Brad's looking after him for me in London. I know it sounds daft, but it's for sentimental reasons, rather like your ring is to you. I suppose the chimp is a reminder of my much younger days, as the others are of more recent years.'

Emma stopped walking and gave him a look. 'Others?'

'Quite a few actually,' he admitted. 'There's an extremely realistic life-size chimp called Buddy, which I bought on Pier 39 in San Francisco. He's got two baby chimp brothers, which came from a former magic shop in Hollywood, as did an orangutan and gorilla. They are all hand puppets.

As they proceeded towards the beach, Emma continued to try and understand his until then unrevealed collection. 'You should have brought them with you,' she said in fun, 'and hung them in the trees. They would have looked cute.'

'There are far too many of them,' he acceded. 'There must be at least 350, some of which are battery operated and so actually move and make sounds.'

She was astonished to hear of such a number. 'What an unusual horde.'

'They're far more interesting than some of the other things people accumulate,' he felt. 'Many came from the souvenir shops in zoos and monkey sanctuaries around the world, so there's a story behind nearly every one of them.'

His love of monkeys and apes was abundantly clear, but she had a burning question. 'Were you ever tempted to get a real one?'

He shook his head decisively. 'I would never consider it. The keeping of primates as pets should be banned. When a baby chimp is caught in the wild for example, it's necessary for the poachers to kill several others, especially the mother. Monkeys and apes do not make suitable pets and it's cruel to keep them as such. I do however have an adopted chimp called Athena, back in England at Monkey World, the primate rescue centre in Dorset. I'm also a member of the Orangutan Foundation and support charities like the Gorilla Organisation and the Wild Futures' monkey sanctuary in Cornwall. Brad takes care of all the subscription renewals now of course.'

Although the sanctuaries and charities he described sounded good, she was less sure about zoos. 'Should monkeys and apes really be kept in captivity?'

'Only in the finest zoos,' he specified, 'especially if the primates have been rescued or bred in captivity. The best zoological organisations have improved so much over the years and now do vital research and conservation work for endangered species, along with important educational programmes. Visitors and particularly children, get the chance to observe them closely, in their specially designed enclosures.'

'But there are some inspiring wildlife documentaries on television,' Emma pointed out, 'where the animals can be observed in their natural environment.'

'They make great viewing and are highly educational,' he was the first to admit, 'but it's not the same as seeing them close up, with your own eyes, to really appreciate them. How many parents have the means to take their children to remote areas of central Africa, to then trek for hours in a rainforest, in the hope of briefly spotting a gorilla or chimp? Anyway, with so much of their habitat being destroyed by mankind's greed, unless it's remedied soon, only rescue centres and zoos will be able to save the animals from extinction. Nearly 40 years ago Jane Goodall, the ambassador for chimps, first founded *Chimpanzoo*, which is dedicated to the well-being and understanding of chimps in zoos and captivity. It will be difficult to save the mountain gorilla however, as none have ever been successfully bred in captivity.'

'It sounds as if gorillas are your favourite,' she guessed.

'I like all the primates,' he made plain, 'but the great apes fascinate me the most, especially the chimpanzee and bonobo. It's probably because they're our nearest animal relatives, sharing nearly 99% of our DNA.'

Until this unexpected topic of conversation, Emma had been totally unaware of one of the species he was talking about. 'What's a bonobo? I've never even heard the name before.'

'It's hardly surprising,' he reassured her. 'They were only discovered in 1929, when a German anatomist was examining a skull in a Belgian museum. As the head was small, he assumed it was that of a young chimp, but then realised it was an adult, which suggested it had to be another kind of ape entirely. This is the reason why bonobos were originally, but wrongly, referred to as pygmy chimpanzees. Now we know better.'

Their arrival at Tern Bay was more than obvious. The birds seemed to be welcoming them with a mighty fanfare of cacophonous screeches.

'Let's spread our towels on the sand,' Ollie suggested, 'and get some more suntan lotion on. There's a particular aspect of bonobo behaviour which you are going to find really interesting.'

As they settled down, the terns were busy doing the opposite. If anything, they were noisier than ever.

She mimicked them. '*Heech,* h*eech-heech, grrri-grrri, heech.*'

'They're making enough racket already,' he protested, having to raise his voice, 'without any help from you.'

She laughed. 'Well, you'd better give them one of your quotes on silence then. Perhaps it will shut them up.'

He had a quick think, as they watched them circling above and plunge-diving for fish. 'This one's from Mother Teresa, the Catholic nun and missionary who was made a saint: '*See how nature — trees, flowers, grass — grows in silence; see the stars, the moon and the sun, how they move in silence.*''

They watched the birds closely for a moment to see if it had made any difference, not that they expected it to.

'It's a shame Teresa hadn't added: '*See how the terns fly through the air in silence,*' Emma hoaxed. 'Then it might have miraculously calmed them down.'

Ollie doubted it. 'If anything, they've taken a *tern* for the worse!

She laughed again at his play on words.

Lying flat on her back she enjoyed the heat of the sun on her bare body. 'I think you'd better stick to telling me about bonobos. Have you ever seen any in real life?'

'Yes. In San Diego Zoo,' he enthused. 'They only live wild in the Democratic Republic of Congo, where they're classed as endangered. There are so many killed by hunters, only to be eaten, or traded as bushmeat. Others are kept as pets or used as an ingredient for a Congolese sexually enhancing medicine.'

She was horrified. 'Hearing this takes me back to what you were telling me this morning about cannibals.'

'In many ways it's almost the same,' he alleged, 'being as they're one of our closest animal relatives. This is why education is so important. Bonobos are even clever enough to make their own medication, without the use of human ingredients. They have the skill to blend several plants and make successful remedies. They walk upright on their legs like we do for some of the time when they are on the ground. There is one big difference between them and the other great apes, however. It is female bonobos who take charge of their groups. They affiliate with other females to control the males where necessary.'

'They've got the right idea there.' Emma championed. 'Bonobo girl power!'

Such a comment did not surprise him. 'It's also the female who takes entire charge of the youngsters.'

On this point Emma was not quite so sure. 'I think it would be fairer if the dads played their part too in looking after the kids, rather than leaving it all to the mums.'

'It would be rather difficult,' he put forward, 'as most often the mother has no idea at all who the father is. You'll understand why when I tell you how much bonobos love sex. It's the whole key to their social life. They become easily aroused, making love for all sorts of reasons, with their own sex as well as the opposite. As it's not just for reproduction, the females seem happy to have sex even when they can't conceive.'

Emma could see nothing at all wrong with that. 'They sound just like women. If we decided to only do it when we wanted babies, you men wouldn't half complain.'

He did not doubt such an observation. 'Bonobos often use sex to defuse tension between rivals,' he went on. 'It's as if they're practising the famous 1960's protest movement slogan: *Make love not war.*' Sex also comes into play when they are anxious or annoyed, as a bribe or a reward for food and also as a means of climbing their social ranks. Like humans, bonobos can make love face to face in the missionary position and can use their tongues when kissing. They are also into genital touching and rubbing, massage and even oral sex from time to time.

'Now I can now understand why you say they're so closely related to humans,' she reasoned. 'It sounds like they have a great sex life.'

'They do,' he recognised. 'Although they have a lot of sex, it's not all of the time and there is a downside. On average, their copulation only lasts about 13 seconds.'

She kept him in suspense for a moment before making an expected comment. 'It sounds as if they go for quantity rather than quality,' she deemed, giving him a saucy look and running her foot up his leg. 'I'm more interested in the latter.'

He shook his head in utter disbelief. 'Don't say my description of the bonobo's sex life has turned you on?'

'Actually, I've been feeling horny all day,' she let fall. 'Sometimes hangovers have that effect on me. It's as if my body knows an orgasm will make me feel better, even if only for a while.'

'I'd be only too pleased to help out,' he offered, 'but you'll have to wait until we get back to the cabin.'

She sat up, giving him a stare. 'What's wrong with here? There is only the two of us, not just on this beach, but the entire island.'

He managed to resist her tempting invitation. 'Sorry, but I'm feeling a little uneasy. With even innocent nudity being illegal in public here in Fiji, the authorities are definitely not going to like sex on the beach.'

'I'm not so sure,' she disagreed. 'With such a gorgeous mixture of vodka, peach schnapps and cranberry juice, a *sex on the beach* cocktail is scrumptious.'

'I'm being serious,' he told her, managing to keep a straight face.

'It didn't seem to bother you before,' she recalled. 'Anyway, it's your own private island and so we should be able to do what we like on it.'

He took a deep breath. 'I don't think the authorities would see it the same way. You probably won't understand, but I've got an uncanny feeling. It's as if I'm being warned to be extremely careful. I think we'd better head back to the cabin.'

She got up and shook the sand from her towel, folding it over her arm. 'I'm beginning to wish you were a bonobo. From what you've told me about them, you'd have had no inhibitions at all.'

'I'm sure you're right,' he granted, enjoying her wisecrack. 'Which reminds me of something else bonobos can do. Just like us and the other great apes, they can have a nice big laugh when they're having fun!'

23

Their routine the next morning started normally but was to take an unexpected turn.

Ollie and Emma had watched the sunset and done their meditations, before returning to the cabin for breakfast. He had then gone back to Benny's beach for another meditation session, the plan being for her to join him there a little later.

He was sitting on his beach towel, deep in silence, when he suddenly became aware of the sound of an engine.

His eyes opened to see a motor launch heading for the jetty.

Being naked, he instinctively got to his knees and wrapped his towel around his waist. Standing up slowly and shielding his eyes from the sun, he peered at the approaching vessel.

As it manoeuvred to dock, he could tell it only just had enough draft. Had it been any larger, its keel would have scraped the bottom, the water being quite shallow.

At first, he thought it might be a boat chartered by island hopping holidaymakers, but its stark grey paintwork suggested it had a more official purpose.

Thinking quickly, he unscrewed the top from the bottle of mineral water he had with him and splashed the contents over his upper body. His intention was to make it appear he had been swimming.

Cautiously, he took a few steps across the sand, watching as a young man jumped from the launch. Dressed in a white shirt and black shorts, he held a rope in his hand, which he used to secure the stern of the boat to one of the jetty's cleats. He did the same at the bow, with a second rope, thrown to him by an older looking man, who then also stepped from the vessel. Two other people could be seen, but they remained onboard.

Ollie was approached by the senior man, who wore a crushed dark suit. He was dabbing perspiration from his brow with a checkered pattern handkerchief. This was hardly surprising, the wearing of any type of jacket being unnecessary and uncomfortable in the growing heat. He carried a battered faded-brown leather briefcase, which looked long overdue for retirement.

'This is a private island,' Ollie made him aware in a deliberately stern voice, 'and I don't take visitors.'

'So I believe,' the stranger assured him. 'You must be Oliver Longbridge.'

Ollie was taken aback at the man knowing his name. 'That's right, but who you are?'

'I'm Thomas Chand,' came the reply, 'and I'm an inspector from the Government's Department of the Environment.'

Ollie's first thought was that someone must have spotted him and Emma without any clothes on and had made a complaint. If this had been the case, however, it would have more likely been a police officer he was facing.

Even so, he thought it best to explain the way he was

dressed. 'You'll have to forgive my appearance in this towel, but I've just been for a swim.' He hoped the inspector would assume he was wearing wet swimming trunks or shorts underneath.'

'I don't blame you,' Chand said rather enviously. 'I'd much rather be in the water myself, but unfortunately I have work to do. I'm here to check there have been no unauthorised building developments on the island.'

Ollie was relieved to hear this and that the visit had nothing to do with their naturist lifestyle. 'Are you aware I bought this island on a lease?' he asked him. 'Full permission was granted for the few buildings here.'

The inspector opened the briefcase, taking from it a bundle of paperwork. 'Of course. Fortunately, I was involved in your original application, made on your behalf if I recall by a Mr. Brad Lithtrop.'

Ollie nodded, indicating this was correct. 'He's my personal assistant, back in the UK now, but I still retain his services.'

'A wise decision,' Thomas considered. 'He was most efficient in setting everything up for you. I don't expect there to be any problems, but we do need to carry out these periodic inspections. It is to ensure no constructions have been erected, except for those authorised in your lease. We are particularly concerned about anything on the foreshore.'

Ollie pointed along the beach. 'There's nothing here at all, apart from the jetty.'

The inspector cast his eyes across the length of sand. 'As I can see. We checked the other two beaches on the island from the boat on our way here and I doubt you'd want to build anything amongst the mangroves.'

'They'd be no point,' Ollie perceived, 'and near on impossible in such a waterlogged environment.'

'Don't you believe it,' came the more expert view. 'They've managed in some places. The structures are prefabricated, using timber from dead mangrove trees, which sit on pile footings to protect them from strong currents.'

Ollie was not aware of this. 'Whatever their reasons were for doing so, I've got none here.'

'I did say it was unlikely,' Chand reminded him. 'I just need to check there have been no further developments around your bure, or cabin as you English tend to call it.'

Although Ollie was reassured, he hoped the real motive was not to snoop on him. 'It's just a routine inspection then, which shouldn't take long?'

'I just need to take a quick look,' the inspector told him, 'and I should be away in half an hour at the most. You being the only person here makes things easier.'

Ollie thought it best to make him aware of Emma's presence on the island too. 'There's also a young lady here. It's a long story, but she wasn't originally intending to come here at all.'

'She'll be none of my business,' Chand established. 'Although we were told you would be living alone, it's entirely your prerogative. You can have who you like here, providing there's room for them in your cabin and you don't try to turn the place into a holiday resort.'

'There's no chance of anything like that happening.' Ollie made clear. Knowing the reason for Thomas's visit had put his mind at rest, but not for long.

He suddenly remembered Emma was due at the beach any moment and all she would be wearing was suntan lotion.

She would not even have a towel with her, as he had brought it down earlier.

Determined to keep his composure, he tried to think quickly of how to avoid what was sure to be a difficult and embarrassing situation. Fortunately, what he hoped was a plausible plan came to mind. 'Would you care to wait here, whilst I pop back to the cabin and change into some dry shorts? It'll only take a moment and then we can commence your inspection.'

Unfortunately, his request seemed rather illogical to the inspector. 'I need to go to your bure anyway to check around it. There's no point in me waiting here on the beach, whilst you make your way there and then come back for me.'

Ollie was unable to argue. 'You make a good point and I know exactly what you're getting at. There is admittedly no sense in my doing any unnecessary walking in this heat.'

It had not been Ollie's wellbeing the inspector had been concerned about at all. He stuffed the papers back in his briefcase. 'I need to get away from here as soon as possible. I have another island to inspect today and it's one I might find problems on. I must go and check your buildings straight away. You can then go inside and change whilst I'm doing so.'

Ollie did at least manage to come up with one more possible delaying tactic. 'Shouldn't you first tell your crew on the boat what you're planning to do, so they won't worry about where you've gone?'

Thomas looked exasperated. 'My men know perfectly well what I have to do and want to get away from here too. They'll be far more concerned by seeing us standing here chatting, as if we've got all the time in the world.'

Ollie gave up. He could only hope Emma would still be

inside the cabin when they got there. At least he could then get her to put something on before the inspector saw her.

He was beginning to see why he had felt so uneasy the day before and had been so reluctant to make love in the open on Tern Bay as she had wanted. He wondered if his Holy Guardian Angel had foreseen the inspector's visit and had been warning him to be careful.

As they made their way across the beach, he tried to make polite small talk. It proved to be difficult, as the inspector's sole interest in life seemed to be his job.

Just as they reached the path, Ollie to his horror caught sight of Emma approaching. As expected, she was completely nude.

Pointing to a bush, he quickly tried to direct Thomas's line of sight to it. 'This will amaze you,' he declared with an over-the-top flourish. 'Emma lost her grandmother's gold ring, but we found it at this very spot. We were so lucky, as there's hardly any space at all beneath the bush. You'll see what I mean if you put your hand down there and feel.'

The inspector did not share Ollie's euphoria for the fortunate find, but reluctantly complied with his request. Bending down, he ran his palm over the sandy earth.

Whilst he was doing so, Ollie signalled frantically to Emma, waving for her get back to the cabin.

Unfortunately, she misinterpreted his gesture. With the inspector crouched down and out of sight, she saw only Ollie and waved back at him happily, increasing her pace.

Thomas stood up, wiping sand from his hands and off the briefcase he had dropped whilst pointlessly feeling beneath the bush. Mumbling to himself, he continued making his way towards the cabin, determined there would be no more hold ups.

Suddenly he stopped in his tracks, his jaw dropping in utter astonishment. He had caught sight of the beautiful naked young woman coming towards him.

As his eager eyes took in her shapely figure and sexy swagger, his first thought was that she must be an hallucination. Never had he seen such a delightful, captivating vision. He could only stare, focusing in turn on her gorgeous face, long flowing blond hair and delicious feminine breasts. His gaze travelled lower, admiring the indent of her waist, the rounded curves of her hips, her perfect slender legs and, at the juncture of her inner thighs, her most secret place. There he gaped, as if frozen in time.

Emma was as equally shocked to see him, a sweaty middle-aged man in a ridiculous-looking crumpled suit. She took in his thinning greying hair, his sagging obese tummy and the confused expression of longing on his chubby face.

She managed a smile. 'I see we have a guest. What fun!'

Chand was too stunned to speak, so Ollie spoke for him. 'This is Thomas, an environmental inspector. He's hoping there are no unexpected erections.'

Emma began to laugh, misconstruing his words. She had not the faintest idea he was actually talking about unplanned buildings.

It was only the look of despair on Ollie's face which helped her control the giggles.

She shook their visitor's hand and gave him her most innocent look. 'I'm so sorry if I've embarrassed you, by appearing in such a state, but a terrible thing happened on my journey here. All my luggage went missing. Every single bit of it. All I was left with was the tiny pink dress I had on when I first arrived. I've been wearing it ever since. Having nothing else, I finally washed it last night and unfortunately, it's still damp. Had you come to the island yesterday daytime, or tomorrow, I would have been dressed. I can only apologise for making you see me like this.'

'There's no need at all to,' he said without hesitation, surreptitiously thinking how fortunate he was to have chosen today. 'It should be me, asking for your forgiveness. I couldn't warn you in advance about my inspection because it's officially meant to be unexpected.'

He turned to Ollie. 'Perhaps you could possibly lend her one of your shirts to cover her modesty?' Doing himself no favours, he added, 'Preferably a long one.'

'What a superb idea,' Ollie feigned. 'I should have thought of it myself. I'll fetch one immediately.'

He disappeared up the path to the cabin, relieved it would also give him the opportunity to discard the towel around his waist and slip into a pair of shorts.

As they stood waiting for Ollie to return, the inspector could feel himself getting more and more flustered. With such a stunningly attractive naked woman in such close proximity, his heartbeat had gone into overdrive.

Thinking he had better say something, his attempt to do so was an utter failure, his incoherent words coming out as sheer drivel. 'I …err …probably …yes, but on the other hand … didn't expect …but who would?'

'Could you say that again please?' Emma requested politely. 'I didn't quite catch your meaning.'

Neither had Thomas himself. He tried something else. 'It's …err …certainly good weather for it.'

'For what?' she asked still confused. 'For me not to be wearing any clothes?'

He felt himself blush, fearing his face must have turned bright red. 'No …no,' he stammered. 'Not at all. I was merely suggesting it's nice and warm for your stay on the island. It's dry too, unlike when it rains. When it does it tends to get wetter.'

Realising his attempts at making a coherent conversation were a disaster, he sought to free himself. 'Please, can I go now?'

'But you've only just arrived,' Emma reminded him.

'To the cabin,' he indicated. 'I have to check nothing illegal's going on around it.'

'What kind of thing,' she asked, thinking as Ollie had initially done, he must be referring to their naturism.'

'My inspection is solely to make sure no additional buildings have been put up,' he clarified.

Emma finally understood the reason for his being on the island. 'Of course. You should have said so sooner.'

By the time they got there, Ollie was dressed. He handed her a white shirt, which she put on.

Having got so used to being nude, it never occurred to her to button it up at the front and so it did nothing at all to hide anything.

Preferring not to comment and trying hard to avert his eyes, Thomas opened his briefcase. He carefully studied the diagram of the cabin and outbuildings, counting how many there should be. He then pointed to each with his finger to ensure they tallied.

Although there were so few, he lost count twice, the distraction of Emma's lithe young body being too much for his senses.

'It's all looking good,' he finally managed to say. 'I can be on my way and leave you to it.'

'You're welcome to stop a little longer if you'd like,' Ollie offered out of politeness. 'I've got some nice cool beer.'

'Not when I'm working thank you,' the inspector said.

It reminded Ollie of the similar response he got from Benny whenever he offered him one.

'There will be no need for me to disturb you again until about the same time next year,' Chand informed him, 'but I'm not permitted to say exactly when however.'

'Of course not,' Ollie agreed a little sarcastically. 'State secrets and all that.'

'It'll give us something to look forward to,' Emma suggested in a more friendly tone. 'You've been our only guest, except for the pilot who flies in our food.' She was tempted to jovially add the dead dolphin, but wisely thought it might complicate things. 'For now, I can see you back to your boat if you like?'

The last thing the inspector wanted was for his crew to see him emerge onto the beach, accompanied by an almost completely nude woman. 'No. I can make my own way thank you,' he decided.

He scurried off but being unable to resist one more look at her, stopped and turned his head. 'Your luggage going missing was rotten luck for everyone concerned.'

*　　*　　*

When he was out of sight, Emma and Ollie creased up with laughter.

'How we got away with it I don't know,' he said.

'It was thanks to my fast thinking,' she hinted, 'about losing all my clothes.'

'Yes,' he agreed.' 'It was very clever, especially as you didn't know the reason why he was here then, but I'm still surprised he fell for it. There is just one small thing I need to mention however.'

'And what might it be,' she wondered.

He pointed towards her. 'The shirt he suggested I lend you. It does nothing to hide your most interesting bits.'

She glanced down at herself, realising her error at not buttoning it.

Taking it off, she handed it back to him. 'He's gone now, so I don't need it anyway. You can remove what you're wearing too.'

He was a little more cautious. 'I think we'd better play it safe and wait until he's definitely left the island. We'll get lunch ready in the meantime.'

By the time they sat down at the table outside the cabin, Ollie had checked the boat had gone.

He opened a couple of beers. 'Cheers! Now we are back to normal, at least by our standards.'

'Why do you think nudity is illegal in Fiji,' Emma pondered, as she served them both some fruit.

'Cultural differences,' he pointed out, 'and probably a misunderstanding of what naturism is really about. As any composer will tell you: *A harp is but a naked piano.*' Many Fijians are Christians, which I am sure has a lot to do with it.'

'Why then didn't the inspector make more fuss about the situation,' she queried.

'It might just have been politeness,' Ollie reckoned, 'as Fijians are generally considered to be courteous. It was also obvious he couldn't take his eyes off your body and we can't really blame him for that.'

'He got a freebie then,' she claimed. 'With my glamour modelling, I usually get paid for people to look at my natural assets.'

'Not all of them,' he pointed out. 'As someone once said: *If only our eyes saw souls instead of bodies, how different our ideals of beauty would be.*"

24

Ollie opened his eyes to find it was already light. He must have overslept, which was most unusual for him.

He turned his head, expecting to see Emma asleep in bed beside him, but she was not there.

Raising his body, he swung his feet to floor and stood up. 'Emma?' he called.

As there was no reply, he glanced around the cabin and then walked over to the door and looked outside.

There was no sign of her there either and he supposed she might be in the toilet or taking a shower.

He had no idea what the time was, without a watch and having put the alarm clock away in a box, the day after he first arrived on the island. As he was completely free to do whatever he wanted, time was of no importance to his lifestyle. With the exception of this morning, he had always arisen early enough to watch the sunrise and had gone to bed at night whenever he and Emma were tired.

Glancing up at the position of the sun, he guessed it must be about 11am. The toilet door was open, so he relieved himself and then checked the shower. There was no sign of her there either.

It then occurred to him that she had probably awoken when they usually did and had gone on to the beach by herself, expecting him to follow. He thought it strange though, for her not to have returned for breakfast by now.

Perhaps she had fallen asleep, lying on her towel during her meditation. If so, he only hoped she had first applied some sun lotion. Although she by now had a good tan, it was still possible to burn, even in the morning.

Going back inside, he was surprised to see her folded beach towel and the lotion still on the table. Concerned, he picked them up, grabbed a bottle of water and his own towel, then headed straight for the beach.

He thought it likely they would come face to face on the path, but this was not to be.

His eyes searched the beach and he called out for her. 'Emma? Emma? Are you here?'

The only sounds were those of the waves, as they gently washed the footprint-free sand, accompanied by the call of some curious birds, flying overhead in formation.

He walked to the water's edge and peered at the sea just in case she had gone for a swim. It was unlikely, for he had tried to put her off risking it.

Turning, he gazed at the palm trees and other flora which lined the beach. With still no sign of her, he shouted again. 'Emma? Where are you? If you're playing hide and seek the game's over. I give up.'

He was starting to get worried and found himself studying the sea again. What if she had gone swimming after all and had been dragged out by an undercurrent and drowned? He tried to put the thought from his mind. It was too dreadful to contemplate, even for a moment.

Making his way up the beach, he stopped at the bush, by the start of the path. The plant had taken on a rather bizarre significance, since they had found her ring beneath it. He brushed his hand through it fondly, just as she had done, in gratitude for it looking after her lost piece of jewellery.

His hopes of finding her innocently rocking backwards and forwards in the hammock outside the cabin by the time he reached it had been in vain. What he would have given to have her laughing at his unwarranted disquiet, telling him she had simply woken before him and gone for a stroll.

He went inside and sat down. It was then he noticed her snorkelling mask was missing. It had lain unused in the corner of the cabin since her arrival.

Getting up, he checked carefully to make sure it had not just been moved.

Finding no sign of the mask brought even more unease. There was good reason why he had deliberately told her about the perils of the sea. By exaggerating the dangers which lurked there, he had hoped to dissuade her from going swimming. She in turn must have thought it strange he never bathed in the sea but was unaware of the reason.

Out of shame, he had never mentioned the time he was in Gran Canaria several years ago and had nearly drowned. It was off the coast between Playa del Ingles and Maspalomas. He had been stupid enough to ignore the red flag warning and had been swept out to sea. It was a miracle the brave rescuers reached him in time. Never since had he been tempted to enter what he considered might potentially become a watery grave.

Knowing she had enjoyed their visit a couple of days earlier to the beach he had dubbed Tern Bay, he considered it possible she had gone there. It was admittedly unlikely she would have gone off by herself, without telling him first, but she did like watching the birds and mimicking their calls.

He covered himself in more suntan lotion and set off, taking just his towel, water and some fruit. Having not had any breakfast, his rumbling stomach noisily demanded nourishment.

All the way there, his mind questioned repeatedly why she should have gone off anywhere without letting him know. It was not as if there had been an argument between them the night before. They had laughed all evening about the excuse she had given the inspector for her nudity. After a nice dinner, they had made passionate love, before falling asleep. Having shared every day together since she first arrived on the island, her disappearance made no sense at all.

His heart sank as he reached Tern Bay to find it empty, at least of any human form. There seemed to be more birds than ever, busy with their weaving, diving and screeching.

He yelled her name several times. 'Emma! Emma! Where are you? Emma!'

Only the terns heard him, some perhaps giving him a quick glance, as they continued their search for food.

He unrolled his towel and sat down. Swallowing a mouthful of mineral water, he unpeeled a banana. It was heart breaking to be there without her. Although she had disrupted his initial intention to meditate several times a day, she had more than made up for it by her irresistible company. He was deeply in love with her and she had expressed similar feelings towards him. He had to find her.

For more than an hour he carefully checked amongst the flora at the top of the beach and then the seashore.

It was a huge relief not to discover her body floating in the water. He was aware most bodies do so face down to start with, because of the weight of the arms and legs, but excess fat in the stomach, or breasts can cause them to float face up. He remembered too of it often taking several days for a drowned person's corpse to float anyway. Initially, as the air in the lungs is replaced by water, the body begins to sink. Eventually, as it decomposes, gasses are excreted, which accumulate in the body's cavities, causing it to rise to the surface.

He tried to displace such gruesome thoughts and to remain positive, to search somewhere else.

It took him some time to re-find the third beach, the hidden Distant Sands, as he called it. He had only been there twice, once by himself and once with Emma. He pictured in his mind her doing a little dance of joy, when she had first stood on its perfect white soft sand. She had thought it so idyllic.

He unrolled his towel and sat down for a moment to rest his legs, just as they had done together. The sea had been so still, that they had pretended the waves were asleep and thought it fun to each make a wish. She never revealed what hers had been and by now he had forgotten his own. Even so, he was sure it must have been about the two of them.

He decided to make another one right away. It was simply

to be able to find her somewhere safe and well.

He rose to his feet and continued the search, just as he had done on the previous two beaches. Checking amongst the flora and then the coastline, he called all the while, 'Emma! Emma! Where are you Emma?'

With no reply and not a sign of her, he reluctantly accepted she was not there and thought it best to return to the cabin. It would take some time, but he set off with the hope still in his heart of finding her there waiting for him, with some easy and plausible explanation.

It was getting dark by the time he got back.

As he approached the cabin, he bawled her name several more times, but only silence answered. It was the very opposite to the inspirational spiritual silence he so loved. The one he was aware of now was no friend, but a cold empty silence, which implied something was wrong. It was like the unhelpful silence of neutrality in a situation when it is morally essential to act. Doing nothing in such a circumstance can be as harmful as hate.

He hurried into the small hut, hoping the satellite phone might miraculously be working, so he could summon help.

It was still just as dead as the extinct flightless dodo. Benny was not due back to the island for a few days and he cursed himself for not asking for a replacement phone sooner.

The battery was at least working in the small hand torch he kept there and so he made a search of the grounds all around the cabin. Several times he thought he saw something, but it was only the shadows playing uncalled for games with him.

Ollie had to force himself to eat some dinner. His worry

about her had his stomach churning in nauseous knots, which even a brandy failed to control. What he would have given right then, to have had Emma sitting opposite, sipping her beloved Prosecco. If she turned out to be alright, he vowed to buy her a hundred or more cases of her favourite sparkling wine and construct a massive storeroom on the island to keep it in.

Recalling then the environmental officer's inspection the day before made him change his mind about putting up any additional buildings.

Without warning, what had turned out to be quite a humorous incident now set his pulse racing. A nagging thought suggested she could possibly have been kidnapped by the inspector. Although the man had given his name, he had never offered any formal identification. There was the possibility he was not even an environmental inspector at all. He could have been anyone.

In Ollie's worried mind things became distorted and exaggerated. As he pictured the bewildered gaze on Thomas Chand's face, as he had taken in Emma's perfect feminine curves, it transformed into an expression of sheer uncontrollable lust. What if he had come back in his boat and taken her from the beach? He could have cruelly raped her, before sharing her with his crew and then disposed of her body out to sea? What proof would there ever be? No one would ever know.

Fortunately, something once said by the inspirational speaker and author, Esther Hicks, saved him from such unlikely and horrid speculation: *'Worrying is using your imagination to create something you don't want.'*

25

Sleep was impossible for Ollie that night, or at least initially.

Physically, he was exhausted, but his brain was more active than ever. His mind's eye had cruelly decided to screen a film for him, featuring a full depiction of his depressing day. It ran nonstop and on auto repeat. He could only watch the mental images in torment, as they pictured his futile attempt to find Emma. Although the scenes moved from beach to beach, without any sign of his missing co-star, it was a very lonely one-man show.

Seeing all this again made him even more anxious, filling him with self-doubt and questioning. What if he had failed to spot her, perhaps as she lay crumpled and dying on a stretch of sand? What if he had missed her in the sea, struggling out of her depth? What if she had cried out to him, but he had disastrously not heard her? What if he had overlooked some vital clue? What if? …What if? …What if? … He surely had no other option, than to accept defeat.

Mercifully, a line came to him from Shakespeare's play, *Measure for Measure*: '*Our doubts are traitors and make us lose the good we oft might win, by fearing to attempt.*'

Determined to slow his unwanted thoughts as he lay in bed, he took a deep breath, filling his lungs with purifying air. Holding it in for a moment, he then let it go, mentally instructing himself to relax. Repeating this several times proved enough to slow his excessive pulse, allowing a much-needed calmness to drift over him. Counting down slowly from five to zero, he had intended to enter a hypnotic meditation. Instead, extreme fatigue finally brought the curtain down, sending him into a deep sleep.

A soliloquy from another Shakespearean play drifted through his dream state. It was spoken by *Hamlet* starting with the famous phrase: *'To be or not to be – that is the question'* and continued a little further on with: *'to sleep – perchance to dream.'* The prince had been contemplating suicide and death. It was the sting of the latter which now plagued Ollie's night-time hallucinations.

As if in a horror movie, he found himself back in Gran Canaria again, battling the mighty Atlantic Ocean. This time however he was all alone. There were no courageous rescuers to save him.

First came the sudden surprise and then full realisation of the difficulty he was in, which turned to absolute fear. Instinct told him to keep calm, but with his body now in a vertical position, uncontrollable panic set in.

He tried for dear life to shout for help, but his paralyzed throat made it impossible.

Gasps for breath rapidly became gulped mouthfuls of salty seawater.

Fighting his impending death, he wrestled against the undercurrent, but unlike him it was indestructible. Hopelessly, he struggled to stay afloat, his extended arms pushing, grasping and flipping, thrashing pointlessly in every direction.

A split-second before his mouth sank below the surface, he somehow managed to spew water and take a final breath.

Descending lower and lower, with aching determination he tried to hold on to that precious last gift of air, but the tightness in his chest, lungs and abdomen became unbearable.

Will power finally failed him.

His life-ebbing body jerked involuntarily several times, then went rigid and was completely motionless.

Despite the collapse of consciousness, he was strangely aware of everything which was going on. As he glanced around, everything seemed to be moving ever so slowly, within a dreamy, muffled near-silence.

Looking down, he could just make out his feet, which had reached the seabed. Even though his descent had been slow, it had made the water murky. It was as if he was standing in a giant bowl of milk.

Without even considering the possible implications, he dared to open his mouth and take a breath. That he was able to do so, without taking in a single drop of moisture, should have alerted him of something being wrong.

It failed to. Instead, the water cleared a little, giving him better vision, which allowed him to notice the fish. Most completely ignored him as they swam by, but others were more curious and circled him inquisitively. Weirdly, they all had a great big grin and began laughing at him, one after the other. A large plump silver-coloured species swam right up to his ear and whispered, 'You'll like it down here.'

It pointed with its fin. 'Look over there.'

Turning his head, Ollie was astonished to see a mermaid swimming towards him. He recognised it immediately from all the timeless depictions he had seen in paintings. Until then, he assumed the half-human, half-fish sirens were mythical. Her extremely attractive face and upper body were unquestionably those of a woman, yet below the waist she had a bright blue fish-like tail. Her long blond hair floated in long curly waves and from her mouth came a sweet but haunting song. Although he could not make out the lyrics, her tone was so blissfully enchanting, irresistibly inviting and sexually tempting.

Only then did he recognise her. He was awestruck, for it was Emma!

'What are you doing down her? he managed to ask. 'I've been looking everywhere for you.'

The smile she gave him was one which would melt the most sceptical heart. 'This is my new home,' she told him so convincingly. 'I wondered how long it would take you to join me.'

Unable to think clearly, he struggled to make sense of what she was saying. It was illogical.

'We are supposed to be on an island in Fiji,' he reminded her, 'not on the ocean floor. You went missing.'

She held out her arms, wrapping them around his neck and pulled him closer. 'And now we're reunited. We can be here together for eternity.'

He broke free of her passionate hold. 'No!' he retorted. 'It's not meant to be like this. We should be back on our island, watching the sunrises together in the morning, with you enjoying your Prosecco in the evening.'

She looked at him questioningly. 'What is Prosecco?'

He glared back in disbelief. If she had no idea what Prosecco was, she could only be an imposter, out to deceive him. In such a dire situation a warning came to him: *'She is a mermaid but approach her with caution. Her mind swims at depths most would drown in.'*

Any doubt about her identity was washed away that instant. This was not his Emma.

Such stark realisation was enough to make him realise he was having a lucid dream. It was nothing more than a nightmare, which he did not like at all.

He ended it immediately, by waking himself up.

Ollie took a deep breath, relieved it was air he was inhaling and not water.

Rubbing his eyes, he got out of bed and walked outside. He needed to clear his head.

It was a full moon and he stood staring at it for a while, admiring its splendour. He observed how it illuminated the table, almost as a spotlight would, where he and Emma usually sat.

Recalling the moon's relationship to water and its gravitational pull which creates the tides, he contemplated the context of his unpleasant dream.

The moon had long been thought to have an influence on behaviour, emotions and moods. Its connection with the mermaid was clear, for both were symbols of sacred femininity and were linked with water. Whilst mermaids had many favourable aspects, they also represented the destructive side of nature.

Astrologically, the moon was a symbol of the soul and

rebirth through reincarnation, which he very much believed in. Likewise, being immersed in water suggested transformation and rebirth too. It also pointed to challenging emotions and overbearing stress, which he was most certainly suffering from.

The smiling fish indicated he was hindering his own spiritual growth. The one which talked signified the need for him to improve his communication, but with whom?

He was not expecting a quote, but an anonymous one surfaced anyway: *'Dive deep for the treasure that you seek.'*

In an inspirational moment of truth, he knew without any hesitation that the time was right for him to contact his Holy Guardian Angel and seek its help in finding Emma.

Pulling one of the seats from the outside table, he positioned it so as he would be facing the moon. There was no specific reason for him to be in such a direction. It just seemed right from his interpretation of the preceding dream.

Sitting down, he closed his eyes and as he was accustomed, took several deep breaths. Utilising his by now almost perfect hypnotic meditation induction, he quickly entered a deep state of trance.

As his mind stilled completely, he entered the silence. From this sacred portal he reverently summoned his Holy Guardian Angel.

All the devotion and practice he had put into his spiritual quest and all the efforts he had made to find Emma were recognized, it seemed. He had anticipated being given a vision of where she might be, in a similar way to how he was shown the whereabouts of her ring. Instead, for the first time ever, he heard what could only be described as *a whisper in the silence.*

'Oliver.'

He had never heard a more tender or beautiful rendition of his name. It could only be the voice of his angel.

'Oliver.'

It was not an actual sound, but more like an immensely powerful thought, albeit from an external source. This was no dream, but the actual spoken word of his Holy Guardian Angel.

Humbled, but so thankful and relieved, he began to ask for help in finding Emma.

There was no need for him to, for the entity already fully knew of his desperation. 'She is trapped amongst the mangroves,' his angel revealed, 'where you have yet to look. I will guide you to her at first light, but now you must rest.'

Sensing such a brief but precious communication had ended, Ollie opened his eyes.

As he had not been told otherwise, he could at least assume Emma was still alive. Even so, he was disappointed at having to wait until the morning.

The thought of her all alone in the mangroves was almost unbearable, but he could accept the extreme danger of searching for her there in the dark. He had to be patient and follow the instructions he had been given by his Holy Guardian Angel.

26

It was still dark when Ollie awoke, but he wanted to get going as soon as possible.

He ate a light breakfast and gathered the things he thought he might need. As his Holy Guardian Angel had told him Emma was trapped among the mangroves, he thought a small axe and a coiled length of rope might be useful. As she had probably not eaten or had anything to drink for hours, he made sure to take some food and water in his rucksack.

From his one brief visit to the small, but challenging mangrove area of the island, he decided that shorts, a shirt and sensible shoes were necessary. It felt strange to be putting these on, having mostly been living a naturist lifestyle. He thought it highly unlikely Emma had taken any clothes with her, so added a pair of her shorts and a T-shirt to the things he was taking.

As he set off at first light, he could not help wondering yet again why she had gone to such an unpleasant part of the island in the first place. When he had told her about it initially, she had decided a day on the beach at Tern Bay would be preferable, watching the birds. He did however seem to recall her saying she would like to see the mangroves for herself one day. It was inconceivable nevertheless why she had suddenly ventured there alone, without even a mention. Just as surprising was her being able to find the location, having only been to the beaches with him.

Being in such a haste to get to her, he mistakenly took the wrong track at some point and ended up on a piece of rocky sealine. It was remarkably similar to where they used to sit and watch the sunsets, but much further from the cabin.

He retraced his steps for a while, hoping to get his bearings again. His Holy Guardian Angel had said it would guide him to her, but he was beginning to think it meant when he was in the mangroves, rather than on his way there. Even so, he sat down on the sandy grass for a moment and entered the silence.

Almost immediately, the shrill sound of screeching terns disturbed his peace. Opening his eyes, he noted the direction the birds were flying towards. He had the strongest feeling he needed to go the opposite way, which made sense, as the birds were most likely heading for Tern Bay.

Whether it was a mere hunch, or guidance from his angel, but it had been the correct decision. After walking some distance, he could make out what looked like the tops of mangrove trees.

Getting nearer, the unpleasant smell confirmed he was at the right place. The terrain was treacherous, which was why he had not gone any further when he had first come across it. Having been naked at the time, he had been worried about the possibility of sustaining cuts and scratches, or some more serious injury.

Tentatively, he carefully made his way through the outer

vegetation. The going was extremely difficult, especially when he reached the black mangrove trees, with their large leaves. It was almost as if their tangle of elbow roots had been purposely designed to make his task as difficult as possible. Grazing his lower leg on one protrusion made him regret not having worn long trousers.

With the mud getting thicker at each step, his progress slowed and became even more of an effort. Rationally, he had to be heading to where the mangroves bordered the sea. Although he was confident his Holy Guardian Angel would be guiding him the right way, he still called aloud Emma's name several times, in the hope she would hear him.

Every so often, he stopped stock still, to catch his breath and listen intently. He so yearned to hear her reply, but none came.

All the while, the odious smell of the hydrogen sulphide gases and smelly black water got worse. Although the odour level was feasibly not high enough to cause him any lasting harm, the stench was enough to put him off eating eggs ever again.

Eventually he saw the red mangroves ahead, recognisable by their characteristic stabilising prop roots.

Reaching these and the fact he was by now nearly up to his waist in slimy water, suggested he had to be extremely near to the shoreline.

After only a short distance it was necessary for him to take off his backpack and hold it above him with one arm, to prevent its contents being soaked. This made the going even more difficult.

It was gruelling even trying to keep his balance, as he squeezed between the trees, their awkward jutting roots and thick wet waxy leaves forming a natural obstacle course.

He shouted for Emma once more, but there was still no response. Instead, the buzzing sound of mosquitos seemed to be getting louder, their presence confirmed by the itchy, puffy red bites on his uncovered arms and legs.

Stopping again to get his breath, he made a quick study of the flora and fauna which surrounded him. There were strange-looking spongy creatures on some of the trunks and roots and even weirder ones with tentacles. Also attached to some of the roots were what he assumed were barnacles, along with large and small snails, with different types of shell. Between them and fungi ran crabs, on the lookout for whatever the last tide had left behind.

Although the mud had made the water extremely murky, there were some deeper but clearer areas, where he detected the movement of fish. The mangroves were undoubtedly doing vital good for the environment and the blue planet's ecosystem. His only desire, however, was to find Emma and get out of this decaying, bacteria-filled swamp as quickly as possible.

He bellowed her name as loud as he could. 'Emma! Where are you?'

At first, he heard nothing, but then perhaps something, although it was incredibly quiet.

He closed his eyes to concentrate. The intermittent crackling, snapping and popping sounds coming from the trees was distracting. So too was the chorus of insects and bird calls.

He did his utmost to blank these out and to silence his

mind of his own thoughts too.

Only then did he hear the recognisable whisper of his Holy Guardian Angel. 'She is here. Cast your eyes about you and you will see.'

With renewed optimism, his eyes darted in every direction.

Initially, all they could see was mangrove tree after mangrove tree.

Searching more slowly and looking downwards caused him to spot an object which seemed to be out of place in this terrain. Bright blue, it was shaped like a tube of some sort and had an orange end.

Beneath it, appeared to be a dirty, matted mess, which could possibly have been hair and what looked like a mask of some sort.

To one side, he could make out a trembling human hand, which was grasping a root.

It was Emma! He had found her!'

Wading around a tree, which separated her from him and wedging his bag between two exposed roots, he clasped her arm.

There was no movement or response from her.

Removing from her face what he now realised was her snorkelling mask and air pipe, he tried lifting her, but she would not budge.

Several more unsuccessful attempts did at least cause her to stir.

Ever so slowly her eyes opened. Focussing, they looked up.

Seeing him there, she began to sob with relief, tears trickling down her cheeks.

Her mouth opened and she managed to speak. 'I can't move,' she gulped. 'My right foot is caught between two of the submerged roots.'

He looked down at the murky water, reluctant to lower his face in it. 'Do you know which ones?' he probed, pointing to the stems above the surface.

'I think it's this thick one,' she gasped. 'The root I'm holding on to and the thinner one next to it.'

Grasping the latter, with both his hands beneath the water's surface, he tried separating it from the other. Although there was a little flexibility, he could tell it was not enough and so opening his bag, he took out the axe.

Seeing it, Emma screamed, wide-eyed in panic-stricken terror. 'No! No! Please, not that! There must be another way.'

Realising she had mistakenly feared it was going to be necessary for him to set her free by cutting her leg off, he quickly reassured her. 'Don't worry. I'm only going to try and chop the thin root, to separate it from the tree. The axe is going nowhere near you. I promise.'

Trusting him, she took a deep breath to calm herself. 'Is there enough space?'

He shook his head. 'Not at the moment. I need you to give me more room. Let go of the other root and twist your body away as far as you can.'

She did her best, but almost lost her balance.

He grabbed hold of her. 'Hang on my waist.'

She clutched at him as if it were a matter of life or death, her fingernails unintentionally pinching into the flesh beneath his shirt.

He winced, but raising the axe, brought the blade smartly

down onto the root.

Either the chopper was blunt, or the root exceptionally tough, but it took four blows to sever it.

He put the axe back in the bag and then with both arms pulled the now detached upper part of root away from the thicker one. Although the other end was still securely embedded in the mud beneath the water, he hoped it would bend enough. 'Can you free your foot yet?'

She tried moving it from side to side, to wiggle it free. 'It's not wedged as tightly as it was, but it still won't slip through.'

Thinking of an alternative plan of action, he took the rope from the bag and unravelling it, tied it around the cut-through root. 'Hang on to the other one as you were before, so you don't fall over. I'll tug this one the other way.'

Wading out into the water, he hauled as firmly as he could on the rope. 'Have another go at moving your foot.'

She shook her head. 'It's still not enough. You need to pull harder.'

He tied the end of the rope into a loop, to make it easier to yank. 'Try again, but only when I tell you to.'

Holding it securely, he heaved with all his might.

'Now!' he shouted, throwing all his weight backwards.

Emma twisted her foot and then by lifting it as high as she could, managed to squeeze it through the slightly wider gap.

'Yes!' she shouted with joyous relief. 'It's free! We've done it.'

He waded back to her, coiling the rope as he went.

Lifting her from the water, he carefully sat her down on the thickest root of the next tree along and examined the foot which had been trapped. 'It's scratched and swollen I'm afraid, as is your lower leg.'

She had been expecting it to be. 'I'm not surprised. I've been trying to work it loose for hours. I'm exhausted.'

He fetched her a bottle of water from his bag. 'You'd better drink some of this. You'll be dehydrated.'

From the speedy way she gulped it down, it was obvious her body had been desperate.

'What on earth were you doing, trying to snorkel amongst the mangroves?' he was anxious to know.

His question baffled her. 'What made you think I was doing that?'

'It was pretty obvious,' he presumed. 'You had your mask on.'

Realising he had misunderstood her actions, she thought an explanation might help. 'I woke up early yesterday morning and not wanting to disturb you, went for a walk. I know you warned me not to go into the sea, but I took my snorkelling things just in case I felt it might be safe. After some time, I came across what I realised were the mangroves and thought I'd have a quick look. The atmosphere intrigued me. It was so quiet and eery, almost like something out of a cult movie. You were right about the dreadful smell, but it wasn't quite so bad if I breathed through my mouth.'

She took another swig of mineral water. 'As I went further, I lost my bearings and realised I was lost amongst the trees. I seemed to be going round and round in circles and ended up down here, near to the sea. Then the tide came in and I was afraid I was going to drown. I pulled myself up out of the water by the tree's roots and clung to the trunk for hours, until the tide turned. I was terrified, especially in the dark. It was when I scrambled back down again into the water that my foot become caught.'

It all made sense to Ollie, except for the snorkelling gear. 'But why did you put the mask with its breathing tube on?'

'Realising I was trapped and knowing the tide would eventually come back in again, 'she informed him,' I thought they would give me a few more minutes before I drowned.'

Ollie gave a sigh of relief. 'Thank goodness I found you when I did.' He could see she was completely naked and was covered in mosquito bites.

Taking her clothes from his bag, he handed them to her. 'Put these on, as they'll offer you a little protection. I've got to try and figure how we're going to get out of here.'

With such a swollen foot, it was obvious he would have to support, or carry her. Wading out into deeper water and along the shoreline was out of the question and so their only chance was to return the way he had come.

He handed her the backpack. 'There's food in there, but it'll have to wait. We need to go now. Use my shoulder to take the weight off your ankle and try and keep the bag out of the water.'

Lifting her down he turned to move.

'Hey!' she objected. 'You're forgetting my snorkelling things.'

He shook his head in disbelief, but obligingly shook the water from them and put them in the bag she was holding. 'It's highly unlikely you'll ever use them, especially after your misadventure here.'

Although he did not say so, he had already decided that nothing would come as a surprise to him anymore.

It took them a considerable time to make it through the mangroves. Her exhaustion meant he had to carry her on his back for some of the way. To lighten the load, he disposed of the axe and rope, knowing Benny could always replace them.

They were tremendously relieved to eventually be safely out in the open again. Moving away from the stench and into the sunlight brought them renewed hope.

They stripped off their wet clothes, to rest and eat.

'Did you call out for me,' she asked him, 'when you were searching?'

'You bet I did,' he made clear. 'I yelled your name more times than I can remember.'

She was grateful. 'I think I must have been almost unconscious, or else I'd have heard and shouted back.'

Ollie thought of his Holy Guardian Angel and the help he had been given in safely finding her. His successful communication with the entity had necessitated the exact opposite to noise.

Knowing how much she enjoyed his quotes, he gave her something that had once been said by O. A. Battista, the Canadian-American chemist and author: *"There are times when silence is the best way to yell at the top of your voice"*

27

When they finally arrived back at the cabin, Ollie helped Emma take a shower and then had one himself. It was good to wash the unpleasant smell of the decay-filled swamp from their skin and hair.

Concerned about her swollen foot and ankle, he was thankful to find an elasticated bandage in the first aid box. Before fitting it, he made sure to apply some antiseptic to the minor wounds she had sustained. Finally, he applied ice from the freezer, wrapped in a moist towel.

'It'll help if you elevate your leg,' he advised, positioning some cushions.

By now, her mosquito bites were really itching, as he could tell from all the scratching she was doing.

'I know they're annoying,' he sympathised. 'Mine are too and you've got a lot more of them than me. If we can leave them alone, they'll heal more quickly.'

'Is there any antihistamine amongst your first aid things?' she asked hopefully.

He checked but without success. 'It seems Brad didn't think it was necessary. There's a natural remedy which will help however.'

He disappeared into the food store and came back brandishing a banana in each hand?'

Emma laughed. 'Are you kidding? Eating a banana isn't going to help.'

He passed her one. 'You just try and then I'll explain.'

She could hardly swallow it quickly enough, expecting him to come out with one of his witty quotes.

Instead, he took the skin from her. 'Natural oils within the banana peel are really good for mosquito bites.' He rubbed it against her leg, flesh side down. 'In a short while you'll find the itching disappears.'

He applied more to her other bites and then to his own.

'Good heavens!' she remarked just a few minutes later. 'Either you're telling me the truth, or I'm just imagining it, but they're far less itchy already.'

'Just think,' he mused. 'Most people eat a banana and chuck the bitter tasting skin away, without ever realising what they're wasting.'

She tried to relate what he was saying to the primates she knew he was so fond of. 'What about monkeys and apes? Do they do the same?'

'When given a banana, they probably don't find the skin too appetising either,' he thought likely, 'but they might sense it's good for them. The skin contains important nutrients, such as antioxidants, dietary fibre, polyunsaturated fats, amino acids and potassium of course. Monkeys eating bananas in the wild is a misconception, unless they happen to be near human habitation, where bananas are growing or lying around loose. Not all bananas are good for primates anyway, including humans, as the kind intended for our own consumption have often been grown using pesticides. They also have more sugar, so giving them to monkeys and apes is like feeding them bags of sweets.'

'I wonder if they'd enjoy a glass of my Prosecco?' she asked in fun.

He surprised her. 'Quite possibly. Chimps have been observed drinking naturally fermented palm sap, using leaf sponges, from the trees the local people harvest palm wine from. It's quite weak stuff, but it's thought some chimps might consume the alcohol equivalent of a bottle of wine.'

'Talking of which,' she hinted.

Ollie went to open a chilled bottle of her favourite tipple. He was amazed at how quickly she seemed to be getting over the trauma she had been through. He was bone-weary, but she had clung to a tree trunk for hours without any sleep and then been trapped in muddy water up to her chest.

'You must surely be totally exhausted?' he declared, bringing her a glass.

Her eyes were closed. She was fast asleep.

Ollie was careful not to disturb Emma when he awoke the next morning. He meditated sitting in a chair in the cabin, rather than down on the beach. Watching a sunrise alone, without her, had little appeal.

He did successfully manage to contact his Holy Guardian Angel again, thanking the entity for its help in finding her.

The sound of movement indicated Emma had finally awoken.

He opened his eyes to see her sitting up in bed yawning.

'How did you sleep last night?' he asked, hoping she had manged to get a good rest.

'Deeply,' she replied. 'How about you?'

'Fine.' He rather stated the obvious. 'We were both extremely tired.'

She could remember well enough. 'It's not surprising, after all we've been through. I even dreamed about it. I was back in the mangroves, clinging to the tree and there were the sea snakes you once told me about. They were slithering up the roots from the water towards me.'

Ollie found this interesting. 'Can you remember what colour they were?'

She tried to describe them. 'I think their skin was covered in bands of black and white.'

'They would have been sea kraits,' he supposed. 'The ones which come ashore. They can spend a good 15 to 30 minutes underwater, before surfacing for air. They are also highly venomous.'

'How fearsome!' she gasped. 'They were really long and crawled all over me, their forked tongues darting in and out of their mouths. They didn't bite me though.'

'Which is just as well,' he cautioned. 'Their venom is twenty times stronger than any land snake. Fortunately, they don't usually attack humans unless provoked.'

'I hadn't the slightest intention of antagonising them,' she established, 'but it got worse. After I climbed down into the water and got my foot stuck, I suddenly had a load of hungry looking sharks swimming right up to me.'

'They would probably have been whale sharks,' he purported, 'as the mangroves provide them with essential nourishment. Fortunately, they are not a danger to humans. Swimmers have even been known to take a ride on them. On the other hand, they might have been lemon sharks, which live in the shallow waters of the mangroves, but they're not a great threat either.'

'There's one small problem with what you're saying,' she objected. 'I wasn't to know what sort they were and whether they were going to attack me or not.'

Ollie was beginning to think Emma was a little confused. 'Were the snakes and sharks you're talking about just in your dream, or there for real whilst you were trapped?'

The more she thought about it, the less certain she was. 'I'm not so sure now. What I saw in the dream and what I really experienced seems to have all blended into one. They could have been there, or I might have just been imagining it.'

He had certainly not seen any sign of such creatures when he had found her but wanted her to know he had done everything possible to find her. 'I searched for you on all the beaches for hours the day before.'

Emma looked rather sheepish. 'Oh. I didn't know that.'

'I went to Benny's beach first,' he explained, 'thinking you might have gone there. I looked from top to bottom, all along the shore, among the palms and other foliage and of course out to sea. With no sign of you, I then went on to Tern Bay, in the hope you had gone to see the birds again. They were there of course, but sadly not you. I even went as far as Distant Sands, but again found nothing. By the end of the day, I had almost given up hope of finding you alive.'

She got out of bed, walked over and put her arms around him. 'But in the end, you did.'

*   *   *

They kissed and then she recalled something she had been meaning to ask him ever since he had come to her rescue. 'What made you realise I might have vanished in the mangroves?'

Ollie considered it important for her to know the truth. 'Do you remember who helped us find your grandmother's ring when you lost it?'

She had not forgotten. 'Yes. You told me it was your angel.'

He gave her a fond smile. 'That's right. My Holy Guardian Angel gave me a vision of where it was. This time the entity did even better, telling me where you were and leading me to you.'

'I think I owe your angel a huge thank you,' she insisted appreciatively.

'We both do,' he agreed, 'and I've already expressed our gratitude. In a roundabout way, I am also indebted to you.'

She gave him a blank look. 'How do you mean?'

'Good can emerge from even bad experiences,' he explained. 'It was through calling for my angel, at the point of sheer desperation, that I heard its voice for the first time. It's something I've been waiting for ever since I came to the island. To finally hear the whisper of my angel in the silence was a humbling, but magical experience.'

'I'm so pleased for you,' she marvelled. 'Perhaps it was fate. Maybe I was supposed to go missing.'

He was not so convinced. It was something he needed to contemplate. 'It certainly proved our vulnerability. You almost perished. In future, let's not take unnecessary risks but instead just appreciate the splendours of life. We should follow the good advice of Marcus Aurelius, the Roman Emperor: *'When you arise in the morning, think of what a precious privilege it is to be alive – to breathe, to think, to enjoy, to love."*

28

It took a few more days for them both to fully recover.

Ollie had made Emma a crutch, so she could walk without putting too much strain on her ankle. He did this by cutting the hard bristles off a broom head, binding it with cushioning and then shortening the handle to the right length.

'All you need now,' he teased, 'is a parrot on your shoulder and you'll look like the pirate Long John Silver, from Treasure Island.'

'Yo-ho-ho and a bottle of Prosecco!' she imitated back.

'They were actually singing about rum in Robert Louis Stevenson's novel,' he mentioned.

'Yes, but I'm a girl,' she justified. 'Drunken men attacking and robbing ships is what I'd call a rum deal!'

Ollie was pleased she still had her sense of humour, for the atmosphere had changed since the near disaster in the mangroves. Although their daily routine of watching the sunrise and spending time on the beach had resumed, things were not quite the same.

He deliberately avoided making any further comments about her going off alone, but secretly hoped she would take things a little more seriously from now on. As Ancient Egypt's Amenemope had put it: *'The ship of fools gets stuck in the mud. The ship of the silent sails with the wind.'* Truthful words, but wisely not ones he would share with her.

'There's going to come a time,' he said, as they sat outside the cabin having lunch, 'when you'll have to make a decision about your lifestyle.'

She misunderstood what he meant. 'You know I love naturism. It's healthy and fun.'

'I was actually talking about you being stuck on this island with me,' he explained. 'I know we've discussed it before, but there's also your modelling career to consider.'

'I'm still on holiday,' she reminded him dismissively. 'Although it wasn't supposed to be on this island, I had planned from the start to take a two-month break.'

'Which will soon be up,' he tried to make her see, 'and what are you going to do then? Your agent has probably got more work lined up for you already.'

This was indeed something which had occurred to her, but she had put it to the back of her mind. 'If we had a mobile signal on the island, I could check with her and find out.'

'There is a satellite phone,' he admitted to her for the first time. 'When I came here, I made the decision not to have any contact with the outside world, but Brad convinced me it was a sensible idea, in case of emergency. The problem is that it doesn't work. The battery's flat and it won't charge. After you arrived, I meant to ask Benny to get me another one but forgot.'

Emma was disappointed he had not mentioned it to her before, but even more so that it was not working. She had a solution, however. 'With Benny due tomorrow, we can add it to our next order.'

He sighed. 'I wish it were so simple, but we need to address the whole situation. It was my decision to live like a hermit, cut off from everything, not yours.'

To hear him say this saddened her. 'Are you suggesting you don't want me here anymore?'

He took her hand from across the table and kissed it tenderly. 'Not at all. I love you and treasure every moment we're together, but it's denying you a normal life.'

What he was saying did ring true. Similar thoughts had crossed her mind quite often in the last few days. Whilst her career was not overly important to her, seeing her parents and friends again one day certainly was. It was a problem with no easy resolution though, as she could not imagine life without him. 'I love you more than anyone in the world,' she assured him unreservedly. 'If it means spending our future on the island, then so be it.'

'I'm touched at your willingness to make such a huge sacrifice,' he admitted, 'but I don't think it would be right for me to let you. There is an alternative. We could leave the island and go back to civilisation as a couple.'

Emma was astonished at what he was saying. 'Would you really be prepared to give everything up for me?'

'Without question,' he told her wholeheartedly.

'But you bought this place for a reason,' she wanted him to recall. 'You hated your work. You detested the city and most of all the noise which came with it. You came here to shut out all the pandemonium which surrounded you. Your sole aim was to find seclusion from it all. In its place you sought a spiritual life, somewhere where you could go into the silence and grow closer to your Holy Guardian Angel.'

Although she was right in all she said, he appeared to be seeing it differently now. 'I have to some extent succeeded in what I was after. Things have changed and I don't have to selfishly just think of myself anymore. I quite rightly have to be mindful of you as well.'

'But it's so peaceful and beautiful here,' she emphasised. 'It's paradise. How could you ever bear to be in London again?'

'We wouldn't have to be there,' he imagined. 'There are endless possibilities and much quieter cities. Zurich, in Switzerland is supposed to be the least noise polluted in the world, with Vienna, Oslo, Munich and Stockholm next. The downside is that Zurich is also on the list of the most boring cities, being so overly clean and tidy. It's why some people find it sterile. The quietest place on Earth officially is a research laboratory in Redman, Washington, owned by Microsoft. It has an incredibly quiet anechoic chamber, used for testing audio devices. There are similar ones in Minneapolis and even at the UK's Salford University.'

'I don't think we would be allowed to live in any of those,' she rightly supposed.

'I wouldn't want to,' he established. 'The quietest outside place in England is Kielder Mires in Northumberland. It's the country's largest area of blanket bog, with no roads or flight paths near it. America has the Hoh Rainforest, in the Olympic National Park. There's hardly any noise in Antarctica either, without any towns or villages, but it would be far too chilly for us. A better choice might be to live in a cave. They've always had a certain appeal to me and there's plenty throughout the world.

In fact, thirty to forty million people in China are believed to live in cave dwellings known as *yaodongs*.

'I think we'd miss the sunshine too much,' she suspected.

'You're right,' he agreed. 'So, it's back to England then, which does at least have quieter rural areas where we could live, with lots of sleepy little villages.'

It occurred to her that he had forgotten something important. 'What about our naturism? Even if we chose to live by the seaside, we could hardly walk down the High Street naked on our way to the beach.'

'To do so we would need to live in the naturist village of Cap d'Agde in France,' he foresaw, 'or the Vera Playa naturist resort in Spain. Both are massive, with public streets and hundreds of apartments, plus hotels, shops, and restaurants. There's nothing similar in the UK, except for small residential naturist clubs, such as Spielplatz, near St. Albans. Times are changing though, thanks to the efforts of British Naturism and other organisations. Within a few years, especially with climate change, there will either be a lot more naturist beaches, or most will become clothing optional. It will be recognised as a human right to swim and sunbathe as you will, either in unhealthy textile swimwear, or completely free of clothing, as nature originally intended.

'All the places you've mentioned seem very nice,' she envisioned, 'but after having a whole island to ourselves, wouldn't they feel overpopulated?'

'Probably,' he concurred, promptly coming up with another option. 'With all the money I would make from selling the island, we could live in an enormous country mansion somewhere, with lovely tranquil private grounds and a huge, heated swimming pool. It would be perfectly safe for you to swim in, with no nasty sea snakes or sharks to spoil our enjoyment. Wherever we chose, we could still be within a reasonable distance of your friends and even for you to do some modelling work.'

It all sounded very tempting, but Emma was still not convinced it was what he really wanted. 'If I hadn't turned up and you were still alone, would you be thinking of leaving?'

'It's not a fair question,' he objected. 'You've changed everything for the better, taking an interest in the things most important to me and encouraging me to share their secrets with you.'

She knew he was mainly talking about his hypnotic meditation techniques, as a means of going into the silence. 'I'm working on those because you've persuaded me that it's good for me spiritually.'

'Not to mention physically and mentally,' he added. 'Silence relieves stress and tension and remedies anxiety disorders. It regenerates brain cells and improves the way our brain functions. By encouraging us to get rid of nonessential information, we can think objectively and better focus.'

'If that's so,' she proposed tongue in cheek, 'I need to put in plenty of overtime!'

Something else occurred to her. 'What about the weather? It's going to seem appalling after what we've been used to here.'

'Quite possibly,' he had to agree. 'There will have to be compromise, but it's an obstacle which we could easily overcome. With so much money and without the need to work we can follow the sun. When it's cold in England, we could lap up the warmth somewhere else, simply travelling the world to create an endless summer.'

Emma pictured it in her mind. 'It sounds fun, but after a while we would tire of globetrotting, with long journeys and waiting around at airports. It would be much simpler to just stay here, where it's lovely and warm."

'We've talked about the climate before,' he recalled. 'It's not surprising as it's one of the reasons why I bought an island in Fiji. We've been enjoying the weather at its best and have yet to experience the rainy season and the possibility of damaging cyclones. They can even occur before November and after April, with abnormal weather caused by the ocean's warming in El Niño years.'

She tried making light of what he was saying. 'Thanks for giving me another weather outlook. Perhaps you could do the shipping forecast next?'

She expected at least a smile from him, but he did not seem interested in humour. It really concerned her. 'You really are serious about all this aren't you?'

'I am,' he made clear. 'I think we should pack everything up today, so Benny can fly us to Nadi tomorrow. We can take it from there.'

Emma never thought she would hear such a proposal from him, but providing it was what he wanted, she would follow him to the end of the Earth.

Was this Ollie's true desire, or was he simply pretending it to be for her sake? As the writer, Gary Chapman, had put it: *'Love is something you do for someone else, not something you do for yourself.'*

29

It took three journeys with the trolley the next morning to get all their things down to the beach.

Emma was taking nearly everything she had brought with her, but it was necessary for Ollie to be rather more selective. He was fully aware that space on the plane would be tight, especially being half full of provisions.

As Brad Lithtrop had sourced and installed nearly everything on the island, prior to Ollie's arrival, most of it could be left behind. The personal assistant could sort it all out later. The last thing Ollie wanted was the environmental officer to come chasing after him.

Having sorted through the things he had originally brought with him, he had safely packed his copy of The Book of the Law and some Aleister Crowley books in his flight bag. In there too were his noise cancelling headphones, which he would need for the journey.

As he gathered a few bits and pieces of sentimental value, he came across the small guidebook of Fijian flora and fauna, which Brad had given him. It had proved most useful and he had really enjoyed being able to identify nature's treasures from it. Although he could easily buy a replacement copy, he chose to take it with him as a memento of his short time on the island.

Apart from what he would wear for travelling home and a spare change of attire, the rest of his limited wardrobe would stay. He fully intended to buy new clothes anyway once he was back in the UK.

A more difficult decision had been over the provisions in the storeroom. There were several bottles of his beloved Cognac and red wine, although Emma had managed to get through nearly all her Prosecco. There was no point in taking any of the alcohol, he concluded, due to liquor import restrictions on their onward flights.

Another dilemma was what to do about the power supply, refrigeration unit and so on. If he turned them off, the perishable foods would soon rot and in time reek the place out. He hoped Benny would be able to advise him on this and perhaps make a solo return flight if there was anything he would like.

Despite Ollie's apparent resolution to leave the island, as they sat on the sand awaiting the plane, there was much sadness in their hearts. Neither was aware of the other's precise feelings, however.

He was trying not to show his, for he did not want Emma to suspect his real motives.

She on the other hand did not really know what she wanted. Whilst looking forward to seeing her parents and friends again, she would still be with the man she had fallen in love with. It would have been the best of both worlds, had it not meant giving up their naturist way of life on such a lovely island.

The necessity for them to dress before leaving the cabin

had been challenging. Emma only handled it by picturing again her dreadful time in the mangroves when she could so easily have died.

Ollie was downhearted for another reason. It was the depressing feeling of defeat and failure in everything he had planned. Trying to be less pessimistic, he relished his success in perfecting his hypnotic meditation techniques and his communication with his Holy Guardian Angel.

Now though, he was about to return to the world he had been so eager to escape from, freely leaving the lifestyle he so loved, on an island which at times had been his personal paradise. Such a circumstance was another meaningful reminder that heaven and hell are not places reserved for the dead, but states of mind for the living.

Through his mind ran the words of Omar Khayyam, the Persian astronomer, philosopher and poet: *'I sent my Soul through the Invisible / Some letter of that After-life to spell / And by and by my Soul returned to me / And answer'd I Myself am Heav'n and Hell.'*

The sound of the plane cut sharply into their thoughts. Looking up, they watched Benny's seaplane circling overhead as it prepared for landing.

'He's in for rather a surprise,' Emma predicted.

Ollie agreed. 'He'll probably think I'm stark raving bonkers.'

'Perhaps,' she accepted, 'but not quite as much as had you been standing here stark naked, juggling half a dozen terns in the air!'

The seaplane's landing was as smooth as usual.

Standing up, they waved to him as he steered alongside the jetty.

After switching off the engine, he emerged through the cabin door, immediately noticing all their luggage piled on the beach.

He had no idea what to make of it. 'I thought I was supposed to be delivering to you, but it seems to be the other way around.'

They met halfway, at the shoreline.

'Sorry,' Ollie apologised. 'I should have warned you, but there was no way. We've decided to leave the island and head back to England.'

Benny was astonished. 'Why would you want to do that? You have everything you could want here. There's peace and solitude, gorgeous powder-white sandy beaches, glorious sunshine and the perfect temperature. You also have irresistible cuisine and all your favourite beverages flown in on demand.'

'You're sounding more like an editorial from a travel brochure,' Emma kidded.

The pilot looked concerned. 'Maybe, but I only hope you two haven't had a lovers tiff.'

'Not really,' she made out, 'but he's keen for me to get back to my job and friends.'

Benny turned to Ollie, who was trying hard to hide his gloom. 'You were so looking forward to your future life on the island when I flew you here a few weeks ago. You must be smitten with Emma, to want to leave so soon.'

Ollie's attempt to look cheerful only managed to produce a half smile 'It's complicated, but for the best. We talked it through last night and decided to leave straight away.'

Benny took another look at their piled-up possessions. 'I'm

not going to get both of you and all your luggage on board, along with everything I was expecting to offload.'

Ollie had already worked out the best plan. 'We can't leave any food, or plastic wrappers here on the beach. It'll get washed out to sea and cause pollution. The mineral water and booze can be offloaded though to make more room.'

Emma overheard him. 'You don't mean we have to leave my new supply of Prosecco behind?'

'Sorry, but I'm afraid so,' he apologised. 'With the exception of food, everything else will have to come off the plane, to make room. I'll be leaving all my Cognac, wine and beer too, if it's of any comfort.'

It took them some time to get those things off the plane, making sure they were left on the path, a good distance from the high tide mark.

All the while, Emma could be heard to mutter, 'What a waste,' over and again.

'You can always fly back here tomorrow Benny,' Ollie offered. 'You can take anything you want, from the island. As well as all this alcohol, there are quite a few bottles up at the storeroom and some food. Perhaps you could then turn everything off. I'll be sending Brad out in due course to sort it out.'

Benny thanked him and loaded the bags and cases. 'Are you sure you don't want to go back to the cabin for one last look?'

Ollie shook his head decisively. 'No. Let's just get going.'

They helped Emma aboard the plane, Ollie sitting in the seat behind her.

Benny closed the door and took his place upfront, starting

the engine.

At that precise moment Emma burst into tears. Ollie tried to console her, but her crying only got louder, until even Benny heard it and stopped the engine.

'Are you alright?' he checked.

Ollie undid his seat belt and knelt beside her. 'What is it?'

She wiped her eyes. 'It's my snorkelling gear,' she sobbed. 'I must have left it in the cabin by the bed.'

By now, Benny had come back to see what the problem was.

Ollie could only look at him and shrug, before trying to comfort her. 'Don't worry. It's not of any great value. I'll buy you a brand new snorkelling mask once we're back in England.'

'They sell lots of them in Nadi, should you need one sooner,' Benny added, trying to be helpful.

'Why would she need one for our flights back to the UK?' Ollie questioned. 'I know airlines put a life vest under the seat for emergencies, but not a bloody snorkelling mask! Most passengers wouldn't even get the vest on properly before the plane crashed, let alone one of those.'

'Point taken,' Benny agreed.

Emma was still extremely upset. 'It's not just any snorkelling mask. It's the one I put on when I was trapped in the mangroves.'

Benny looked inquisitive.

'It's a long story, so I'll tell you about it later,' Ollie promised.

'When you do,' Emma was sure, 'he'll realise why the mask is so precious to me.'

Ollie sighed. 'Sorry Benny. I'm afraid you're going to have to wait, while we pop back to the cabin for it.'

Emma stopped crying. 'We'll try not to be too long.'

*   *   *

'It's a nuisance you didn't remember to pack your precious mask,' Ollie muttered, as they made their way up the path.

Rather than comment, she just quickened her pace.

It was only when they reached the table outside the cabin, that she insisted he sit down. 'Now we're here, let me tell you that I have no intention whatsoever of going inside to get the mask.'

He wondered what on earth she was talking about. 'Why ever not?'

'Because we're not going anywhere,' she told him stubbornly.

'We're not?' he questioned. 'We talked about it last night and we came to the mutual decision to leave the island and head back to England.'

'What you're saying is not entirely true,' she corrected him. 'You suddenly surprised me out of the blue by saying you wanted to leave. I tried to make you see sense, reminding you just how much the island means to you. I went through all the reasons you came here in the first place, but you claimed you were seeing things differently now. I pointed out how much you hated London, with all its noise and how awful the weather would be compared to here. What was your response? Well, let me refresh your memory. You did your best to confuse me with lots of *Guinness Book of Records* style facts about the noisiest and quietest places on Earth. Even when I brought up naturism, which we both love so much, you started listing alternative locations where we could practise it. As I suspected from the start, the only reason you mentioned us leaving was because you feel bad about me missing my friends and parents and even my modelling career. The truth is that I do, quite often, but not nearly as much as I will miss the island. I want to stay, to continue living here with you and if I ever change my mind in the future, you'll be the first to know. Until then, we are not going anywhere, so you'd better get that into your head! We are going to carry on our relationship, as lovers, which means everything to me. You're going to continue helping me with my meditation and astonish me with lots more fascinating things, like sacred sexuality, the occult and all the other stuff I'd never even heard of until I came here. You are also going to keep me constantly entertained and amazed, by reciting all your wonderful quotes. This is all I want, nothing more.'

She took a breath and then added, 'Apart from my Prosecco of course!'

This was the first time Ollie had ever experienced Emma in such a determined assertive mood, but what she was saying delighted him.

He was only too pleased to show it. 'Your will shall be done.' he promised, giving her a kiss, 'but why didn't you tell me all this before, down on the beach, or even when we were on the plane?'

'Because it's private, between you and me,' she let him know. 'I would have felt awkward, saying what I had to in front of Benny.'

Ollie could understand her sentiment. 'We had better get back down there and give him the good news then.'

'What do you think he'll say when we tell him we've changed our minds?' she wondered, rather concerned. 'It's rather like the time you were going to send me away, but changed your mind at the last minute.'

'If necessary,' he decided, 'I can quote to him the words of

Bernard Shaw, the Irish playwright: *'Those who can't change their minds can't change anything."*

Surprisingly, Benny took it well and only laughed when they revealed what was happening.

'You're the customers,' he reminded them. 'At least it means I'm still going to be flying in your supplies. It's my favourite job.'

He helped them take everything off the plane, including their luggage and all the food. He even offered to assist in getting it back to the cabin.

'We can manage,' Ollie insisted. 'You can get away. We've kept you long enough and I know you're a busy man. There is one favour I'd like from you, however. I need two brand new top of the range satellite phones and chargers please. I have a service provider already, but get in touch with Brad in England, so he can sort out the technical issues. Your office has his number. Give him my regards and tell him the old phone doesn't work. Hopefully, you'll be able to get the phones to us in a few days' time. I'd be really grateful.'

'Not a problem at all,' Benny was sure, 'but why do you need two of them?'

Ollie pointed to Emma. 'One for her and one for me.'

Emma was thrilled to hear this, knowing she would at last be able to talk to her parents and chums.

'Same provisions as today?' the pilot checked.

Ollie nodded. 'But double up on the Prosecco.'

'It sounds like you're intending to have fun,' Benny anticipated.

'Tell me something,' Ollie quizzed him. 'Have you ever heard of Bernard Shaw, the playwright?

'Of course,' he replied. 'I studied literature at college. They adapted his *Pygmalion* into that old Broadway musical, *My Fair Lady*.'

Emma was expecting Ollie to repeat the quote about changing minds, but he had something else up his sleeve.

'To put things into perspective,' he suggested, 'I have a quote for you from his one act play, *Annajanska, the Bolshevic Empress*. It goes like this: *'We don't stop playing because we grow old; we grow old because we stop playing.'*'

Benny gave him the thumbs up. 'I could hardly argue with that. I'll leave the two of you to carry on growing younger.'

They waved to him as he boarded his plane and took off.

'I've grown quite fond of Benny,' Ollie reflected.

Emma was of the same mind. 'He's an alright guy and until the satellite phones arrive, still our only contact with the outside world.'

It took four trolley loads to get all the new provisions and their luggage back to the cabin and storeroom. With Benny gone and it being hot, it was a relief to get out of their clothes again.

They ate dinner by the cabin that evening, beneath the stars and a full moon, with just the soothing sound of the gently snoring sea, as it slept in the distance.

Life was once again perfect.

Afterwards, they went inside and celebrated, by making love.

Before going to sleep, she asked him for an inspirational goodnight thought.

He had the perfect one. It was from Luciano De Cescenzo, the Italian actor, director and writer: "*Each of us are angels with* only one wing, and we can only fly by embracing one another."

30

Early next morning they were back on the beach, awaiting the sunrise.

On previous occasions they usually sat slightly apart, so as not to distract the other from their thoughts. Today they were together, as close as they could be, his protective arm around her.

Although they were focussing on the horizon in anticipation, they stole a moment to turn and gaze momentarily into each other's eyes.

Slowly, their lips met in an intimate adoring embrace. For those few sacred seconds, time froze. It was as if they had the entire planet Earth to themselves.

Reluctant as they were to break such a treasured moment, the morning twilight directed their attention back to the awaited splendour.

"There is a time in the day, just before the sun rises, that is silent. All you can hear is the creation of the universe," he whispered to her. The words were anonymous, but as always appropriate.

Gradually, the cloudless sky grew brighter and, in the serenity, transformed a florid pastel orange. Rising slowly, the breathtakingly beautiful yellow sun disk made its glorious entrance.

As its powerful golden rays cut through the sky, a lone but mighty beam of lifegiving light swam gracefully towards them, across the surface of the mirror-like sea. Such a magical and spectacular resplendent majesty blessed their love forever.

Taking his arm from around her, they both straightened their backs in preparation.

He reminded her again of the techniques she should use, to enter the silence through hypnotic meditation.

Closing their eyes, they breathed deeply. They could at least both share this moment, despite it being a spiritual necessity for them to seek ultimate tranquillity individually.

Using the method which by now he had perfected, Ollie entered the silence quickly, bathing in the ultimate bliss of nothingness.

Emma took much longer to calm her unwanted thoughts. They came and went, only to reappear in another guise. Like demons, they tried to torment her with negativity and doubt, but she remembered Ollie telling her not to fight them. Having heard what they had to say, she let each one drift away. Recognising this more positive attitude, the invading conceptions eventually accepted defeat and retreated. Her mind was at last at peace and for the first time ever she drifted into self-induced total silence.

It was the sweet music of birdsong which finally brought her from the stillness.

'Welcome back,' Ollie remarked. 'How was your meditation?'

Her face beamed with joy. 'I finally made it, into the silence, just for a while.'

He was overjoyed to hear it, knowing how much she had feared the absence of even external noise, when she first arrived on the island. 'Did it feel good?'

'Although this might sound rather strange,' she anticipated, 'it seemed like I was back home. I don't mean in England, but somewhere from a long time ago. I was in a kind of nothingness. To start with I felt slightly uneasy, but then I just let it wash over me. Does it make any sense?'

He nodded his head knowingly. 'Absolutely. You must remember though, that nothingness does not imply nothing, for there is always something. One day you'll find contentedness, peace, fulfilment and eventually enlightenment.'

'Perhaps I will also be able to contact my Holy Guardian Angel,' she aspired.

'I am sure you will,' he encouraged,' but it's vitally important to keep working on it. Only through silence can we connect to our higher self, which is our true spiritual self. As I have stressed before, this is not the same as our Holy Guardian Angel however, for the entity is separate from us. Only in the silence can we hear the whisper of its voice. Should we fail to hear it, then we must listen again and again, or call to it gently once more and patiently await its reply. Once the link has been made you will eventually hear its angelic guiding voice.'

'I'm not quite there yet,' she accepted, 'but even getting this far is down to you. If I had not come to this island by mistake and met you, I would still be sitting around with pop music blaring from my smartphone. You've proved to be a great teacher.'

'I'm not the only one,' he insisted. 'There are two tutors on this island.'

She was unclear what he meant. 'Who's the other one then?'

He took her hand. 'You, of course.'

'I'm flattered you think so,' she said in response, 'but in what way have I taught you anything?'

'You've brought home to me the importance of true love,' he shared. 'When I came to the island, I rejected everybody and everything, leaving them behind. All I thought I needed was solitude, in which to try and find real silence. Whilst we are all on our own unique spiritual journeys and can only complete the Great Work hermetically, you've made me realize how precious it is to have a soulmate for company at least to the final crossroad in life. There was a Roman philosopher and statesman by the name of Seneca, who said that: *'Love in its essence is spiritual fire.'* I'm not sure of the context he meant it in, but you've convinced me that love plays a huge part in spiritual transformation and divine transcendence. It also makes our fleeting existence on this tiny planet even more wonderful. As Sophocles, the Ancient Greek dramatist put it: *'One word frees us of all the weight and pain of life. That word is love.'*

Ollie had told her several times how much he loved her, but only now did she understand the true depth of his feelings. His use of the term *soulmate* had made her tingle with happiness.

'For once, I've got a saying for you,' she enthused: *'The most beautiful clothes that can dress a woman are the arms of the man she loves.'*

He was deeply touched by what she said.

As they embraced, he added, 'And being a naturist, they're

the only garment you'll ever need!'

31

A couple of days later Emma noticed him sitting at the table outside the cabin. He had a pen and was busy scribbling something down on a piece of paper.

'What are you up to?' she asked out of interest.

'I've decided to write a book,' he disclosed, 'as you once suggested I should. I rather wish I'd brought a laptop to the island now, but never thought I'd need it.'

'You can ask Benny to get hold of one,' she suggested.

'A good idea,' he agreed. 'It will make things a lot easier.'

She was inquisitive. 'What's it going to be about? An anthology of all the inspiring quotes you've memorised perhaps?'

'I can certainly include some of them, but it's going to be a novel,' he had already decided.

A slightly disappointed look appeared on her face. 'You're going for fiction then?'

He corrected her. 'Faction actually. The story might appear to be a figment of my imagination, but for the most part it will be factual, about my time here on the island. I'm going to use fictional names however, rather than my own, for the central character and the author. The reader will never know whether it's a true story or not.'

'If that's the case,' she ventured, 'will I be in it too, or are you leaving me out?'

'Emma will definitely be included,' he promised, 'even if I change your name. *'Someday when the pages of my life end, I know that you will be one of the most beautiful chapters.'*

She gently kissed the top of his head. 'That was lovely?'

'But not my words,' he confessed. 'Mine come to me when I'm least expecting them to. They started entering my head this morning and so I'm getting them down on paper, before they vanish again. There's something I want you to know. It was your love which has inspired me to write. As Plato, the Athenian philosopher, put it: *'Every heart sings a song, incomplete, until another heart whispers back. Those who wish to sing always find a song. At the touch of a lover, everyone becomes a poet.'*

Emma again admired his uncanny skill for producing a perfect quote seemingly out of thin air. This time she wanted more. 'I want to hear your own words now. Read to me what you've written.'

'Not much so far,' he admitted, 'but it's a beginning. Take a seat and I'll read it to you.'

Knowing he had her undivided attention he began: *'Noise! The dreadful droning sound of the seaplane's turbine engine and spinning propeller escalated. As it prepared for take-off, Trevor quickly reached for his noise-cancelling headphones. Turning them on, he placed them over his head and adjusted the cans to effectively cover his ears. Leaning back again in his seat, he gave a sigh of relief. Silence had been restored—'* Unfortunately, his recitation was disturbed by the approaching sound of an aeroplane.

'It must be Benny,' Ollie assumed. 'He's probably delivering our new satellite phones.'

Dashing into the cabin, he slipped on a pair of shorts. Emma settled for just a T-shirt, which was fortunately long enough to reach down over her thighs.

'I can't wait to phone my parents,' she told him as they hurried down to the beach.

The seaplane nearing the landing stage was not what they had expected. Rather than Benny's de Havilland Otter, it was another type of aircraft.

Emma recognised it almost immediately though, for it had *Paradise Pleasure Flights* painted on the side. 'They're the company who flew me here,' she reminded him.

Even more surprising was what happened next. The door opened and two young men stepped onto the jetty. Both casually dressed and wearing identical sunglasses, they made their way to the beach, followed by the pilot, who was clutching a couple of large suitcases.

As they spotted Ollie and Emma they gave a friendly wave. 'Great weather for a holiday,' one of them exclaimed, a huge grin on his face.

'Let's hope it stays like this for the next three weeks,' the other added. 'We can party 24/7.'

The word *party* jarred with Ollie, just as much as it had when Emma first arrived.

He made a halting sign with both hands. 'I'm sorry to disappoint you, but this is a private island and I've no idea what you're doing here.'

The two strangers gave him a look, then stared at each other, before glancing back at the pilot. He just put the cases down and shrugged.

'This is the right island isn't it?' the younger of the two asked.

'What exactly were you expecting?' Ollie delved.

'The *Pink Parrot* of course,' the other qualified. 'It's a gay resort.'

Emma saw the funny side but managed not to laugh. 'Who did you book with,' she asked, anticipating their reply.

'A company called Over C Travel,' came the answer, just as she had predicted.

Ollie sighed. 'I'm afraid you've fallen for a scam, just as Emma did a few weeks ago. It's all one big con, with people being sent all over the place to non-existent destinations. On this island there's just one cabin, which Emma and I share. I can only suggest you fly straight back to Nadi and sort something out from there.'

There was a reaching for mobiles.

'Sorry,' Ollie apologised, 'there's no phone signal here, no wi-fi, no anything. There's only silence.'

The pilot turned, beckoning the two disappointed party hopefuls back towards the seaplane.

They climbed back onboard, but just before the cabin door closed one of them had a question. 'Don't you get bored living here in silence?'

'Not at all,' Emma assured him. 'Silence isn't empty. It's full of answers.'

Ollie was amazed. 'Did you just make that up?'

'No,' Emma revealed. 'It's something I read years ago. Since being on the island with you I've come to realise it's true.'

From the same author – the historical occult novel

FROM MANHOOD TO GODHEAD
The Many Lives of Jean Vassar

The compelling story of Jean Vassar's journey through many lives, as he discovers the hidden secret doctrines of *reincarnation, sacred sexuality, magick, initiation, alchemy, ritual, Masonry, Qabalah, mysticism, Egyptian Freemasonry* and carefully explained *occult symbolism.*

Through the miracle of rebirth Jean's ever evolving soul travels all over the world and far beyond. Encountering many real-life historical characters, including the *Cathars*, the *Knights Templar, Paracelsus, John Dee & Edward Kelley, Elias Ashmole, Count Cagliostro, Count de Saint-Germain, William Blake, Eliphas Levi, Paschal Beverley Randolph* and *Aleister Crowley*, their vitally important teachings are brought to life once more, mainly in their own words.

★ ★ ★ ★ ★ *Impressive beyond words*

'The most extensive research must have gone into the making of this book. This has been written by someone who is more than competent in his subject. It is filled with information and illumination.'

★ ★ ★ ★ ★ *Magnificent*

'A magnificent piece of Work. Inspiring, gripping and thorough, this novel brings to life our occult history and weaves it into a rich tapestry allowing the reader to appreciate the important connections between the great thinkers of our past.'

Printed in Great Britain
by Amazon

65985064R00165